Table of C

CW00493237

Warrior of Zandar

Drak System

May Doyle

Table of Contents

Chapter 1

What was she doing watching a group of Horde warriors approach her on the dusty plains? She could hear hoof beats reverberating in her head.

Holding tight to a *Guyipe*, her hands were fisted. Her dad said it was like a horse, though she had never seen one before.

She wasn't born on earth, she hadn't stepped foot on it, or felt its stiff grass. Her eyes had never seen a bright yellow sun so bright it would blind her. Zandar was her home planet.

Earth colonists who settled there over a century ago had been stranded, and the Zandian's had allowed them to land. Earth's elders begged the nearest planets for help. The king in the east, the Zandian's leader, agreed only if they followed a bunch of immovable rules that were harsh laws.

And she had broken one.

Her small form huddled into the *Guyipe*, trying to hide but failing. There was nowhere she could safely reach before they got to her. When she saw them, she spun to run, but the shout that rose was a warning to stay put.

So, there she was, facing the approaching Horde warriors.

There were ten Horde kings; the biggest, meanest, and fiercest warriors that fought to win their position. During the year, they paid tribute to the king once, moved with the seasons, and traded among themselves. Zandar had fifteen moons, but her dad, who was sort of a historian, said a year on earth was twelve.

It was because of him she was outside the gates.

Out of fear, they were huddled behind gates because Horde warriors passed every moon, inspecting and taking resources. They'd only do it if they thought the colony had too much. Humans never knew what they did with the resources. Did they use them or throw them away? She didn't know.

She watched as her *Guyipe* shifted nervously on its feet, its thick fur standing on end - the same thing happened to her hair. Star's eyes danced frantically like *Guyipe's* four eyes, skirting nervously over Horde warriors as she watched them approach warily, sweat rolling down her back.

After learning the language of her home planet, she could speak with them. However, her throat tightened as the most enormous warrior drew closer, and she realised she was looking at the Horde's king.

Scars all over his body were the first sign he was the Horde King. Compared to other warriors he had more - A Horde's strength was determined by its king. If they weren't leading their Horde into battle or across the plains, the kings were considered weak.

Taking in his broad shoulders, her eyes swept over them, his muscles were bigger than anyone in her village. He was breath-taking.

When the Horde king stopped before her, she took in the beads and braids in his hair, intricately done and twisted close to his head at the front. She hadn't noticed the decorations until she was close enough to see them. She was fascinated by his hair. On Zandar, warriors never had short hair, unlike her dad and brother.

The only thing on his chest was straps for his weapons. He flexed his thick muscled thighs as he moved to the side to see her better. The thick fur that covered his lower parts fell to mid-thigh, so it covered everything.

His skin was much darker than hers, which was naturally pale. It was pearly white like a ghost. His features weren't that different from hers. His ears were elongated and pointed, his brows were sharp and angular, and his bones were strong, not like her fragile human bones.

There were no whites in his eyes like hers, and she couldn't tell if he was looking at her or not, but it was as if she could feel the prickly sensation of his eyes on her. When she realised how little she was wearing, she winced.

When she heard her father's scream, she jumped from her bed. She had on a white shift that reached her knee. A blush spread across her cheeks. It was decent but more than any man had ever seen.

He jumped off his *Guyipe*, his big legs thumping as he hit the ground. As his boots crossed the short distance, dust kicked up from the dry land.

With a command, she quieted her *Guyipe*. "*Ayat!*"

He grabbed her chin in his warm hand. His rough fingers were too strong on her sensitive skin when he pinched her chin, tilting her head left and right. It made her eyes water. The sharp tips of his nails brushed against the back of her cheek. She was pretty sure his eyes followed his hand, but she could be wrong.

"*Trokko?*" His demand dried up her mouth.

She couldn't find air, so how could she tell him her name? She had no moisture to wet her mouth. Because of the dry, hot plains, there was a lot of heat between their bodies.

There was a difference in the way his eyebrows moved. Annoyance made them move to the side. She knew she should answer him, but her fear stopped her.

"*Sako Immani,*" he told his warriors, his grip tightening. Her eyes watered as they laughed.

He had just told them she was a stupid human or a stupid alien. As they didn't have a word for humans when they settled, the word meant the same thing.

She never saw herself as *Immani*, so it infuriated her that these Zandian's did. Despite her eyes watering, which he seemed to find strange and fascinating, she ripped her chin from his hands and spoke in his language. "*Nen,*" she tried to sound tough and firm, but it came across as wispy and rough.

"*Nen?*" he asked, his eyes blinking slowly.

She took that as a surprise because she'd never been near a Zandian, not so close to seeing their eyes. He must not have expected her to know Zandian. It was easy to read humans. She'd watched them her whole life, but not Zandian's. She stayed away when the Horde came.

Her mouth was dry even after wetting her lips. She touched her bottom lip with her tongue, and his black eyes seemed to shift. She hadn't talked to a Horde warrior before, let alone one of their kings.

There wasn't a single person in the colony who had.

She should be showing respect, bobbing down and lowering her head. A respectful greeting to give a Horde king. He should be greeted like that by those who weren't his equals. If she tried to bob down, her legs would turn into jelly, so she kept talking and hoped he wouldn't kill her.

Before she could mention her name, he commanded, "*Vao*," and then one of the warriors jumped down beside him, passing him water.

The Horde king handed it to her, and she drank it gratefully. She was unnerved by the warriors' silence as they watched her drink. When she handed back the flask, the Horde king flipped it over and laughed when he saw it was empty.

Unsure but determined and frightened, most of all frightened, she held his gaze. In a clear voice, she said, "Star."

"Star?" he asked. There was a twitch in his brow, a flat line to his lips that she took as confusion.

"My name," she clarified.

"*Immani* Star, what are you doing out here? Leaving your colony comes with punishment," he said as if she were a child and wasn't aware of the rules.

He called her human Star, and that wasn't a name she wanted to be called by. She was a Zandian.

"*Seya*," she agreed. "I know."

"So, what are you doing here?"

"My *Fathar*," she said, shivering and licking her lips again. She looked beyond the *Guyipe's* and six warriors astride them to the bare, dry dust with nobody around. "I was woken by a thumping sound. I went to check on him, but he was gone. Blood trails led out of the colony."

"You decided to track him yourself?" he laughed, and his warriors joined in. The fact that they laughed at her dad while he was in trouble made her head pound. Usually, she was even-tempered, but this made her angry.

Before she had a chance to think, she raised her hand. She thanked the lucky star she was named after that he caught her hand before she could land a blow. Honesty, she wasn't even sure he was paying attention to her, but now he was.

There was a moment of silence among the warriors. The Horde king held her hand next to his cheek. His eyes moved from her hand to her flushed, angry face. As much as he was trying to figure her out, she was trying to figure him out.

The insult was repeated, "*Sako Immani.*" Her face got hotter. Whether she found her father or not, her life was on the line.

It might have been because she insulted him and the Horde warriors who looked less than impressed by her. By hitting him, it meant that she viewed him as inferior and by association, his Horde.

"Perhaps," she said, watching the warriors twitch again. "Let me go; let me search for my *Fathar*," she requested, wanting to escape this rough, battle-hardened king who looked intrigued by her.

Her goal was to find her father and bring him home safely. Having heard grunts and seeing him disappear so quickly, she feared he had already slipped beyond her grasp.

It was impossible to look away from him when his eyes feasted on her. After holding her hand for a moment, he gently let it go, lowering it slowly, eyes locked on hers. Before she could ask again, he bent down; he knelt in front of her.

She was shocked when he quickly parted her legs. Caught her off guard, she yelled. He slapped her arse, and her eyes widened. She bit her lip at the contact, trying to remain silent, as his hand came down on her arse and stopped her squirming.

Despite his action, his warriors didn't blink; one grunted something in an unknown language and dialect.

She was worried for a moment that the king intended to rip her shift with the sharp nail he trailed along the edge. She relaxed when he only felt the fabric.

There was nothing soft or velvety about her shift. There were no fine fabrics available. She wore a dress made from the fur of a small herbivore who wandered through the colony. The covering was rough but better than nothing, though it felt like sand rubbing against her soft skin.

Upon feeling her legs, he let out an exclamation. Was there something he was trying to find?

When his head disappeared under her shift, his warriors chuckled. She really lost it at that point. She struggled to move away from him, smacking his head and thumping him again when he lifted her shift. As if they had been given a signal, the warriors turned away.

There was no covering below to conceal her. This would never have been done by a man from the colony. The worst part was that it was in full view of others. Flames engulfed her face, and instead of killing her for hitting him, he smacked her arse again with a chuckle, "Fierce *Immani*."

She was in a state of shock; her eyes closed tightly, and her hands clenched. As long as she kept them closed, she could pretend it wasn't happening - Pretend away his hot breath on her most intimate parts. It was a place no one had ever touched or seen before.

His hand left her arse after rubbing it once.

Her muscles tensed under his scrutiny, she kept her hands still when he placed his fingers on her folds. Only a whistle of air and a quick inhalation could be heard from her. Having felt his hold on her chin moments before, she expected him to be just as rough and that; once he was done, there would be bruises. The way he touched her, however, was gentle.

Spreading her folds and circling her entrance with big fingers, she was mortified at being inspected in public.

Her concern about her father had been eclipsed by another concern. While she was untouched, she wouldn't stay that way for long if he did whatever he wanted. A few men did that in the colony and were hanged for rape.

His head lifted from under her shift. He licked his fingers, much to the amusement of his warriors, who heard his actions.

"*Fhok his's nwale*," he stated.

Her mouth dropped open. Several warriors grunted in return, perhaps as an acknowledgment. He said, "Fuck, it's velvet," confusing her since she had felt velvet before and wasn't sure if she had the right fur to feel like velvet.

In a flash, he grabbed her by the waist and sat her on his *Guyipe*. As she held on to handfuls of fur with her fingers, she froze, her thighs clenching tight against the furry beast's sides.

"You ride with me, *Immani* Star."

That word again, *Immani*. There was no room for compromise in his gruff commanding voice. In other words, it was a king's decree. Since she was a human, she was not permitted to say no to him.

"I am Zandian," she told him, just so they were clear.

"*Nen*," he declared, swinging behind her. In spite of the fact that having a male body pressed against her was shocking, she considered this polite after what he just did. Squeaking, she thought, maybe not, as he grabbed her breasts. Then he dragged her against him. It was the hard outline of his cock between her arse cheeks that made her face flare once more. "I have decided I like *Immani*."

It made her feel faint, and instead of confronting him, she thought it would be more productive to find out where the Horde king was taking her. Furthermore, she'd find out how she would be punished for being outside the walls.

"Ride," he commanded. They were flanked by the warriors as he headed away from the outskirts of the colony on his *Guyipe*.

When he got the beast moving faster than she had ever experienced before, her thighs became painfully tight on the *Guyipe*.

"Where are we going?" Star was worried as she looked ahead at the brown trees and the bare outcrops of rock.

"To find your *Fathar, Immani*," he answered.

Honestly, she didn't expect him to believe her or even dare to imagine a Horde king would help her search for a human. There was no sign of surprise among the warriors. After rushing out of her home without thinking about where she was heading, she felt hope for the first time.

If anyone could find her father, it would be a Horde king.

"*Behku*," she thanked him. His arms tightened around her, his fingers tracing circles through her shift. "Your name?"

"Avayu," he said, making her scoff. She knew it meant king, but it wasn't his name. Suddenly, she lost track of what she was thinking as he whispered in her ear, "You can call me *Avaye*."

My king!

Somehow, she didn't think he wanted her to call him "My king" because of his title; it had more to do with power and sex. Those were two areas where he had the advantage in this case.

It was possible to spin the title *Avaye*, which meant my king, in many different ways. *Avayak* meant Horde king and *Avayu* meant simply king. The term *Avayeak* meant my Horde king and was less commonly used.

His eyes moved over the ground as they made their way through the rocky outcrops. The trail he was following appeared to be the same one Star had taken. Her eyes were drawn to a brown tree covered in blood. In the early morning light, it shone starkly. It was evidence that her father had been dragged in this direction.

She let out a small cry. The muscles in his arms tightened minutely. Although she didn't know why he did it, she liked to think it was because he knew she was hurting.

It was one of his warriors who called out to him. His attention turned to that direction as he turned the *Guyipe* they were sitting on. She felt her *Guyipe* brush her legs as they passed, as if it thought Star was leaving her. As the warrior pointed through the trees, she stretched to see over their heads. Her arms suddenly gripped her tightly, bruising her.

Star swallowed hard as a gap opened, and she saw what lay beyond.

There was a party of Jutin. True *Immani*. Alien invaders who come for one purpose only, to take planets, exploit their resources, and move on. Zandar was too powerful for them; they had no luck against the Hordes. The strong bones and might of the Zandians meant the Jutin's thin arms and tough scales were no match for them. Despite that, the Jutin continued to try season after season.

Even though she wanted to know why they took her father, she couldn't ask questions and give them away. Afraid of the Jutin, Star grasped the Horde king's thigh and pushed herself back into his chest. His thighs bracing her no longer felt so demanding or frighteningly overpowering. Now they felt like a promise of safety.

Even though the Horde kings rule the planet with its king, she wasn't truly scared of him yet. She feared that her colony could be destroyed since the Jutin were taking what they called brides from the outer edges of the colony. They were taking what they thought they deserved.

The number of humans were only a few thousand. There was a daily decline in numbers at the outer edges of the colony. In an effort to stop Jutin from grabbing them, humans at the edges had begun moving into the center.

The Jutin wanted brides for only one thing...to pass on genes to the next Jutin. Their science made it possible to eradicate human DNA and use them as vessels. In addition, brides served the Jutin by breeding for them. It was a fate they all hoped to avoid by gathering close.

He was speaking. It took a moment for his words to penetrate. The fear she felt at seeing her father in Jutin's hands and for herself almost drowned out everything else. Then, "...protect you, stay here, *Immani* Star."

Although her lips curled, she nodded her head, ignoring his use of *Immani* because she knew she could not fight a Jutin or even a Horde warrior. She lacked the muscle mass of his warriors. She had no strength like the Horde. It was impossible for her to keep her people safe. Her only tool was her hands, so she made music with them. She didn't fight.

It was surprising how quietly he dropped his *Guyipe*. His giant palm circled her waist, bringing her slowly to the ground. Her body brushed the front of his, and while she might be filled with fear, she enjoyed the press of his body.

His body liked the idea of a fight. His cock was ready for bedding, the outline pushing against his fur. Her mind blanked. She struggled to determine if she was intimidated or impressed by his size.

"Don't *Fhokien* move," he ordered. His casual use of the 'fucking' was a shock. She didn't hear it often. Her mother would clip the men's ears if she did.

The Horde king placed her on top of a rock, lifting her as if she weighed nothing at all. Even though her body was small, she still had curves like the other women in the colony. Having never seen a Zandian woman, Star was unable to compare their similarities.

When he didn't move, she told him, injecting sincerity into her voice, "I won't move." His black eyes remained fixed on hers until he had that promise. With a nod, he stepped forward in front of his warriors, taking the lead.

The shouts of Horde warriors rang through the trees as they approached the Jutin. In surprise, the Jutin holding her father dropped him. Star winced. She saw his eyes flutter and was filled with hope.

Seeing Jutin climb the trees, she grew worried.

Jutin were born to climb their home forests, they were excellent and skilled fighters in the trees. According to the accounts of human elders, their home planet was full of tall trees with little water and one lone river around the equator.

Above the Horde king, long limbs swung back and forth. For some reason, her heart clenched when one managed to cut a line down his arm, but he just grinned.

Mad, he's mad!

He grabbed the Jutin by the throat on his next swing, still grinning. The Jutin's eyes widened, but the Horde king was too fast, and before the Jutin could do anything, his head left his shoulders. Her stomach rolled at the sight. Her arms were wrapped around her knees, and she pulled her feet up under her.

She was surprised by a tickle on her neck, turning away from the warriors decimating the Jutin. She stared into the red eyes of the Jutin devil himself. She was being pulled up by a Jutin that was swinging above her. It was using her hair like she was a fish on a hook and reeling her up.

Hanging ten feet above the earth wasn't so terrible, but as he began to climb higher, panic took hold. Once they reached the treetops, he would be able to get away easily.

In a fit of fear, she yelled "*Avaye*," using the name without hesitation.

Curses began to reach her as the sounds of battle below stopped. A crash through the trees showed her the Horde king standing on the back of his *Guyipe*. As he took hold of Jutin's foot, he balanced without fear.

With a mighty yell, he ripped the Jutin from the tree and with it, her.

As she tumbled down, she expected to land on her head and never get to see her father open his eyes again. She closed her eyes, glad she had at least saved his life. She landed with a mighty oomph. A pair of arms caught her mid-air.

It was one of his warriors.

There must have been a tremendous amount of coordination going on between them. He trusted his warrior to get his *Guyipe* under her and catch her.

As the Horde king dismembered the Jutin above them, a shower of black blood fell. He let out a challenging roar. It was frighteningly intense, something she had never seen or heard before. The Jutin fell in pieces around her, and she felt herself pale, clutching the arms holding her.

In a single motion, the Horde king slid his legs down the side of his beast. He stared at her with black eyes, and this time, she could tell he was unhappy. In favour of fury, he had abandoned the desire to fight and bed someone. Perhaps he didn't like Star seeing this side of him because he turned away with a curse. Suddenly, he changed his mind, storming over to take her away from the warrior

"Get *Immani* Star's *Fathar*," he instructed with a curt head bob.

She could see her father stirring, and from what she could make out, his wound was mostly from the head. As her younger brother visited the healer frequently, she knew head wounds bled a lot. Seeing this, she no longer felt concerned when she saw him try to sit up, despite the fact that his eyes were still closed, and he appeared to be feeling groggy.

'*Fhok*," he muttered as he and his warriors began to return to the human colony.

Star was unable to speak because most of her upper body was still covered in Jutin's blood. There was a thick layer of it in her golden hair, and there must be a fair amount of it covering her right side since it was heavier there.

Blood always made her feel faint, but Jutin's blood decorating her made her stomach turn. She fought to keep the remnants of last night's dinner down because it would be a waste to throw it up.

Star hated violence, which was almost hilarious, considering they lived on a planet where violence was present, inside and outside their gated colony. Her father's moans reassured her, and she hugged herself, trusting that the Horde king would hold her. With her *Fathar* beside her, she was able to let out a few tears quickly, the tension leaving her quickly.

The muscles in her limbs felt almost floppy, her heart was beginning to beat normally, and her hands were still shaking. The Horde king covered her hands with one of his own, enveloping them both. His heat surrounded her and the smell of sweat and *Guyipe* filled her nostrils.

It was not unpleasant.

She was distracted by his whispering in her ear, "Say it again." She looked up to see the colony on the horizon.

"What? I don't understand." She was puzzled. Despite her best efforts, her brain kept recalling bits of Jutin floating around her like petals from a Jillipe flower. Jillipe flowers climb tall to reach the suns. Their dark blue, almost black petals absorbed the heat of the twin suns.

"Say it," he commanded.

Her face flushed as she recalled what she had said last. She frowned, her lips parting. The thought of keeping her mouth shut seriously crossed her mind. Suddenly, she was reminded of his roar and his frightening ability to kill so easily. Her hope wasn't that he would kill her, at least not yet...but she would do as he asked.

"*Avaye*," she whispered, hoping none of the other warriors heard.

She blushed as his arms tightened and his chest vibrated against her. "Again," he commanded, moving his hand under her breasts and over her heart.

"*Avaye*."

He sighed, so he must be satisfied. After that, they continued their journey in peace, his hand over her heart and his other hand guiding the *Guyipe* along with his strong thighs. It felt like her skin became hyper-aware of everything he did, every shift of his legs, how his hand was warmer and rougher than hers. She was attracted to the contrast of his skin, wanting to examine it more closely.

She suddenly felt a strange sensation in her chest, warm and cold at the same time, pushing out of her in a long sigh. His hand became still when her breathing became faster, and his head appeared beside her face. She could have sworn he was looking down at her heaving chest with satisfaction in those black eyes.

"We'll have your *Fathar* settled soon, *Immani* Star," he tried to reassure her with a smile. It didn't look natural on him. He was clearly trying for her benefit. She appreciated it but wondered why he bothered.

It was unnecessary to reassure her. He had done what she never thought any Horde king would do. In the end, he saved her and her father from a terrible fate. It was without a doubt in her mind that she would have turned herself in if her father's release was at stake.

Ultimately, she would have become a Jutin bride and perhaps saved her father, or gotten him killed, or both of them might have been captured. They would have both become casualties of the Jutin - An all too familiar story.

"He's old for an *Immani*, no?"

"He was old when he met my mother. They had us later in life," she told him. It wasn't that unusual in the colony to meet someone older or younger to pair with.

"Us?" he asked, stroking her thigh absentmindedly with his hand. It left a warm tingly feeling in its wake.

"My *Brathar*," she answered, knowing that the Horde warriors consider each warrior their brother once they were accepted into the Horde. "My true *Brathar*," she corrected herself. "My *Mathar* was thirty when she had me, my *Fathar* was approaching fifty, and they had my *Brathar* eight years later," she explained.

"Hmm," he rumbled against the top of her head. She was suddenly stilled by his hand clenching down tightly on her leg. Star had been trying to shuffle around so she could look at him. Grunting, the Horde king gripped her leg almost bruisingly.

One of his warriors spoke, "My cock needs my *bryd*."

His fellow warriors groaned and laughed at him. The Horde king gripped her tighter. For the Horde, bedding and fighting were the norm, so his words might sound crude to Star, but it was the norm to Zandian's.

"Tell me, *Immani* Star, do you have a warrior?"

She replied, "I have none." He grunted again, which could mean anything or nothing at all. With his pure black eyes, it was hard to tell what he was thinking. She still preferred to look into them to try and figure out what he was thinking and feeling.

Just as they reached the colony gate, her father's eyes opened.

"It's okay, *Fathar*," she spoke loudly enough for him to look up at her. For most of the ride, he had been lying across the *Guyipe's* back. After realising she was sitting with a Horde king, his eyebrows drew together and his eyes widened in fright. He swallowed, visibly trembling.

"They do not open the gates, *Immani* Star?" the Horde king growled in her ear. It was hard to contain her shudder, or was that a shiver of delight?

"They are frightened. The Jutin attack our borders often, and I'm covered in blood along with your warriors," she explained carefully.

"It's disrespectful," he pointed out.

"May I go down and speak to them?"

His hand tightened, and his breath shuddered out of him. "*Nen*," he growled in a low and thunderous voice.

Okay, so that's definitely a no.

"Could we ride up to them? They may calm down when they see you're a Horde king." They would let him in, eventually. What worried her was that he was still high on bloodlust from the fight. That much was obvious. It made her hair stand on end when he refused to let her down.

He clicked his tongue, and the *Guyipe* began to approach the gate.

Two human guards stood at the gate. Star only knew one of them. "Simon, I need to come through. I bring news, and my *Fathar* is injured.

The Horde king let out a rumble of warning when Simon stared at him for too long. In an instant, Simon bowed, then stepped back up with a lowered gaze. His hands fumbled with the control for the gate. Sweat gathered on his lips as he struggled to operate the mechanism.

The colonies didn't have much, but once a year, they could buy things from the Zandian market. There were ten representatives from the human colony allowed to attend and carry back everything they could on *Guyipe's* and carts.

For thousands of people, it wasn't enough. Nobody dared to push for more, for fear they would stop allowing it.

After the gate opened fully, she patted his hand in relief without thinking. It caused Simon's eyes to widen and the muscles in his cheek to twitch. Star waved at him, and with that, they headed through the gates.

They arrived at the *Guyipe* barn first.

"It might not be much, but the barn owner will water and feed your *Guyipe* if we leave them here," she offered.

It would require money, but the Horde didn't have any money. She would have to dip into her savings pot she kept at home. In exchange for performing live music, the colony paid her. Depending on what was requested and how long she had to spend, she travelled to different parts of the colony and stayed the night. Having gathered closer together recently had made it easier.

Less travel, less time away from home.

Thank Zandar's God, Satur. It would have been different if she wasn't there. What would have happened to her father? Would he have been killed or worse, maybe used by the Jutin in some way?

Except for one warrior who stayed on his *Guyipe*, the Horde warriors dismounted. Star took the *Guyipe* into the barn. The Horde king crossed his arms and watched her go back and forth, gathering and tying up their *Guyipe*.

Her father sat with his head between his knees. His colour had returned by the time he looked up.

As she kneeled beside him, taking his cold hands in hers and blowing on them, she asked, "*Fathar*?" The Horde king shifted. Her eyes flitted to his, where he was watching her intently.

A smile spread across her father's face. "You have always been such a good girl," he breathed. Suddenly, his eyes rolled back, and she cried out in alarm.

Seeing him on the floor, the Horde king lifted him. Star leapt after him, but he stepped away. He spoke to his warrior quickly.

"*Immani*, where is your home?" asked the warrior. She didn't respond. She was fixated on her father. He shook her. "*Immani*, your home?"

"Yes, yes," she replied, her feet hurrying along the dusty well-travelled road. There was silence, likely because everyone was hiding from the Horde warriors. They hadn't yet realised she had a Horde king with her.

"This way," she instructed.

There wasn't much to the house in the end, but it was one of the better ones. They had four incomes. Hers, her brother, her mother, and her father. Father only gathered now. In recent years, however, he had reduced evening gatherings as he headed toward semi-retirement.

Chapter 2

The door burst open before she could open it. Despite the king's status, a small woman with grey hair and blue eyes ran down two steps to the Horde king. It was her husband's cheek she grabbed. "Gunther," she said fearfully. After receiving no response, she looked up and noticed everyone around her.

Star ducked slightly behind the Horde king. His eyebrows rose, and he glanced down at her with amusement, she thought.

Star's mother did a bob for the Horde king, but when she came back up, her eyes were fixed on Star. Her mother took in the blood covering her, and her mouth thinned.

"Come out from there, child," she commanded. The fact that her mother could still make her feel like a child despite her maturity was beyond comprehension.

As she shuffled her feet, Star began with a very reasonable, "*Mathar*, I can explain."

Her mother's arms crossed, and she pointed at the house. Grimacing, Star did as she was told and saw the Horde kings' eyes follow her every step.

Her mother joined her in their small living area. Apparently, her mother expected the king and a warrior to enter the house because she didn't comment when they followed them in. Instead, she rounded on Star.

Star put her hands up in surrender.

"You will be the death of me. What possessed you?" Star opened her mouth to reply to her mother but... "Nope, no, *nen*, I don't want to know," her mother snapped, her hands hitting her hips. In the next instant, she contradicted herself by saying, "Well, come along and tell me what happened."

Star squinted her eyes at her mother because...ahh.

She caught the Horde king's eyes, and he appeared to be trying not to laugh. Star frowned as his warrior chuckled. He put her father on the flat bench as she exclaimed, "*Mathar*!"

"Don't you *Mathar* me! Now, come on. What possessed you to chase after him with no protection?" she asked again.

While her mother waited for an explanation from Star, the Horde king nodded his head in agreement behind her. Poking her tongue out, she wondered how it had suddenly become her fault and why she felt like she was apologising to him as well?

"I woke up, found him missing, so I took a *Guyipe*..."

"*Nen*," her mother interrupted, looking furious and fearful all at once. "Never mind. I don't want to know."

The whiplash Star was getting from her mother's indecisiveness was giving her a headache.

The warrior laughed aloud this time, and the Horde king slapped him on the head as her mother turned on them with furious eyes. Star almost laughed when the warrior backed up a step. Yes, mothers everywhere always had this control, she thought with amusement.

"What happened to your father?" her mother asked.

Her mother wanted to know but didn't want to hear it from Star. She wasn't even going to try and explain. A burst of air left her, and she pointed at the Horde king, sticking him in it. "He knows, he rescued father."

His smouldering black eyes promised retribution for this sudden turn of events. She shrugged as she escaped into the bedroom she shared with her brother. Each of them had a bed of their own. Many families didn't, so it was a nice luxury.

In preparation for paying the *Guyipe* barn owner, she took money from her pot once the Horde king left. Her father was sitting up and rubbing his head when Star came out.

A furious tirade from her mother was blistering his ears, fuelled by fear of losing them both. It was clear that both the Horde king and his warrior were trying to back away from *Mathar*, obviously not wanting to attract her attention.

"There is something we need to discuss, *Immani* Star," the Horde king told her.

She frowned because she had no idea what he could want. Suddenly, she felt herself sway because she remembered, and it was as if a pit of despair had opened up in her heart. Humans were forbidden to stray outside the gates for whatever reason.

That was about her punishment!

That was what he wanted to discuss. Star nodded her head to let him know she understood.

While still berating her father, her mother snapped, "Not dressed like that." Her *Mathar* was a scary woman, so she nodded.

When she said, "I'm going to change," the Horde king's expression intensified and heated.

She swallowed, hurried back to her room, and grabbed a dress. Having become accustomed to her near nudity around the Horde, she hadn't thought of that. Although her mother noticed the blood, she refrained from saying anything since she was unharmed. After fourteen years of her brother's mishaps, her mother had developed an uncanny ability to know when to worry about spilled blood, which was why her father was still getting a lecture.

She tossed down her shift, grimacing at the thought of everyone who saw her in it on the way back, she grabbed another scratchy dress. Being a day dress, this one fell below her knees, covering her arms completely with a cape and hood. Until she could bathe, she could throw it over her blood-soaked skin for now. It could get unbearably frigid and was meant for the cold seasons. People were even reported to lose limbs if exposed to low temperatures without appropriate clothing. Even in their homes, human leaders recommend cuddling around a fireplace during the winter.

Horde warriors were made for the cold, and their furs were of
high quality. The creatures from which it came had thick fur, unlike
the thin fur of the small creatures from the south. The Hordes traded
and spun clothes all year round with other Hordes and other supplies
the human colony didn't have access to.

She sighed and pushed the cape down as she walked towards
the Horde king. She was prepared to take whatever punishment he
deemed appropriate.

Upon entering the room, he scowled at her clothes. Despite
looking down, Star could not find anything wrong with it. A frown
spread across his face. Biting her lip, she tried to figure out what she
had done to offend him.

Oh right! With her eyes on the floor, she bobbed down once,
then came back up. She figured he wanted a proper greeting.

It was a mistake.

The Horde king walked over, lifted her chin, and chuckled, "It's
a bit late for that, *Immani* Star." He touched the edge of her cloak,
frowning at its texture.

Her mother appeared slightly scandalised, seeing he had touched
her so intimately. If only she knew!

Star had little incentive to admonish him over such a small touch
now, not after he'd been under her shift, inspecting her.

She blushed at the thought.

As he caught sight of it, he muttered under his breath. Then,
stepping outside the front door, he tipped his head in the direction
of Star, who was following him.

His feet led him back to the *Guyipe* barn. She assumed she would
receive her punishment there. Once that was done, goodbye, Horde
king.

It was a shame because she hadn't spoken to a Zandian or even
touched one. There was no way she could forget him looking at

her or touching her in an intimate place that only females had seen before.

"My warrior will send a message to the Horde," he said as they walked.

The dusty streets were still empty, but curious faces peeked through windows and doorways. In the back of her mind, there was a mischievous urge to call out, "Hello," but she controlled the impulse. Keeping her smile hidden, she ducked her head.

"What message?"

"That we need a new *tepay*," he said. He wouldn't meet her gaze with his strange, enthralling black eyes. As they approached the *Guyipe* barn, he looked straight ahead. Her hand slipped into the folds of her dress. Hidden in the fold of her dress was a sack containing money for the barn owner.

She wondered why he needed a new *tepay* and why he was telling her. These were the only homes the Horde had, and they took them with them. The tree trunks that made the frames were strong, like mostly everything on Zandar. The homes were easy to erect, take down, and transport. The covers over the frames were made of thick leather, tied at the bottom to keep the cold out.

She had never seen one before, only heard about them. Unfortunately, she hadn't seen much of her home planet.

When she didn't respond, his mouth dropped. When he turned to the *Guyipe* to murmur to it, she discreetly lifted her hand and put down the pouch of coins.

She jumped when a hand covered hers.

Hearing her squeak, the Horde king froze, turning his head. His eyes flicked to her hand, where his warrior was taking the pouch from her. He frowned at them; his eyes blazed as he focused on the point of contact between their skin.

Her skills in covert work were not particularly strong. Her assessment was that she stunk at it.

"What is this, *Immani* Star?"

Star was becoming less and less irritated by being called human or alien Star. Was it the deep voice he used? It was possible.

Her instincts were to run out of fear because she had added to her punishment.

Her punishment could be hard labour in their Horde. She could be lashed for leaving and worse, for putting a Horde king at risk. The Horde had a right to her punishment. Her thumb was rubbing repeatedly over the fabric of her rough dress as she fiddled and fumbled with the sleeves.

Initially, the Horde king's black eyes appeared to focus on her hands before moving to the warrior's outstretched hand. He took her bag from the warrior and inspected its contents. A blush spread across her face. Mortified, she turned to look at the *Guyipe*, wondering how this day went so wrong and when she might be able to breathe deeply again and bathe. She could feel the hardened blood sticking to her skin.

"What is this?"

Hunching, she shrugged and hoped he would let it go. The warrior growled at her. For a moment, she squeezed her eyes shut. The Horde king didn't berate her. He held his hand up to his warrior and growled. The sound must have had some meaning because his warrior inclined his head and left them alone.

"*Immani*, what is this?" He asked in a stern tone that made her cringe. His hand gripped her chin, once again, handling her.

Wetting her lips, she cleared her throat and held his intense gaze. She felt his fur brush against her stomach. He invaded Star's personal space without caring if she wanted him there.

"The *Guyipe* barn," she said nervously, filling the silence. While she licked her lips, his eyes followed the path of her tongue. When his hold became more demanding, she swallowed hard. Trying to explain, she said, "We have to pay the master."

"But not me," he said, handing the bag back to her. "Where did this silver come from?"

"I play strings," she told him. At the outer edges of his eyebrows, there was no movement, but the middle came down. She took this as genuine surprise or shock, although it was difficult to tell if it was mixed with a sense of delight or not.

The strings were an instrument that fits in her palm with a small, thin piece of wood that was easy to rest on the inside of her thigh or a cushion. Playing was possible by tightening and loosening the strings over a hollow point with her other hand.

Star was sought after for her playing, and she sometimes played when people passed. She was proud to do it. In earth's past, her father told her, music was played through a system that only required a musician to play once, then everyone could access it without the musician. It was impossible for Star to imagine such a thing.

"This is your silver?"

She replied, "Yes." Did he think she had stolen it? She tried to keep any offence she felt from her voice. Apparently, he heard it because he grinned.

"Disrespectful *Immani*," he murmured.

Incredulous, she wondered if this would add to her list of criminal offenses.

He said, "Relax." His eyebrows made the annoyed expression again. She was sure that as more time passed, she would recognise Zandian expressions.

"You can't order someone to relax!"

"I am *Avayak*, and you will do as I say," he said. When she saw his eyes, she found herself standing rigid, for what she really wanted to say was, 'He may be Horde king - *Avayak* - but he was not her king.' But that would be foolish!

She had done enough stupid things today. Keeping out of trouble was something she really needed to work on. If she kept scaring her aging parents like this, they wouldn't last long. To be fair, what else was she supposed to do?

She needed to tone down her thoughts before they tumbled from her and got them in more trouble. Her insubordination could encourage the Horde to plunder, and they could take whatever they wanted.

"Give this silver to your family," he said, placing the little bag back in her hand and closing her fingers over it. His rough palms closed over hers. That strange, hot, cold feeling in her chest made her take a step back.

Maybe she was getting ill. Oh, Satur, if she killed a Zandian with a human illness, a Horde king at that, they would surely kill her whole family.

"I believe I'm getting ill," she whispered faintly. That movement was definitely a frown, she thought, as his hand came up to touch her, but he stepped back.

"Why do you think you are ill?"

"I feel hot and cold. I have goosebumps on my arms and odd fluttering in my stomach."

His eyes widened, and his nostrils flared. The black orbs shadowed by dark lashes lifted in astonishment.

"When do you get hot and cold?"

"When we were on the *Guyipe*, and just now, I'm afraid I might make you ill."

She didn't want to answer to his whole Horde if she killed him because of some human disease that she didn't know about.

His hand touched her cheek as he moved into her. Hot. As they stood there, she felt it again, but this time with a full stomach roll that accompanied it. Taking rapid breaths, she felt her chest heave as she moved away from him.

He smiled at her. "I have the cure for this," he said, his smile fixed firmly in place.

"You do?" He knew what it was! What a relief.

"Yes, but you must come with me to collect it," he said suddenly, breaking her happy mood.

"I cannot," she answered immediately.

"You will," he ordered.

While shaking her head, she stared at him, hoping he would agree it was a bad idea and let her return home. Once again, his gaze roamed her body. She knew where they stopped on her body because an almost tangible touch followed the line of his eyes. The tops of her thighs, her collarbone, her breasts, her waist, and her hips.

"I will speak to your *Fathar*. You are coming with me."

"But...but my life is here," she argued weakly. A Horde would not need someone like Star. "I am needed here," Star replied.

"*Nen*. You will travel back with me," he decided before she could argue more. In a confident voice, he began shouting orders at the Horde warriors.

Her short stride slowed her down as she rushed to catch up with him. He reached her home before she could. Outside, her father waited on the steps, no doubt thinking the Horde king would depart soon. His eyebrows rose when he saw the Horde king coming up the dusty path with her, frantically following, trying to keep pace with him.

He said to the Horde king when he stopped before him, "I have my daughter and you to thank for saving me today."

"I did my duty," he told her father. Standing off to the side, she wondered if she should run. However, the Horde king would find her. The colony wasn't large. If he asked her people, they would show him where she was hiding out of fear of reprisals.

"*Nen*, you could have left me there," he said. His grey gaze shot to Star; the Horde king's eyes followed. "You didn't have to save her."

The Horde king replied, "I didn't save her. She was fine."

"We both know she would have found her way to me and died or worse," her father said. The Horde king inclined his head. "I will take whatever punishment is necessary for both of us."

"*Fathar*!" she objected.

There was a look of consideration on the Horde king's face. Once again, she rubbed at a spot on her sleeves frantically as her breath came faster. Her fear for her father or her mother if he was hurt. Was she going to be silent and let it happen? She wasn't sure, but she didn't think so. She knew some brides strayed, but not *Mathar* and certainly not *Fathar*, their love being well-known throughout the colony.

"*Nen*, she will come to the horde for punishment. I saw her first, so it will be hers to take."

Shocked, her father's eyes flashed. In no way did Star imagine that the Horde king would take her. They both thought their punishments would happen in the colony. Her father's hand fisted. His eyes were filled with a loud 'no,' even though he didn't say it.

The Horde king could come and take whomever he wanted. They had no right to refuse, none. No Horde king had ever demanded her, and no warrior had ever asked for humans.

He explained to her father out of pity, even though he didn't have to. "I won't harm her. While she's a member of the Horde, she has the protection of all the warriors," he said. That made her heart shift a little. A Horde king who could do as he liked was taking the time to reassure her elderly father.

Her father still looked hesitant. "And under my protection," the Horde king added. His tone dared her father to say anything about his protection, and Star's gaze begged him to leave it.

So far, he had been generous. Star didn't want things to go bad if he was taking her. She didn't want her family hurt, and if she refused, she knew her father would fight for her.

"I will go," she announced suddenly, frightened by the silence and the sadness on her father's face.

Her father stood and hugged her tightly.

"*Fathar*," she whispered, her heart aching. "After my punishment is over, I will return." Her father's eyes misted more, and he swore savagely as he returned inside the house.

"Do I have time to say goodbye to my *Brathar*?"

A nod from the Horde king prompted her to rush inside and tell her mother. She was already sobbing in her father's arms. Alarmed at this, she approached her and touched her shoulder. "It's okay, *Mathar*, the punishment is mine to take," she told her with no fear.

At the entrance, the Horde king stood behind her. She could feel his presence.

"You are too young for this," her mother cried.

"*Mathar*," she said, exhausted by this argument. "We've been over this plenty of times." Gripping her shoulders and grinning at her, trying to get a smile to appear, she reminded her what she always told Star. "I am no babe running around my *Mathar*'s skirts with my bum hanging out of my trousers."

A watery chuckle escaped her mother's lips because Star had once run around her and lost her trousers exactly like that. Due to a growth spurt, her waist loosened in the cold season. Therefore, when she ran around her mother's legs, the trousers fell to her ankles, and she tripped. The quiet sound of the Horde king shifting behind them drew her attention.

Suddenly, Star saw hatred in her mother's eyes, which shocked her since she was accustomed to her mother's gentleness. Her eyes were filled with loathing as she stared at him now. Taking her child was obviously a line you did not cross. She looked at Star again, took her hands in her smaller ones, the same long delicate fingers Star had, with the same pale skin. Her father described them as pale as moonlight.

"You will be fine," she said, but it seemed to be directed not at her but at the Horde king. Her gaze constantly drifted over to him. "I know you will be fine because you are my baby and strong." She breathed deeply and reiterated, "You have always been strong."

"Yes, *Mathar*," Star frowned when she refused to let go. The Horde king let out a sharp, trilling sound with a click at the end. The language could be harsh, and it was hard for a human to speak. Since their tongue muscles weren't as flat as Zandian's it could be challenging to copy their sounds. She understood it meant to hurry.

After letting go, her mother ran back to her father, who had her winter fur in a bag.

"She will need nothing from here," the Horde king said, and they froze.

"A drawing then," her mother tried, waiting for permission. She then hurried over to the bag and searched through it for the drawing of her family. Their drawings were done in a substance made from a rock in the West that transferred to the paper they used without rubbing off. "Here," she said triumphantly, tucking it into her hand.

"Thank you, *Mathar*."

"Come," he said, tugging at her dress, his hands fisting at his sides.

Her mother sobbed.

Her eyes pleaded with her father to take her mother out of the room, her heartbreak too much to bear. None of them thought the day would start with her father being taken and Star being punished by the Horde. Despite her desire to be brave, she was trembling inside, filled with fear regarding what the Horde king would do.

Was it his right to administer punishment? Or did the right belong to his Horde? Star still didn't know and was afraid to ask anything. The journey to his horde would be difficult. If she knew her punishment, the journey might be terrible. She figured it was better not to know for now.

"My *Brathar*?" she asked as they descended the steps.

"I have not forgotten, *Immani* Star." Taking her arm, his finger brushed the sleeve of her dress. He muttered under his breath. She frowned, wondering why he kept doing that.

"He shouldn't be far from here."

As she said that, her brother came bounding around the bend. While he rushed to greet her, his thin arms whirled, and his breath burst forth with exuberant glee. He surrounded her with his arms, his fourteen-year-old frame not yet large enough to have muscles. Although he wouldn't be as big as a Zandian, he would grow, and she just hoped she wouldn't be gone too long.

"*Sithar*, where are you off to? I heard rumours you had arrived with the Horde warriors," he said, stepping back to look over her. As her head turned, she expected the Horde king to be behind her, but instead, he was off to the side, giving them some privacy. Her tentative smile warmed his black eyes.

"You heard right," she told him. Then worried he might make things worse with his hot head, she forced a big smile for him, grabbing his hands and squeezing. His eyes strayed to the blood still coating her hair. It looked like the chance to bathe might be a long way off. "*Mathar* and *Fathar* will explain when you get home."

"Explain what?" His eyes flickered to the side, and he stiffened. Crushing his hands with her own, she pulled his eyes back to her. "Why are you with the Horde?" he asked.

"*Brathar*," she whispered softly, her gaze moving over his features. He looked so much like her, and now his young face was filled with confusion and tight with tension.

She frowned at him as she rubbed the spot between his eyes. "You know I wouldn't leave you unless I had to. You know I love you, *Brathar*."

This alarmed him even more. His wiry frame wrapped around Star as he hugged her. "You don't have to leave. Stay." A tear streamed down his cheek as he pleaded with her to stay.

"I will be back soon, *Brathar*," she promised, her voice full of confidence that she didn't actually feel. A strange dynamic always existed between them. Occasionally, Star was a playmate, and sometimes she was an older sibling with parenting responsibilities. Unconsciously, they seemed to understand the delicate balance at play.

Today, she was a much older sibling, and her tone warned him not to voice the fury swimming within. The realisation that she was leaving finally dawned on him.

"What do you mean you'll be back?" he asked, his voice shocked, his blue eyes wide and uncomprehending.

"I made a mistake; I must pay for it."

Clearly and concisely, she outlined everything that had happened. When she told him about the Jutin, his unhappy features darkened. "Surely he will let you go now that he knows you didn't do anything wrong?" he pleaded desperately, his eyes flinching as they took in the blood. "Your hair is stained with blood. The terror of the attack must have been punishment enough."

"You know the consequences of not doing as we're supposed to. It's not up to me to bargain."

"This is bullshit!" he cried out. In panic, she turned her gaze towards the Horde king. He was watching their exchange with narrowed eyes. "Please, what if you don't come back?"

"*Brathar*," she breathed out, bringing her hand up to touch his unruly golden locks like hers. Out of the corner of her eye, she noticed the Horde king shifting uncomfortably. There was no escaping the black gaze of the Horde king.

"*Teyae*," her brother pleaded in Zandian.

As if to signal her, the Horde king stood tall. As she exhaled, she was trying to conceal her panic and prevent her brother from getting himself killed. If he thought she was uneasy about returning with the Horde king, he would react.

She didn't want to go anywhere with a man who inspected her. A blush tried to rise. She fought hard to keep it from showing on her face.

"You have to accept this, Black." She rose quickly before leaving, sneaking a kiss on his cheek.

"*Sithar*," he called as she turned away from him, tears in her eyes. As the Horde king approached, she kept her head down.

Strong! Ha, she thought with sadness. She didn't feel strong; her mother was wrong.

When her brother called after her, and some workers stopped him from running after the Horde king, her strength left her. Most likely, her brother would try to tackle the Horde king and do something incredibly stupid.

The Horde kings attention must have been drawn to her sniffles because he stopped between two homes. The gap between them was barely wide enough for a person to walk through.

Her body was engulfed in a hug as he pulled her into the space. The sobs came quickly, and when he swore, it confused her. "*Fhok*."

He pulled back and tilted her head, his eyes searching her tear-stained face. For a moment, he seemed fascinated by the salty tear trails. Watching her shoulders shake with the weight of sadness, a frown appeared on his face. Then when a sob burst free again, he dipped his head down to capture the sound.

At first, she froze as his lips landed on hers. There was something strange about the sensation. She'd only kissed one man, and he wasn't as intense as the Horde king.

She didn't know why she thought his lips would be hard and unmoving, probably because he had a big, solid, and firm Zandian body.

He rubbed his tongue over her lips. She gasped in surprise when he touched her tongue. He must have seen that as an opportunity because the next thing she knew, his tongue was in her mouth. He pulled her against him and up his body with his strong hands.

Her tongue moved against his after some gentle coaxing on his part, and that seemed to energise him.

He gripped her thighs and twisted them around his waist. His cock was firmly pressed against her stomach, the feel of it ignited a strange heat within her, and she found herself not giving a damn who came upon them.

She inhaled sharply when her hands landed on his chest.

Finished kissing her, he pulled back to check her eyes. She felt dazed and couldn't think straight. Maybe he was looking for more tears. She was melting into a puddle, and something had taken over her body. She had never acted that way before.

She never expected him to kiss her. It was the first time she kissed someone like that using her whole body. The experience was strange but exciting. As he dropped her to the floor, her eyelids fluttered. She wondered if that was why everyone her age was looking for a bride or bed partner because of what she felt from a simple kiss from him.

She'd never done it before, never thought of sleeping with anyone but her husband. However, she suddenly thought it was a sound idea because the feeling of wanting wasn't going away.

The Horde king looked as baffled as she was about the kiss. A grimace spread across his face as he adjusted his cock.

Ducking her head, thinking the blush and tear tracks were unattractive. She's never been called beautiful, and perhaps she was even less so to him.

There were a lot of noticeable differences between them, like her flatter eyebrows, thicker tongue, dull nails, rounded ears, and pale skin, then, there's her hair. Zandian's had only two true colours, black or the shiniest dark brown. Star's golden colour screamed different right away. Her fair skin and small body screamed delicate, especially when she was around their huge bodies. Zandian females could be different than humans for all she knew, but her hourglass figure was ideal for humans.

She wasn't sure if she wanted him to find her attractive.

Was he just kissing her because he wanted to stop her crying?

It didn't matter that his cock was hard because he was the Horde king, virile, vigorous, and potent. Their exploits were well known in the colony, and women gossiped about the stamina of *Avayak's*. The stories about the women they bed, the fights they won, and they always won were like a legend come true.

There were several Horde warriors sitting on their *Guyipe's*, ready to go. In the space of one very early morning, her life had changed dramatically. It wouldn't be possible to go out and play the strings to mark birth dates. No evenings spent in homes entertaining husbands and brides as they danced.

As she tried to shake off the depressing thought, the Horde king, whose name she would have to find out, hauled her up on his *Guyipe*. He ignored the frowning *Guyipe* master, who seemed less than pleased to have fed and watered their *Guyipe's* for nothing, even though he must.

A Horde warrior growled something out, and the gates opened. There was muttering in the distance, people coming out of their homes to see Star disappear with the Horde. What would they think when they heard it was a Horde king that walked through the colony?

Punishment was coming her way.

Her thighs clenched on the *Guyipe*, and the Horde king wrapped an arm around her waist. His hot breath fell on her face as he clicked to get them moving. "*Radac*," his shouted order to ride sent the *Guyipe's* sprinting across the dusty plains.

Chapter 3

His warriors kept pace with him. Occasionally, they glanced over. Whether it was because she was being so quiet or because the Horde king had not yet released her, she didn't know.

"Two days ride," he grunted suddenly. She felt his finger brush against her breasts. It might have been an accident, but she doubted it. He seemed to take it for granted that he could touch her wherever he liked. Perhaps he was like this with all women.

"Two days ride?"

"To the Horde," he responded. Her small form bounced a few times due to the beast's speed, causing her to smack into him. His thighs bunched up under her as she landed on him again. In spite of the fact that it was an accident, she was still concerned she'd bruise him, and he'd be annoyed with her.

"I have never ridden for more than a few hours," she replied, wondering if she would fall asleep and how she would avoid falling.

She was almost deafened by his grunt and sharp whistle as he called his warriors close. "We will stop for the night," he said to the Horde.

"*Avaye?*" The warrior who found her bag of coins asked, his tone clearly indicating his surprise.

"We will stop tonight and tomorrow," he said, adding the tomorrow with a frown.

The warrior looked at her, and she met his gaze, wondering what he saw as he scrutinised her with those dark eyes.

"*Seya Avaye,*" he agreed. A frown appeared on his face as his eyes fell upon the Horde king's hand, still holding her tightly to him.

After the warrior fell back with the others, she pondered why the Horde king had stopped.

Because she had never ridden such a long distance for so long, the Horde king ordered them to rest for two nights. She assumed that was why they stopped, which was quite sweet, but she would never say so to such a big warrior. The word 'sweet' probably wasn't used to describe him by his people.

"Three days," he corrected quietly, and a nervous chuckle rose in her throat.

His hand moved up to circle her neck.

He emitted a rumble of sound as she swallowed hard. As he stroked her throat, he made long, smooth lines with his thumb.

The exhaustion of the day, combined with the constant rocking and soothing motion of the *Guyipe*, put her to sleep. The next time she awoke, the Horde king had her cradled on his lap. She didn't wake up when he moved her, so he must have moved her carefully.

As she saw him staring down at her, her eyebrows lifted in question. She was startled for a moment by his black eyes before she fully awoke and remembered everything. Groaning, she hoped she didn't do anything embarrassing like snore or talk during the night. He was looking so intently at her that she was unsure what to do with herself.

"We're stopping for the night," he told her, his voice low as his warriors set up a makeshift camp around the small grouping of abhor trees. The black abhor trees differed from the Silvay trees' brown trunks that grew near the human colony. There was an abundance of yellow fruit on the abhor trees during the summer months.

Star nodded and prepared to slide off the *Guyipe,* so he could get down. With no time to react, he leapt off the *Guyipe* with her in his arms as if she were no weight. Her eyebrows were twitching when she saw how smoothly he landed.

"Eat, then rest," he ordered.

She tightened her lips because she wanted to snap back at him for ordering her around. Her father and husband were the only men she had to listen to. That thought made her grimace; if she ever found a husband.

It was like he could feel her displeasure before he began to turn. Huffing, she thought she saw an eye roll behind his lids as he tilted his head, glancing over at his warriors to ensure they weren't looking at him when he asked quietly, "What is it?"

"Do you have some water to wash off the blood?" Her mouth dried out as she touched her thick, bloody hair. Jutin blood on one side must have left the gold strands almost completely black. There was an overwhelming need to wash it off. She couldn't bear to sleep with it in her hair or spend another two days with it like that or for however long their journey would last.

Her stomach revolted, twisting and turning. She felt pale, and he swore as her legs trembled. Perhaps the stress of the day and the fact that she hadn't eaten yet all combined to make her feel weak.

He lifted her before she could move, saying, "Come." Much to his warriors' surprise, he stalked through the trees with her in his arms. A glance was exchanged before they shrugged and talked among themselves.

Using his shoulder, he drove through a thicket of bushes bunched together, holding her close to his body and shielding her head with his body. A satisfying sound escaped his mouth, and she looked up.

"Oh!"

As she took in the Butar river, he put her down. Her colony was surrounded by small streams, but nothing as wide as this. There were rumours that one of her colony members swam upstream and discovered a large body of water on the other side, but they weren't allowed to enter. The area was off-limits because it was outside the colony's boundaries.

Bathing was usually done once a week. Everyone in the family worked to get water from the small running streams and heat it. The wait was always worth it, especially for her father and brother after working all week. The Horde king didn't seem to realise how enjoyable it was for her to see so much water. She was amazed by the width of the river, and it was the deepest cerulean blue she had ever seen.

Water gently rippled under the glistening white rays of the fading suns.

Taking off her shoes, she strode to the edge and dipped her toe into the water without waiting for his permission. She squealed at the cold and pulled her foot away, frowning. She had thought for sure it would be warmer.

How disappointing.

It was then that she noticed the Horde king staring at her. Her cheeks began to glow with colour. As she backed away from the edge, she fiddled with her dress. "I can wait," she said firmly.

A sharp frown crossed his eyebrows, and she knew immediately that his answer would be no.

"In," he ordered.

It brought on a flush of embarrassment to see him just standing there. Did he expect her to bathe in front of him? Surely, he didn't expect her to get naked while he watched?

The corners of his mouth turned down. She rubbed her arms, the chill of the night suddenly hitting her.

In spite of her initial excitement, she couldn't swim, so she looked at the river with apprehension. The longer she stared at the water, the less exciting it seemed. The water was cold, probably deep, and she had no way of keeping herself safe.

She blurted out, "I can't swim."

In surprise, his eyebrows shot up and to the side. Gritting his teeth, he glared at the water, a sound of discontent and annoyance rising in his throat.

Taking off both weapons and scabbards, he began to mutter under his breath. "*Immani* Star, she can't swim. What happens next?

The *Avayak* jumps in the river," he growled as if she weren't listening to everything he said.

A smile appeared on his face and before she could comprehend what he was doing, he began untying his furs.

Seeing the hint of tanned hipbones, she slammed her eyes shut. His huff of laughter teased her. Moments later, there was a thud, followed by splashing as he entered the water.

Shivering, with one eye opening just in time to catch a perfectly rounded muscular bottom disappearing into the water. Suddenly, her heartbeat accelerated, and her breathing became choppy, which was made worse because he was completely naked when he turned around. Even though she couldn't see anything, she still squirmed when he beckoned her in.

"*Omeya*," his order to 'come' didn't get her feet moving at all. It was as if they were frozen in place. Her toes were still chilled from her quick dip a moment earlier. It was easy for her to see he was focused on her. His black eyes were too intense to disregard.

The idea of going into the river with him naked was something she shouldn't do. Since she started bleeding, it had been drilled into her. Mother would berate her for not being careful enough, but she wasn't as repulsed as she thought she would be by being naked and vulnerable around the Horde king.

No man had ever seen her naked, but he had already looked, so what could be more embarrassing? In spite of this, she tried to plead with him, "*Teyae* turn,"

Whether it was the blushing or the word please, he turned in the river and gave her his back.

She removed her cape and dress, hoping none of the warriors would dare come this way. Not that they would. Unless there was an attack, and even then, the Horde cry would be heard before the warriors could get to them.

When she saw the suns last rays slipping below the horizon, she exhaled briskly. Despite the cold, she walked straight in up to her knees, regretting her request to wash her hair when she shivered.

The water hit between her legs, and all the air in her lungs escaped in a rush, with her shivering intensely. She was shaking like a leaf as he turned at the sound of her panting breaths.

Squeaking in alarm, she dived under the water, crouching, so the water covered her breasts.

The moment she did it, her body shook even more. A high-pitched and sharp sound came from her throat that she had never heard before - Fear and startlement mixed.

Seeing her huddled in a ball in the water, he frowned. When she couldn't handle it any longer, she shot up, much to the Horde king's amusement. A dark chuckle escaped him.

She noticed him eyeing her breasts as she huddled her arms around her tiny waist and hated thought of dipping her head under. Since the cold air had already made her nipples peak, the pink discs pebbled right away when they hit the water. Everything was on display, so he could scan her from top to bottom. In the end, they lingered the longest on her nipples.

Then he stalked forward.

Her fear of what the water would reveal led her to meet him halfway. The water barely reached his waist while it reached above her ribs. There was a tantalising glimpse of hardness below that she couldn't help but peep at.

He surrounded her with arms. There was a moment of panic where she worried about what he was going to do. She dismissed her fear since he could take her whenever he wanted.

In the water, he spun her back to his front, and she gripped him tight, worried about how deep he was going. As her feet rose from the wet sand below, her grip got claw-like. Grunting, he strode deeper into the water, only stopping when it reached his neck.

He tried tilting her head, but her grip got tighter. It was tighter than he expected because he cursed.

"Let go, *Immani*. How am I supposed to wash your hair if you won't tilt your head?" His question had her stilling. She instinctively tried to wrap her arms around his neck out of fear, but now she stopped.

"Tilt your head to the water, I won't let go," he reassured her as her head slowly sank into the water. His eyes met hers, and he tutted when he saw her looking at him. "I promise, I will keep you safe," he continued.

Closing her eyes, she trusted he wouldn't drown her after saving her from a Jutin. The Horde king then washed her like a babe; rubbing her hair with his hands and taking his time to get rid of the blood. Her head started aching, pins and needles tingling along her scalp.

"Cold?" he asked.

She shivered and answered, "Hmmhm." He ran his hands through her hair one last time. Keeping his gaze on her for a moment, he helped her tread water.

His hands roamed her body. She was far too cold to try and stop him. Her only thought was the bone-chilling cold, the way her body shivered even as she tried to stop it. Had she wished to swim in the water? Never again.

He had gritty hands from lifting sand from the bottom of the lake. The sand quickly swept over her body. She thought he was trying to get her out faster. She'd have pink skin, but it'd be clean.

Stuttering from the cold, she asked, "You...your name?"

She was being carried out of the lake by him. She wasn't bothered by her nudity. She could only think of the blessed heat of his body. His body remained warm even after a freezing dip in the lake. The shivering lasted longer than he liked, so he dried her off with his furs to her strangled exclamation.

He stopped between her legs. He flinched, clenched his jaw, then swore and quickly put her dress back on, looking away from her.

"You want my name?"

"*Seya,*" she replied.

"Will it stop you from shivering if I give it to you?" he asked as he put on his fur. She was sitting on a flat cream rock, her form huddled. She tried to nod, but the shivers kept her from doing so.

"I...I will t...try." She hoped to say it slowly enough, so it came out steady because she wanted to know his name. He had been more intimate with her than some humans she had known all her life, so calling him Horde king wasn't enough.

The unsteadiness of her voice didn't seem to convince him, as he murmured, "Mm."

As the twin suns dipped below the horizon, the only thing that remained was a bright ray that illuminated the sky. Soon it would be dark, and she wasn't looking forward to lying on the cold ground and attempting to sleep in the dark.

"Hadak," he suddenly said out of the blue. In an instant, her head shot back up. He was scanning the trees for danger instead of looking at her. "*Maye trokko.*"

His name was... "Hadak," she said with only a faint trembling.

There was a slight stiffening of his body before he inclined his head. In response to her whispering his name, he replied, "Only in private."

Star nodded her head in agreement with that. He helped her get up off the floor, which only increased her shaking. Taking her back to the warriors, he guided her in the right direction.

Despite not being able to see the fire, she could feel its heat. As she saw the flames in front of her, she uttered a desperate cry under her breath. Upon entering the space, the first thing she did when she entered was going straight to the fire to warm herself up. She didn't care about who was watching her or whether or not it was the right thing to do she stole a place beside the fire.

Taking a deep breath, her relieved moan made the nearest warrior's eyes widen.

His warrior spoke the language she had heard them speak before, a roll of s's and harsh words that were rough and from the back of the throat.

"*Huysis ryss roth wuss ims*," he said while adjusting his furs. *

It was the first time she had heard any sounds like it, and she could imagine how difficult it would be for humans to imitate these sounds. It was easy for them to roll the sounds off their flat tongues because of the difference in shape.

A flash of light flashed in the warrior's eyes as he looked at her. From the way he was looking at her, she had the distinct feeling that they were discussing her in particular. It was difficult with their black eyes to tell what they were thinking, but she was pretty sure it wasn't love and warm hugs type of look.

"*Huysis ryss siss ryns*," Hadak snarled from beside her, making her jump. **

A grunt accompanied the warrior's agreement, and his eyes moved away from her. With no doubt in her mind, she knew that whatever they were saying involved her.

She wasn't vain enough to think they thought she was beautiful or that they thought she had anything special about her. They were probably comparing her to the females of the horde. It would be interesting to see what they looked like. She wondered if their females were similar to the males or if they looked more delicate like human females.

Jutins were difficult to distinguish between the sexes, so she didn't bother to try. In the females, the colour of the body only changed to a very slight degree when it was time for mating. It was the only time when anyone would be able to tell which of the two was which.

It was possible that the female Zandian's look the same as the males, or they could be completely different.

"What is the language?" she asked Hadak. There was a moment of silence over the flames when she noticed the warrior stopped sharpening his blade. An additional warrior was in the process of tying up something over the tree when he stopped.

"It's not Zandian?" she asked.

During the long period of silence that followed, nobody answered, making her cheeks burn with discomfort. While they were silent, she was filled with embarrassment as she sat there; a feeling of complete loneliness overtook her.

Would no one talk to her once they were in the Horde? Was there some reason they all stared at her as if she was...well, from another planet? As far as she knew, that was how they saw her. As *Immani*. What a depressing thought.

Hadak grunted a sound as he looked around, and the warriors returned to their business. In front of the fire, the Horde kind sat down. "It's a variation of Zandian from our home range."

"There's more than one language?" she asked. The fact that more than one language was spoken in Zandian wasn't unusual because when the first humans settled on Zandian, they spoke four different languages. She just hadn't heard it before or heard that there was more than one language spoken on Zandar.

In the end, humans lost their languages and only spoke one common tongue among themselves. A few humans caught some Zandian words from time to time, and they began to incorporate them into their day-to-day lives in the colony. In the end, they pieced together the language with help from a book in Zandian which they acquired at the market to help them understand the language.

"Only two," he said. "Zandian and Zande, Zandian is our common language that is spoken by the majority of Zandians. Zande is a dying language," Hadak said, a tight line to his mouth as he spoke.

"Oh!" There wasn't much else she could say to that, and they didn't seem to want to talk about it, so she kept any further questions to herself. It was evident that her curiosity wasn't appreciated by them.

As the food was passed around, she joined in with the eating, but only when she received a bite from Hadak, otherwise, they didn't hand her anything. She never assumed that any of it was meant for her at all, so she was grateful Hadak shared..

There was a time when Hadak nudged her leg with a bit of braised meat that he was holding on to. With a gentle smile on her face, she took it from his hand. As she took the piece of meat and chewed it, his eyes followed the way her mouth moved.

"It's good," she complimented Hadak, wondering at the intensity behind his eyes as he studied her. She heard him grunt as he finished the piece he was chewing on. As soon as he became aware that she was shivering again, he ground his teeth together and pointed to the spot beside him.

There was no doubt in her mind what he meant.

She hesitated for a moment. He let out a growl, and she found herself suddenly being picked up and placed in front of him. His legs bracketed her, she was in the cradle of his thighs and could no longer move. She found herself caged but so unbelievably warm.

Having a blazing fire in front of her and being surrounded by the warmth of his skin behind her had a lulling, drugging effect on her. However, she remained rigid.

"Relax, *Immani* Star, I won't bite you," he grumbled to her, his chest vibrated beneath her, moving her as he spoke. She began to notice that her hair was starting to dry out. She felt deliciously warm, her belly was full, her body was clean, and inevitably, she relaxed.

Lethargic, she lay in his arms as he held her, not caring that his warriors could see him holding her tenderly.

A whistling tune escaped Hadak's lips. It was a tune she'd never heard before. He might have done it because he knew she'd miss music. In this strange new place she found herself in, maybe he was trying to comfort her.

His fingers ran lightly through her golden tresses just once. At least, she thought she felt his touch before she closed her eyes.

It was laughter that woke her up, her eyes blinking rapidly.

With bleary eyes, she saw the dying embers of the flames and the warriors standing guard. It wouldn't be long before the other sun rose. Within an hour, they would have the light of two suns.

When she started getting up, the arms around her tightened.

It was noticeable how prominent, and firm the bulge was against her hip. Through Hadak's fur, his groan of contentment and the way he hugged her tightly made her think he might be dreaming he was back in his bed with one of his females.

No one sounded that content waking up unless they were used to waking up beside someone.

She grumbled at the thought that he thought she might be someone else. She totally wasn't paying attention to the weird spurt of jealousy that gripped her. That wasn't happening. She couldn't be jealous of a Horde king's affection, could she?

His affection might never be hers, and she wouldn't give him hers.

The only reason he held her was... well, she didn't know why.

After shaking off her errant thoughts, she turned her head to see one black eye open.

"Not yet, Star," he whispered.

Taking a deep breath, she swallowed. He called her Star for the first time. Not *Immani* or *Immani* Star.

She didn't know what they were waiting for, but she stayed with him as his warriors left the area. Horde warriors that understood what he wanted without him saying anything.

"Why are we staying behind?" He let her sit up but gripped her chin with firm fingers. Her eyes narrowed at his arrogance. Whenever she moved, his eyes followed her. His hand held her and made her face him. She couldn't even turn away from him if she tried. There was no comparison between their strength.

"*His's nwale*," he whispered. She had no idea what he was calling velvet.

Star began to speak but was caught off guard by his next action. He swooped in and kissed her, his tongue touching hers again in what could only be described as their mouths mating.

There was no stopping his hands. He stroked a sensitive spot behind her ear and pressed his body heavily into hers. The sound that came from her was partly a moan of surrender and partly a groan of confusion.

He stopped, opened his black eyes, and grabbed her bottom lip with his thumb. He looked at her lips again, his eyes soft. "*Nwale*," he whispered again. His mouth collided with hers and his thumb pressed against the corner of her mouth.

Honestly, it felt like he had more control than just holding her chin.

It was like he was taking possession of her pleasure. Like he controlled it. Her excitement was heightened by his.

Although she was inexperienced, she had seen men rut, okay, not men but teenagers. In the colony, horny teenagers had to find places to have fun without their mothers smacking them over the head, so they had their fun publicly, behind houses or in bushes. It always seemed painful and a lot of effort for little reward.

The feeling he coaxed out of her made her remember the path in the colony she wasn't supposed to take. She'd disobeyed and wandered down there, and the sounds coming from the red door weren't ones of fright. It was then that she understood that there were whores in the colony who enjoyed the sport of lovemaking.

She knew she would enjoy it with Hadak. She just knew.

The whores weren't looked down upon. If they weren't happy, some husbands sent their wives for instruction. It always made her cheeks blaze at the prospect of going to the red door and talking intimacies, having to ask questions.

There was no need to ask those questions because if Hadak made her feel this uninhibited, perhaps she could have easily made a living as a whore. The strange, absurd thought was lost as he pulled her onto his lap.

She parted her knees over his thighs. Most of her weight was on his left thigh. His hand brushed over her arse, pulling her close, and her throbbing center fell onto his big thigh.

Her response was immediate. She slumped forward and moaned loudly. It was needy and raw at once, such a wanton sound.

"*Fhok*," his furious curse was as heated as she felt.

He grabbed her hair and brought her face up to see her eyes. The little pants that came from her lips were unattractive, but they seemed to please him. As he took her mouth in another punishing kiss, his hands tightened around her back, keeping her immobile.

"There's no time, we have to leave," he said without changing his tone. The flush of pleasure quickly faded as she frowned.

She had gotten lost in the moment, yet it seemed he could stop just like that.

It was easy to feel his hardness, his tense muscles. There was obviously something between them and she wasn't so naive as to think he didn't feel it.

When he stopped and looked like he was ready to pack up and leave, she thought that maybe he only wanted her because she was available; It was embarrassing for her.

He'd probably return to his wife or partner when they returned to the Horde.

She felt a little let down by the first genuine sexual experience she'd had because she wasn't counting the kiss he used as a distraction when she was in the colony. It wasn't a fairy tale, just like the old tales her dad used to tell. It was more of a horror story, and she should remember that.

Maybe he wanted to pass her around to his warriors. Engrossed in her own head, she hadn't even thought about the consequences.

"What is that face?" he asked.

Feeling blank and empty, she didn't know what to do. She shrugged and moved away from him.

"Tell me," he demanded, and this time, it sounded authoritative. The Horde king was speaking.

"I'm worried about what's going to happen," she said honestly.

He didn't seem satisfied with that. His tongue clicked with a flat sound sharp with displeasure. "Nothing so bad, *Immani* Star."

And...they were back to *Immani* again.

Whatever that moment was, it was obviously an experiment for him. As for her, she really did not feel like being used again, so she was hoping that he got what he wanted from her.

There was only one thing she wanted to know, and that was what her punishment would be; she didn't want to get involved in anything else. Having brief moments of pleasure and then going home, to find a husband she would have no feelings for. No, no way. Better to be ignorant.

"We ride hard today. Will you be okay?"

"I can handle it," she answered with strength.

It wasn't so bad yesterday, with Hadak holding her on when the pace became too rough for her to handle. By holding her like that, he was able to prevent her from falling flat on her face and being trampled by a *Guyipe*. If she had been on her own, she had no doubt she would have been under it being stomped on repeatedly as it barrelled over her.

"I think there is a lot you will have to handle, *Immani* Star. Some you'll like, some you won't," he added with a shrug.

There was a shift in his muscles as he made to move. Tempting, yes, his body seemed tempting now.

If she could just drown out the voice that told her, 'she liked his body very much' and ignore it, then, she would be fine. If she could just shut her eyes for a moment and not see him, then she would be fine.

The moment they reached the *Guyipe*, he swung up and reached for her, grabbing her under her arms. Holding her hands up to grasp his arm, he swung her over onto his lap. It caused her eyebrows to wrinkle. She was confused because he wasn't making her ride astride with him.

"This is my first, Furan," he introduced as he pointed at the warrior who had been sharpening his sword the night before. It appeared that he disliked her presence. Furan leaned in to greet her. He touched his ear to his shoulder, a traditional greeting.

She did the same, hoping that if she followed their customs, he might warm up to her, no matter how short the time she spent with their Horde. There was no way she wanted a sword-wielding warrior scowling at her all the time.

Due to the angle at which Hadak was holding her, she found it difficult to reach her ear to her shoulder. However, she didn't do a terrible job of it, or at least didn't completely make a mess out of it and screw it up.

After a squeeze, she found herself looking at Hadak in question. In response to her gaze, his lips twitched as he looked at her. "In the Horde, he will protect you. He is the person I have the most confidence in with my life, do you understand?"

"Yes," she replied, nodding.

"He's my first because he, above all others, has my loyalty. It would be easy for me to trust him to handle the Horde if I had to be elsewhere. He has proven himself over and over," he said with absolute faith, exchanging a grin with Furan. "It is now his responsibility to keep you as safe as he would me."

"Am I in some kind of danger?"

"The Horde is difficult," he muttered, glancing at Furan with a frown as if he was unsure how to explain it. His grimace deepened. "You will see, they are not as soft as your colony."

His assumption that they didn't have violent humans and criminals was incorrect, and most of the time, their leaders dealt with them immediately. She didn't think for even a minute that either of the strong Zandians would let criminals prosper in the Horde.

"I don't understand?"

"*Immani* Star, I don't think I can explain it, but you should not fear unprovoked attacks," he said. In agreement, Furan nodded.

An unprovoked attack! What in the blazes did that mean?

Now, she was hyperventilating over saying the wrong thing and getting lashed. A look that could offend someone and result in her being beaten. She should have spoken up and asked what she might do that would be wrong, but she was engulfed in fear. Surely, they would have told her if she had made any mistakes when talking with them.

If Hadak saw anything she was doing that was offensive, she had every confidence that she would be told.

"The Horde, will they be..." It seemed silly to ask if they would be surprised by her. It was inevitable that they would be.

He moved his hand under her outer thigh. His fingers skinned under her dress as he stroked her skin. The way he touched her made her feel like he thought he was entitled to do so. There was even a moment when he seemed to forget he was doing it. He gazed at the horizon, the dust plains, and the scattered trees. His hand touched her skin all the time as if it belonged there. It felt natural.

"The Horde," he told her, his eyes seeming to roll for a moment before hardening. "The Horde will do as their *Avayak* tells them."

Her eyebrows twitched at that, and it caught his attention. "They do as their Avayak tells them." With a wide smile transforming his face from handsome to stunning. "Always," he added.

It was evident that he had a sense of humour and was joking with her. Despite the fact that he wasn't human, she appreciated why women in his Horde would want him. Additionally, she understood why they wanted his warriors too; each had a strong and handsome look. Each was designed to defend and protect the Horde.

There was something special about being a member of the Horde.

*Her cunt would warm me
**Her cunt is mine

Chapter 4

The day and night passed without incident. After lying down, she fell asleep instantly. Her sore body was unused to traveling for hours on *Guyipe*. She was awoken by Hadak, and they were heading out the next morning.

Getting to his horde didn't take long.

"Don't speak when we approach," Hadak said in a tone at odds with what she had been getting used to around him.

Her teeth clenched immediately. "Why?"

He grunted, and she got no response. After a while, the outline of *tepay's* became visible. She felt her skin becoming clammy. She felt nervous at the thought of riding into the Horde for the first time, something no human had ever done before. Before that very moment, it didn't seem real, as if she had pushed it to the back of her mind.

"No talking," he grunted again, throwing her leg over the side of the *Guyipe* as he shifted her on his lap. His eyes were as hard as the lines on his body. There was tension running through him, making her wonder what she would be getting into.

Her gaze was drawn to his warriors. It didn't seem to surprise them that he asked for silence. Furan felt her eyes on him, he glanced at her, his black eyes narrowed, slightly different from Hadak's. He nodded. It could be a nod of reassurance, or it could be a nod of agreement with his *Avayak*. Deciding to take it as both, she kept her lips pressed in a firm line.

As she surveyed the rough perimeter with his Horde warriors positioned about his Horde, she couldn't help but wonder why he was so tense. Keeping her hands fisted, her instinct was to run fast.

As if to reassure her, Hadak touched her hand, but all she saw when she looked up was his sharp jawline.

"*Avayak*," a warrior called as they drew closer. There was a similarity between his face and those around Star. Nevertheless, she had begun to observe slight differences in their features and facial expressions.

"How are things with the Horde?"

"We had riders from the *Avayu*," He looked up at her and widened his eyes, stopping for a moment as if uncertain if he could speak freely. When she felt Hadak nod behind her, he continued, "It is time for the Hordes to come together and speak of the Jutin's threat."

Behind her, Hadak stiffened.

"He wants the *Avayak*'s to gather by the end of the season to share their information," he said, his lips drawn back in offense. "He accuses us of not sharing information."

An annoyance-filled hiss escaped Hadak as he tutted. "He claims we have made the problem worse."

As he shrugged, the warrior said, "He didn't say it outright, but he said the problem had gotten worse because..." He paused awkwardly and clicked his tongue.

"What does the *Avayu* say?" Hadak asked with a harsh tone, leaving no doubt in her mind that whoever the *Avayu* was - she suspected it was the king in the east - he was going to piss off all the Horde kings.

He shifted his shoulder in a rolling motion, saying, "Negligence."

The stiff lines of Hadak's body suddenly became rigid as he hissed. "Negligence," he muttered. He nodded at the warrior in thanks. "*Radac*," he urged the *Guyipe*. As soon as the order to ride was given, the beast jolted into action. He guided the *Guyipe* between *tepay's* until at last he came to a pen. In contrast to the human colony's *Guyipe* barn, this had an open area with a shelter in one corner, which could easily be removed by the Horde when they departed.

As he jumped off his *Guyipe*, he was still rigid with tension. The furious look in his eyes made her catch her breath as he dragged her down. After releasing her, he ordered the *Guyipe* master to provide food and water for them. Turning away from her, he gathered his sword from the back of his *Guyipe* before it was taken.

She stood with her hands hanging limply at her sides, tired from another day's ride, blinking heavy eyes as the Horde moved around her. It was unclear to her what exactly she was supposed to do and whether she should expect a whipping.

There was a wide range of sizes among the *tepay*s. She had never read or heard about how the Horde worked. Therefore, she didn't understand why some *tepay* entrances had a splash of paint. She could see a slash of red on one and a black splotch on another. Despite her desperate desire to ask questions, he had ordered her to remain silent. She stuck her tongue to the roof of her mouth to help her remember.

Hadak growled to Furan, "My *tepay*."

Furan stepped in front of her to grab her attention. She raised her eyes and waited for him to speak because, apparently, she wasn't supposed to.

"Come with me, *Immani*, I will get you settled. There's a *fhalah* who will attend you for now," he said and motioned her to follow.

She found herself staring at Hadak for a moment, and she wasn't sure why she looked to him for comfort since he was the reason she had come.

"What is her name?" she asked him in reference to the *fhalah*. Nearby, a warrior tutted at her question. Her shoulders tightened instantly as she realised she had spoken and shouldn't have. "*Kussa*," she apologised.

Furan waved her off, uncomfortable with her apologising.

"We do not speak with other *fhalah*s, except during war and within our families." He thought, then added, "We speak with *fhalahs* in *Avayak*'s family. We want to respect our future *bryds* as much as possible. Each warrior earns the right to have a *bryd*, which is a sacred bond closer to family than our blood. She will become what he fights for and what he returns home to the Horde for. Only she will know his words."

It was a sweet sentiment. She could tell he meant it. It made her wonder how exactly they found a *bryd* without speaking to or getting to know her.

How did the *fhalah*s talk to each other? Down the dusty paths, her friends sometimes called her name, so how would she communicate with the *fhalah*s? A grimace formed on her face. The probability of offending someone was high.

She would remember not to speak to the warriors, but the thought of walking around with all the Horde calling her an alien or human didn't feel right either. "What will you address me as?"

He shifted uneasily as he started down a narrow opening. "Perhaps, you should keep your questions for *Avayak*," he said gently. They passed a door with green colour on it.

Wondering if her questions were intrusive or if they weren't allowed to tell *Immani* about the inner workings of the horde, she replied, "Yes, of course. *Kussa*. I'm curious. The day you saw me was the first time I had left the colony. It's hard to get information about the Horde. We only hear rumours."

Just as she finished speaking, a door opened. Before Star could finish her thought, a hand smacked her across the face.

It was such a powerful and unexpected hit that she fell to the ground in shock.

There was a throbbing in her cheek and tears stinging her eyes. Trying not to throw up, she swallowed convulsively, holding her spinning head.

Following a harsh swear word, Furan dived for the person who had just hit her. This was followed by some Zandian shouts. It was too quick for her to catch. If she wasn't mistaken, there was some Zande mixed in. After a few hisses and harsh k's, Furan crouched down next to her.

As he gazed at her face, he drew his lips downward. "Let's go, no more talking," he told her fearfully.

In confusion, she wondered what had just happened and why the Horde member was just standing with his arms folded across his chest and his eyes filled with disgust.

She nodded and took Furan's hand, though it made the Horde members' faces screw up even more. She instantly dropped it.

Her goal was to avoid being hit again.

It felt like her cheek was numb and falling off at the same time. Silently, she walked beside Furan, gathering the last scraps of her dignity.

As they approached a *tepay* twice as big as any they had seen, she immediately recognized it as Hudak's.

There were actually two *tepay*s attached together. When Furan approached the flap to lift it for her, she hesitated. Trying to figure out if this was a mistake or if she was meant to be given her punishment soon.

Was she being melodramatic? It was entirely possible, but what else could she think? No one had told her how she was being punished.

According to her mother, some people who work off their offenses didn't return.

She pondered her mother's words when she had called her strong, almost sobbing, as she realised how wrong her mother had been.

She wasn't strong enough to survive being hit by a Zandian.

And maybe a hit was the least she could expect.

There was no point in worrying about the future. Only the here and now mattered. With that thought in mind, she took a deep breath and entered the *tepay*, only to have the air explode back out of it.

Even the most prosperous humans in the colony couldn't afford his *tepay's* metals and gems. His casual display of Zandian gems in the corner made her eyes bulge. It was as if they had just been thrown down without any care. There were soft rugs covering the floor, made from some animal fur she had never seen before. To keep the rug dust-free, she flicked her shoes off and dug her toes in.

His bed consisted of a pile of furs atop four chests. This looked like a comfortable, warm, inviting space. As tired as she was, she would have loved to lie in it, but it wasn't hers.

No way was she crawling into a stranger's bed, especially not Hadak's bed. He might interpret it as an invitation. A folding chair sat at an unassuming desk. Although the fabrics and furs were all rich, he had a minimal amount of furniture. On the left side of the bed, another tent connected to his with flaps peeling back, revealing a bathing room with a tub.

Her mouth filled with bile as her head swam. Her knees slammed into the carpet as she stumbled.

The last thing she heard was, "*Fhok*, get *Avayak*," as the rug rushed up to meet her face.

She was awoken by a deep snarling followed by rushed voices.

"You touched her," the snarl from Hadak confused her.

She squeezed her eyes tight, feeling her brain swell. Her thoughts flitted in and out like a sandstorm.

"I did not know she was yours, *Avayak*," the male replied, the voice tight. She vaguely recognised it as the one who hit her.

The growl from Hadak's throat was so ferocious that she feared what he might do to the male.

"You know she is *Immani*; we cannot hit her without causing damage. You wouldn't hit our females with half the force you used on her. It's a good thing my first stopped your arm before you spun her head from her neck," Hadak spat out, his fury coating his words. "Get out. I'm not rational right now," Hadak told him.

Water gathered in her mouth. Her head pounded. In an effort to still the urge to vomit, she breathed through her nose.

In their colony, the last person to react like this had suffered a brain injury due to a fall. However, he slept for at least three days, waking only to throw up when he was moved.

She was awake and aware and planned to stay that way.

"Seya Avayak."

Hadak called his name before he could leave. "Intuk, I will kill you if you ever touch what's mine again," he said without a hint of humour in his voice. Her head pounded, or was that Intuk's booted feet as he marched away?

A gentle touch on the face caused her head to turn. A sharp pain spiked behind her eyes, leaving her fading into darkness.

"*Immani*, you must wake up," a soft voice said, softer than any she had heard in the Horde. Opening her eyes, she squinted at the top of the *tepay*. She vaguely remembered big arms around her waist when she was falling asleep and the feel of steady breaths against her bare neck.

Bare!

Her attempt to sit up failed. It felt like someone was hammering her eyes. Holding her head tightly because it would surely roll off, Star made a wounded sound.

An exclamation at her pained sound caused her to turn around. Her eyes widening as she turned and noticed the person behind the bed was a female, a stark contrast to the Zandian warriors she had previously seen.

There was a slight line under where her breasts or should that be her chest because it looked more like muscle than breasts. It was clear that her nipples were different.

Zandian males had discs like humans, while females had only a nub without any colouring around it, unlike Star's pink nipples.

There were very few differences in features between Zandian males and females. Her eyebrow bones weren't as sharp as Hadak's, but her cheekbones were almost pointy, not curved like Star's.

Her black eyes watched her as she did the same to her. Her eyes flitted to her breasts repeatedly, confused by their size.

"Ah, it's good to see you awake. I've been here all morning. During the night, the *Avayak* was here, so you were not alone," the female said with a warm and friendly smile.

After swallowing to wet her mouth, she smiled tentatively. "I am Star," she told her, then cursed as she considered slapping herself and saving them the trouble. "*Fhok*, I don't know who I'm allowed to talk to."

"You can tell me your name, and we can talk," she laughed. "In any case, I'm here for you. Talking to me won't get you into trouble."

"Oh good," she sighed in relief, hating the idea of breaking more rules or stepping into unfamiliar territory.

"I am Ulla, named after our moon," she said with pride.

She told her, "I was named after the *khkar* in the skies." Her eyes lit up and flicked to the sky. "In my old tongue, it's called Star."

"Ah, *Shtar* translates to diamond here." Ulla pointed to the white gems, and her heart beat faster at the realisation she was still in Hadak's *tepay*. How did she only just notice that?

"How long have I been out?" she asked.

Ulla started rooting around in a bag. She pulled out something mashed into a sticky paste and put a spoon into it. Having placed a significant amount on the spoon, she held it out to Star.

"Take it, *Immani*, it will help with the pain," she said softly.

Grabbing the spoon, she eyed the paste with a shiver of apprehension. "It won't poison me?"

"*Nen Immani*, this will not poison you; others have also experienced this." Her confident voice echoed through the room. It gave Star the courage to stick the spoon in her mouth.

In response to the vile taste hitting her throat, her lips sucked together and pursed. She forced herself to swallow despite the heavy liquorice taste.

"*Kussa*. What happened? I can't remember much."

"Intuk hit you for speaking to Furan," she said.

"Why? Who is Intuk?" Her mind flashed briefly to a disgusted Horde member. "Oh, right, him. It's good to know he should be avoided." Star reached for a cup of water which she saw to wet her mouth. She asked again, "Why did he hit me?"

Was the *tepay* slanting? It must be because her eyes struggled to focus, suddenly rolling on their own, and her limbs became full, heavy, like boulders on her shoulders. The *tepay* was slanting, the sensation similar to falling.

The *tepay* righted itself again. Oh, how curious a shadow filled it too.

Then the shadow spoke. "He hit you because he could," answered the shadow in a distinctly male voice, making her squeak in alarm because she realised A, not only was the shadow alive, but B, her top half was naked and exposed.

As she tugged the furs up, she tucked them under her arms, hoping to contain her breasts. When Hadak stepped inside the *tepay*, she felt her heart seize. He glanced dismissively at Ulla. "Leave *Fhalah*," he ordered.

In affront, she said, "You can't talk like that to my friend." Then she clapped her hands over her mouth as he peered at her.

Ulla stifled a wince, her shoulders shaking. Was she...Yes, she was. She was silently laughing. Definitely silent laughter lay beneath that firm peaceful look on her face.

"*Immani* Star, I'll speak as I please with my Horde, hm?"

His soft question and her name on his lips made her feel as if she were floating. Even so, she did notice Ulla paused when she heard Star's name fall from his lips before she left.

With detachment, she watched him remove his sword and boots as the medicine numbed her. Whatever was in that liquorice goop was good.

"Intuk, why did he...?" she squeaked as his fur began to drop.

Then he stepped out of his furs, unashamedly nude with firmly muscled arse cheeks flexing as he turned.

Seeing his cock, she sucked in her breath. It lay across his stomach. Perhaps, lay was too gentle a word. His cock was standing at attention, angry looking and with thick veins along its length. Seeing it pulse made her eyes widen.

Star frowned as she took in three ridges she had never come across in human anatomy before. After trying to recall cocks when she'd seen rutting, she shook her head because she didn't remember seeing anything like that.

When the images lingered, she shook her head again to loosen them.

Suddenly, the faces in her memory were replaced by her and Hadak with their limbs entwined, heads thrown back in ecstasy. She could almost imagine him thrusting into her, his hands lovingly stroking and petting her body, guiding her, telling her how good it was.

"What do you think, Star?" he asked. With her face hot and choking guiltily, she held back a gasp.

As she contemplated his question, she felt her cheeks turn scarlet as his eyes filled with amusement.

He watched every thought glide across her face. He noticed her blush, observed her bite her lip, and he grinned wickedly.

"Intuk," she repeated, trying to distract herself. "Why did he hit me? Because I spoke with Furan? I still don't understand."

A long sigh escaped his lips as he crossed the divide, tying back the flaps further so she could see him bathing.

She swallowed as one big thigh stepped into the tub, followed by the other. After hearing his groan of relief, she wanted to kick herself for interfering with his bathing. Perhaps she should congratulate herself on getting him talking while he was naked, giving her a delightful view of him, but she felt slightly guilty.

While she was on her side, she watched him grab a cloth and clean his body before he responded. Her eyes were glued firmly on his face.

"You spoke to an unwed warrior outside of a *tepay* with no contract between you," he told her, confusing her.

She shook her head. After a moment's silence, he sighed, trying to decide how to proceed with telling her too much, or so it seemed to her.

"A warrior honours his *bryd* by not speaking to other *fhalah's* as the *bryd* honours the warrior by not speaking to any unmated warriors outside of her home unless she wishes to request a contract with his family or he with hers."

The cloth splashed as it dipped below the water line. Her eyes followed eagerly. She wondered when she had become so bold.

The medicine must be to blame.

"The contract between them allows them to spend time together to test if they'll like each other. While there's no guarantee that there will be a *bryd* at the end, or a warrior for her, most times, they do get mated. Before entering a contract with anyone, we wait a long time and carefully choose who we want to be with. We are guided by our gods to the one who is meant for us. It's inside us." He thumped his chest, spraying water.

"I was disrespectful to Furan because I spoke to him without a contract."

He gritted his teeth and frowned. *"Nen*, not exactly." He licked his lips, his eyebrows caught in the middle as he thought. "Speaking freely was disrespectful, and by doing so, you offered yourself to anyone who was interested in you." He said, "You have this in the colony. My males report this, and others have seen it."

She frowned, trying to figure out what he was talking about. There must have been a problem with the drug because it took her a minute to process it. She snorted. "Whores," she said, eyes wide with realisation.

"Seya, it is like that but without payment. The *cotte* do not have *tepay*s, they sleep in whatever warriors' beds they are lucky enough to find. The king in the east, he's got these, ehh..." Scratching his chin, he shrugged. "...huts that have been set up for them around the city to do their trade, but they would not be able to survive in the horde like that."

He lifted his leg from the tub, flexing the thick muscles as he washed. Was his hand moving slowly over his leg? She was glued to the motion of his hand as he rubbed circles over his skin. There were rivulets of water flowing down his leg.

There was a sudden dryness in her mouth, her stomach clenching tightly.

Then her mouth watered as she wondered if his wet skin tasted the same as it did dry. She licked her lips when his hand moved higher, and he laughed.

Her eyes shot to his, and she found him looking at her while she was watching him. He did it deliberately to see if she would look!

It was a little unnerving to see his knowing expression. It was an unsettling experience for her since she had never watched anyone like this before, not even a human.

"Does Intuk think I'm a whore? Do I need to worry?" she asked, her mouth still dry and trying to steer the conversation away from bedding. His black-as-night eyes became icy and murderous.

"There is no need for you to worry. I told you that I will protect you in the horde; my warriors will protect you." He stepped out of the bathtub, his cock still hard as he brushed his fur over his body. It was quick and perfunctory. Not wanting to miss a single moment, she didn't blink when he stroked the fur up and down his length. "You have a fascination with my cock, *Immani* Star."

Moving back on the bed, she choked and looked up at him with uncomprehending eyes. His eyes were dancing with humour as he smiled.

It made her squirm in an uncomfortable way. Even after she instructed her eyes to look away, they were uncooperative. She was secretly pleased that her uncooperative gaze was drawn to him repeatedly and that it had made him smile and had taken away the icy glint in his eyes.

Grasping at her arm and scratching at it, she ignored his question, and he chuckled when she refused to answer.

The bed furs dipped as he lay on them. When he dragged her into him, she made a noise of surprise at how tightly he squeezed her. Again, he caught the tip of her chin with his fingers.

Rolling her eyes upwards, she met his burning gaze with her own. That was the moment her naked body took notice of his naked body for the first time and burned at the points of contact. He wasn't quite under the fur yet, but her lower leg was in contact with his lower leg.

It was exhilarating.

There was no way she could moan at him for sliding in beside her. It was his bed that she was in.

Her head spun at the thought of moving, of feeling sick once again, and the thought of getting up made her shudder.

He rubbed her arms, thinking that she might be cold. She actually felt hot, too hot for the furs.

She felt too hot for their bodies to be pressed together.

"It was my promise to you that you would be safe, but when I tell you not to do something, trust me. There are different rules that apply to the Hordes than even the king in his city has to follow." He kept his grip on her chin, so she could see every word his lips formed up close. She felt the weight of his words like a physical touch.

"*Seya*, I'll try," she agreed.

"*Nen*, do not try. You have to make sure you do as I ask." He exhaled sharply, closing his eyes. There was an immediate sense of loss at not having his gaze on her.

A frown spread across his face as his eyes flew back open. "I do not like the thought of punishing you in front of the Horde."

This was her opening. In a whisper, she said, "Don't punish me, then."

He chuckled, "*Nen*, if you do something that requires punishment, then just like the rest of the *bryds* or family members here, you will face the punishment with a stiff spine and endure it."

Now she was confused. Was he talking about her punishment for venturing beyond the colony or punishments he thought she might accrue while she was there?

Oh great. Having brought her there completely ignorant of what to expect, she was likely going to end up suffering punishment after punishment, and he would be the one to do it.

"I need to know what I can and can't do," she pleaded with him. However, he was already nodding, and she couldn't help but exhale in relief when she saw that.

"The *fhalah* you met yesterday will return as soon as you are well. She will be able to help you. She'll guide you, and as for your punishment for leaving the colony..." He trailed off, his fingers brushing her chin before disappearing down at his side.

She was beginning to feel the strain of suspense. All kinds of scenarios ran through her mind, from being attacked by a crowd to being whipped to being forced to do hard labour.

It was then that a hot hand snaked under the fur and settled on her arse, making her jump.

Oversensitive skin that felt like it was on fire when his thumb rubbed in a circle. He dipped his hand between her legs and rubbed his finger between her sensitive flesh. As her body suddenly became limp, he was able to move her thighs apart with ease. His whole palm covered her. God...it was too hot.

"You'll let me take your *nwale ryss*?" he asked, referring to her velvet cunt.

Was that the reason he inspected it on the dusty plain? Did he want to punish her with her body?

She could have denied wanting him and received a different punishment, but this wasn't too bad. Nerve-racking, yes, but not too bad. There was no doubt in her mind that the desire she felt for him was genuine. It must be the same for him, or at least that was what she thought from seeing his stiff member.

His body certainly liked hers.

It was as if her body suddenly burned at his words, or did it just burn? The flames had been burning since the moment he stepped into the room.

His hand was pressing on her as if he was trying to remind her what he had asked. Did he ask, and would he take it anyway?

There was no way the Horde king would take anything unless it were given to him. There was no doubt in Star's mind about that. He wanted her to want him. When he teased her, she could see it in his eyes. There was no way for her to know if he liked her naked body. His females look different. The fact that she had breasts may have repulsed him.

What was she even thinking about? Not important right now. His impatient eyes, however, were.

His fingers curled up a little, and one curled in towards her achingly empty hole. A promise, a wicked promise.

There was a sense of tension in his body as he waited for her answer, and hers almost melted beneath his hand when she answered with a shaky nod.

It was like he had a lustful grasp on her body; like he had a direct line to a source of passion that she had never experienced, and he had some control over it.

Her breathy pants resulted from fear of the unknown and anticipation. Right now, would they? Could she? His eyes flickered over her face.

"*Fhok*. Maybe I should give you a taste of what you'll be getting, *maye Immani...*"

He just called her 'his human,' and oh god, why did those words make her happy?

Her *Mathar* never told her about this.

It was an overwhelming pleasure that he was giving her at that moment and if she experienced this pleasure even before he was inside her...

"...by tasting your *nwale ryss*," he finished.

Oh god. It made her feel hot, and she wished he would stop talking since his dirty mouth made her feel overheated.

It felt like her skin was on the verge of breaking; as if there was some intense pressure trapped inside of it.

Because of that feeling, she bared herself and nodded in agreement. A look of surprise swept over his face, and he inhaled sharply when she boldly exposed her body to him.

Was this too quick? She could have waited, but what was the point? This felt good, so if it felt right, that was all that mattered, in her opinion.

Now, it was too late because his hand had already reached her naked breast. His fingers traced the coloured outline of her breast. With his elbow propped up, he could see her other breast, but this one he traced with his tongue.

She let out a sharp sigh of pleasure, and he rolled his eyes up to watch her, assessing her reactions.

It must be different for him, something new to explore.

His interest in exploring her body sent a flare of heat through her, which he teased higher by taking her nipple into his mouth.

He nipped her lightly with his teeth. The small bite of pain lit up her senses.

Her moan had him lifting his head to look at her face as his flat tongue rubbed her nipple back and forth. Her face was flushed with pleasure as she watched. Her eyes were heavy, her mouth open, and chest was heaving.

It wasn't enough for her. She was ready for more now. Twenty-two and she hadn't even kissed a man properly. This was what she was missing out on. Honestly, she wasn't sure if anyone else could make her feel like this.

"Gods! You do want it. *Seya*," he hissed, eyes wide and fixed on her.

He traced a line through her wetness with his fingers, slowly bringing them to his mouth. Before he put his fingers in his mouth, he looked at their glistening tips. She had never seen anything hotter. The Horde king was the height of pleasure; forget the rutting teenagers.

He asked, "You want my mouth on your *ryss, maye Immani*?"

His words. God, his words. She should cover that mouth with her hand.

She wanted his mouth on her. Yes, and she liked it when he called her *maye Immani*. Yeah, she really did. With everything he was making her feel, he was burning her up.

As she nodded, she hoped he would do something to relieve the pressure.

He grabbed her thighs and spread them so she was ready for him. "Say it, you'll only get what you ask for, *maye Immani*," he said intently.

Opening her mouth and agreeing was all she had to do. Her skin felt like it was on fire. She frowned as she realised that she did feel hot.

It wasn't just desire.

She felt incredibly hot.

Was she feverish? She panicked, and wondered how long she'd had a fever? People in the colony died of fever. A lot. When he saw her widening eyes, his head started disappearing between her thighs.

"*Avaye!*" she pleaded desperately. Quietly. Strained.

As her eyes rolled back in her head, his surprised "*Fhok!*" followed her into the darkness.

Chapter 5

After she regained consciousness, she thought he must have been mortified that she passed out while he was between her legs.

For days, she had been in and out of consciousness. She thought she remembered Hadak running in search of a healer. Before he returned, her eyes had rolled back again. Ulla had come by, but she had been sweating and hallucinating by then, so she wasn't even sure her memories were accurate at that point.

She had fainted at some point, and Furan had been standing guard over her, whispering something about how his sister got her warrior when she fainted. He had told her she had to wake up and try again. He told her that she was already tying Hadak in knots without fainting, therefore, she needed to get her arse up and get back to wooing him. Although she laughed internally, she wasn't sure if she was hearing things.

The silent figure of Hadak had been watching her every night, occasionally glaring at her feverish eyes and mumbling something unintelligible. There were times when he looked at her in confusion as if he had no idea what to do. His hands clenched tightly in front of him as he looked at them.

In the midst of waking up from a nightmare that had its claws in her, she let out a choked cry.

"Star," Hadak shouted as he rushed out of the bath, snarling at the warrior who came flying under the flap, sword drawn, alerted by her cry.

Unless he planned to defeat her nightmares, Star was about to tell him to put the sword away. As she recalled the no-speaking thing, she grimaced.

As Hadak watched her, he said, "Go." His eyes were filled with fury, and she parted her lips. "I thought I may have to inform your *Fathar* that you died." Before she could ask what happened, he blasted her with a pitch-black look, eyes aflame and mouth curled up. "When you are injured next time, let me know. I would rather you die accidentally than from neglect." Sopping wet, he left before she could respond.

Besides her cheek, she had no other injuries. Bringing her fingers up, she gently touched it. It was obvious that she had been out for a few days, as the wound was mostly healed, and the swelling had reduced. She could only feel a faint bruise underneath her eye.

As soon as she brought her hand down, she felt a tug under her arm, and when she lifted it, she let out a long, painful breath. She poked at a vicious-angry-looking red scratch, frowning. She developed a fever over such a small thing.

She had seen worse.

Her neighbour fell and received a cut to her knee that turned a very repulsive colour. It oozed and wept. Days after she died, the stench could be smelled in the house. She died quickly as a result of her fever and infection.

She was scratched by the Jutin when he swung her into the tree. She hadn't noticed it at all. When she got a scratch, she always washed it out and applied salve. However, this time she ducked into a freezing river with the Horde king, quickly rose, then spent two days riding and sweating with the scratchy material from her dress irritating her cut. It was no wonder she got sick.

She pursed her lips. Did she apologise to Hadak? He stomped out like a petulant child.

When she thought about it, she grimaced. She was saved from the Jutin by him.

The height of stupidity would be to get rescued from Jutin, only to die from a scratch a few days later. Hadak called healers to save her. Did she have a right to complain? Suddenly deflated, she thought no.

As soon as she saw him, she would explain. Tell him she didn't even feel the scratch when it happened. She'd apologize for scaring him, hoping he'd understand.

Her head tucked in, she sat at the edge of the bed, unsure of what she was supposed to do.

Hadak didn't bring her back here just to stand inside his *tepay* all day. She was fiddling with the sheets because she had nothing to wear. Her tongue flicked against her lip as she wondered if he'd get mad if she looked through his chest for her dress. She knew it had to be somewhere around there.

Her hands tentatively lifted the lid of a chest. She gasped when she saw bolts of silky fabric. There was no way that her dress was in there. Itching to dip her hands into the cloth and pour it over her skin, she swallowed, and shut the lid just as the flaps slapped open again.

"Star, what are you doing?" Ulla asked, stepping nervously into the *tepay*.

"I feel better," she said, waving away her worries. "Is there any way to find my dress?" Her eyes darted to the bathing room. She scowled when she couldn't find it after ducking into there. She noticed Ulla's uncomfortable squirming then.

"What?" she asked with dread.

Ulla's eyes shifted away from her. She knew when those black eyes were avoiding her by now.

There was a lot of nervousness in Ulla's swallow as she said, "He said..."

"What did he say?" A river of worry washed over her.

"He told me to take *Immani* to her *tepay* as soon as she wakes up. To have her..."

"Have me what?"

"Work in the food *tepay*, something about punishment," Ulla said hesitantly.

Suddenly, her mouth dropped open. That was her punishment. To work in the food *tepay*. If he had thought that was a punishment, he didn't know what lengths humans would go to in order to get a decent job in the human colony. Working with food would be hot and sweaty but not too terrible. Although it would be challenging, but as long as she didn't poison anyone, it should be fine. If she didn't know what the ingredients were, she wouldn't touch them.

Actually, it was a relief. Some parts of her wondered if he'd planned this from the beginning. He may have known that her small frame couldn't handle heavy work. She sniffed, shrugging her shoulders. Ulla looked relieved she wasn't annoyed with her.

Star asked, "Okay, but can I get something on before I leave?"

"Don't you have any clothes?"

When she looked under the fur, she found nothing but another layer of fur, saying to Ulla, "I had a dress, but I can't find it."

"They are moving my *tepay* today, so I can't go back there. Otherwise, I would lend you one," Ulla apologised. "We rotate with other warriors on the outer edges of the Horde. My *Fathar*'s in his prime and still a Horde warrior," she said with pride.

"That's great," she replied, unsure what else to say.

A wide, honest smile spread across Ulla's face before she grimaced.

"What is it?" she screamed, twisting her hands in front of her, desperate to cover herself.

Ulla looked at the entrance to the *tepay* with fear. "He wanted you out before he came back," she said. "*Teyae*, we need to leave. I worry the warriors will remove you."

"Why?" she asked with astonishment. What was going on right now?

"Because they know the *Avayak*'s orders and will see you as an intruder, it's best to leave." She eyed the flaps once again.

"But I don't have anything to wear," she hissed.

Ulla twisted her hands as she stared at Star, her nerves evident. She reached behind her, refusing to walk around the Horde naked, and stole the top fur from Hadak's bed. Star tucked Hadak's fur around her as best she could.

It was obvious that it was from a bed, and it wasn't what she would call decent. It was more out of practicality than anything else. Since she had never worn short dresses before, the length made her feel off. She managed to hold it together.

The moment Ulla kindly removed a piece of leather from her silky dress and wrapped it around Star's waist, she almost burst into tears.

Leaving her parents was difficult, but sleeping alone would be strange, as they were usually close at night. While she knew she had technically been sleeping with strangers for the past few nights, it would be strange for her to do so completely on her own. She hoped this *tepay* he had requested for her might house a few Zandian females.

Although her home had never been crowded, her brothers' reassuring snores at night and her parents' shuffling about next door were all things she took for granted. In a desperate attempt to cover everything, she tugged at the hem, licking her lips as she straightened.

"Is it far?" She asked Ulla, trying to appear brave.

Ulla shook her head rather than asking if she was okay, since nothing about this was okay. *"Nen,"* she answered. She squeezed Ulla's hand when it slipped into hers. "Let's leave before too many Horde members wake up and start walking around. *Seya?"*

"Seya," she replied. She was glad she hadn't irritated everyone this morning.

She felt the cold air hit her. As she remembered how cold it was getting, she shivered. It was a quick change of seasons on Zandar. There were five cold seasons, five hot seasons, and five rainy seasons.

Their colony was often flooded during the rainy season. When floods came to their colony, rivers overflowed, and crops died. There were even some Hordes that struggled in Zandar's wet season.

Ulla tugged at her hand. As she marched through the Horde, her stride got longer. Ulla dragged her to the end of the row before she could blink and take it all in.

Ulla showed her what looked like a hastily thrown-together *tepay*. There was one flap that wasn't quite pinned down. The heavy leather would be impossible to manipulate and close, so she'd have to deal with the elements.

As soon as she got inside, her mouth dropped open. The *tepay* may as well not be there. As she walked, dust crunched under her boots. The only thing of hers she still had, aside from her dignity, which she might soon lose. Even though she wouldn't complain, she might get a fever living in such dirty conditions.

It looked like her new home, at least for the foreseeable future, was this dirt pile that may as well not have a roof. There wasn't much she could do with it. The only thing she had was two furs and something that looked like a stool. She sighed, figuring it was punishment time.

There were worse things that could happen, she told herself.

Ulla looked at her with heartbreak, horrified.

Nodding, she gritted her teeth. Ducking her head, she made her way to the furs.

This was what it was like to be a Horde king. The ability to be ruthless. It was almost like those small moments between them hadn't happened. Though they didn't exchange tender words, there was something between them. There was some spark. It was something you could touch, taste, and feel. That's what she thought until now, it turned out she was a fool.

When she looked at the furs, her head dropped to her knees. She didn't expect the Horde king to bed her and keep her. She wasn't sure if she wanted that. She looked around and thought she wanted a little more respect than this.

It didn't bother her to do her punishment. In all honesty, she was glad to do it so she could go home. She couldn't believe he was going to bed her before she got sick and then dump her in this *tepay* afterward.

Her opinion of him shifted.

Since she had arrived at the Horde, they'd only had one moment together. It was hot and sensual. She enjoyed herself a lot. She had been smacked by his warrior or knocked unconscious for the rest of her time there.

It was a new day. After another long sigh, she tilted her head back, surprised that Ulla was still standing, visibly upset.

"Ulla, what is it?" The look on her face made her nervous.

"Why would he put you here?"

"I don't understand. This is meant to be mine. He said he would have another *tepay* built." And it did look as though it had been put up quickly. With just a stool in one corner and furs on the floor, it felt dark and sparse. She wondered how she'd do anything, even wash, with so few contents.

She could clean it up, she supposed.

That sounded fine until she realised she couldn't sweep the dust and dirt that would blow under the gap and around the *tepay*. During the night, it would get on her fur and cover her.

"I'll be fine," she said to Ulla as a cold breeze brushed around her ankles. In despair, Ulla shook her head. "I'm being punished." Star's shoulders tightened, and her mother's words came to mind. She was strong; she could take this.

That's all she had to remember if things got too much.

"It's okay, it could be worse. My time will be spent in the food *tepay*, and when I have finished my punishment, I'll return home," she told Ulla with a forced smile.

How long could it take? Five moons? She'd take fifteen. Just as long as it wasn't years. She shied away from that thought, putting it in the back of her mind.

"*Nen*, this is terrible. You don't have a shelter, the flap is loose, and you won't be warm in the cold season." Ulla's anger rose.

Star watched her pace the bare patch of dirt before she spotted something sticking out of her fur. She frowned when Ulla pulled out a grey silk dress. A loose, flowy dress with slits up the sides that would make moving on a *Guyipe* easy. If she wasn't riding, she'd feel uncomfortable wearing it. She'd wear it if it were hers. She'd worn dresses like that before, and they weren't the most revealing. If it stopped any additional time from being added to her punishment, she'd wear it.

"Now this," Ulla said, looking insulted by the grey silk. If Ulla could shoot fire from her eyes, the dress would have already caught fire.

A smile spread across her face at that thought, and she snatched the dress from Ulla. Shimmying the fur down her hips, she dropped the dress over her head. This silk felt like a thin, light, and unbelievably soft covering against her body. It was the softest thing she'd ever felt against her.

Like her mother's rough velvet bag that she stroked all the time. Up until now, it had been the softest thing she'd ever felt. She remembers being young and thinking nothing would ever be softer than that velvet bag. It was old, passed down by her mom's mom. Over the years, it probably lost its softness.

The grin spread across her face as she swung the dress from side to side, deciding that, if nothing else, she should be grateful she was dressed.

Ulla said, "Oh, Star," with pity in her voice.

Despite the deep probing look in Ulla's eyes, Star shrugged, comfortable with what she had. "My *Mathar* got rid of her old bathing tub," Ulla said. "It was going to be given to a friend in the city. I will get a warrior to bring that here for you and a light."

Oh, right, she hadn't even thought about when it got dark or that she didn't have a fire pit. A sense of determination filled her. If she had to build her fire pit, then she would. She could get back to her family by doing everything from scratch, and the Horde king would see she was committed.

There were no sounds of life coming from the lonely *tepay*. That's the only thing that would get her. Silence. It would have been nice to have her strings. If she made some, she could fill the *Tepay* with sound.

"Okay."

The Horde king's furs on the floor made Ulla scowl. "I think you can keep those furs to throw on the pitiful excuse for coverings they gave you," she said. Ulla reached down and grabbed them, pushing them into Star's arms.

"They're his, I don't want them. Please return them to him with my thanks for the loan." Even if it was only for a short time.

Ulla's face drooped even more - a scowl marked it. Ulla's opinion of him was as low as Star's, but Star didn't want their interaction to influence Ulla's feelings.

"Truly," she told her. "It's more than I expected and not terrible." She smiled. Ulla did ease her rigid stance a little. "*Teyae*, go back to the *Avayak*," she told her.

Ulla frowned. "But I'll bring you that tub and show you where the food *tepay* is," she said. "I think you start tomorrow."

Nodding, Star stepped back from the furs to focus on her morning tasks. Ulla watched her pin the flap down with the stool and pulled it in.

Star said gently, "It's okay."

Even though Ulla didn't seem convinced, she walked out of the *tepay* with tight eyes and a scowl on her face. Ulla wasn't happy.

Ulla arrived back at Star's *tepay* after an hour. There was also a tub with her being held aloft by two warriors. It was a solid silver tub, and the gesture was nice, but all she thought about was how she was going to fill it. Pulling at her lip, she worried Ulla had brought it over, and she wouldn't get full use of it.

For her, not being able to talk to the warriors was weird. There was never a time when she had to restrain herself from sharing something or asking a question.

Uncomfortable with the silence that seemed full of everything, Star wanted to ask. She waited by the flaps with Ulla for them to put the tub next to the stool. As she couldn't open her mouth to say no, she watched with dismay as they put it in the draughtiest spot.

Her small fur caught the attention of one of the warriors, who murmured under his breath. Ulla clenched her fist, and her eyes flared. They left quickly, not wanting to stay too long in her cold, dark *tepay*. Before moving away, the warrior gave her a curious glance.

Ulla murmured, "Come." Ulla gestured out the *tepay* to the path, so she followed.

"What did he say?" Star wondered, curious about the flame of anger in his eyes.

"He said it wasn't fit for animals," Ulla spat. "Nasan is right."

As she passed the *fhalah*s, she watched them whisper together. She was mostly ignored by the warriors, which was fine. After getting hit by one of the warriors, she wasn't looking forward to more encounters with them.

They stopped at a *tepay* with a yellow mark. "What are the marks for?"

"It lets the Horde know which *tepay* is which. Yellow means food. Dark yellow, a shade darker than your hair, marks the eating area. Warriors with *bryd*s don't come here, this is for warriors without *bryd*s," Ulla explained.

"Where do the *fhalah's* eat?"

"In our homes," Ulla replied absentmindedly as a *fhalah* exited the *tepay* with a frown.

Her mouth twisted when she saw Star, and she knew instinctively she wouldn't find any allies here. Star was still worried about cooking for herself. Did she have to take food from the store, and where did she cook it? Having no way to start a fire or know where to get food, she had the added worry that she'd make a mistake.

"No use giving me tired eyes," snapped the *fhalah*. "You will work today; you have no injuries that I can see."

Maybe not visible to the naked eye, but Star had just woken up after almost a week of non-stop terror and fever.

When Ulla defended her, she said, "She needs light work today." The *fhalah's* wrinkles wrinkled in disgust.

When the aged *fhalah* pointed inside the *tepay*, Star nodded. Besides, she was too tired to fight with her when it was going to be her job all day. Ulla held her arm tight, her expression outraged. The *fhalah* lifted the flaps and disappeared under them.

"Ulla, *Teyae*." Please.

Ulla let out a breath reluctantly. "I will come for you later and help get you home."

"It's fine, you've done enough."

Ulla sighed when she saw the stubborn glint in her eyes. "Okay, but I will drop off the light for you. There's no way I want you to be stuck in that *Fhoken tepay* all night without a light."

Before turning around to leave, Ulla watched her duck under the flap.

All the *fhalah*s stopped working to look at Star as she surveyed the activity in the *tepay*.

There were two benches with women folding dough, braising meat, and making something that looked like a sweet. In the bowl, there was melted orange liquid swirling around.

"She comes in silks; does she think she's going to sit and watch us work?" One *fhalah* sneered, and the others laughed. That's when Star realised they thought she didn't know the language. Ulla was the only *fhalah* she spoke with in Zandian.

If she could have found her old dress, she'd have worn it. It would have been better if she had shown up in a dress similar to theirs. It was practical, so Star would have worn it. They seemed to have aprons to protect their dresses and skin, and no one was in a hurry to show her or tell her if she had one.

"*Sako Immani*, too stupid to live."

There seemed to be an attitude among all Zandians that humans were stupid. It could get pretty tiresome pretty quickly.

It was clear to her that these *fhalah* were not inclined to be her friends. There was nothing she could do but do what was told to her in order to get out of there and return home. In those insane moments of madness where Hadak seemed to guarantee her safety, it became all too obvious she was no longer protected by him. It turned out that for whatever reason, she trusted him and that feeling of security just vanished in a flash.

"It is ugly to look at. Take a look at those legs. They are so white. It's like looking at the dead."

"It's cheeks as well! Take a look at them, they are so round, like a ball. How do their warriors stand it? Loose hair, not showing her neck." This *fhalah* made a clicking noise of disgust.

After the old *fhalah* got angry that the *fhalah*s hadn't returned to work, she picked up a wooden stick and smashed it on the surface. "Stop your gossiping, the *Immani* may be *sako,* but that's nothing to do with us. We just have to work with it."

That was great, she wasn't even a human anymore, now she was an 'it.' She had somehow lost her name somewhere along the way on this very fast and rapidly spiralling journey she was on.

"That won't survive in the horde," said one standing over the open fire, hissing at the creature.

"*Nen*, it won't, but we'll use it for now until it's used up."

All the *fhalah's* turned to look at her with sudden toothy grins on their faces as they looked at her. She might have smiled back instinctively if she wasn't aware of what they had just said. However, instead of engaging in any discussion, she simply stood passively with a growing anger in her heart. She had the desire to prove she was as strong as any of these *fhalah's* who must possess ice in their hearts. She felt very sorry for the warriors who were forced to spend their whole lives with them as *bryd*s.

That was the start of her day.

Despite being given many tasks they could have easily done themselves, she did them on her own. Then there's gutting the dinner for tomorrow night as well.

There had only been a couple of times when Star had done that back home, so when guts spilled on the left side of her dress, it was much to the amusement of all the other *fhalah's* present. They didn't give her an apron. It was all part of the fun, they whispered to each other.

The liquid ran down her leg. Luckily, Star was able to wipe it off before it got into her boots. As she bent down, she received a sharp whack on her shoulders, which caused her head to jerk up.

The old *fhalah*, whose name was Ghertun, snapped, "Don't slack in the food *tepay*."

Since she supposedly didn't know the language, she should have no idea what she was getting hit for. Despite her bald-faced lie, Star didn't call her out on it.

After spending the morning with them, she didn't want to talk anymore. She just wanted to finish and get back to where she came from as soon as possible.

"You should be careful how hard you hit it. Their skin splits open like the guts in here," said Illasay, another who found her punishment amusing.

It was Star's native tongue that she used when she asked, "What do I need to do now?"

"There is a thought in its head, I see. There was a moment when I thought it couldn't speak."

"I want you to take this. Tonight, serve the warriors and spare the arms of my *fhalah*. Besides, they will be of more use to you than you are."

She realised then that the *fhalah*s had a deep hatred for her. At least a hundred Horde members sat outside the *tepay*, yet none of them offered help. Their backs were turned toward her.

It was her punishment, she reminded herself. Do it and get home as soon as possible.

Her mind and body froze when Gherturn pushed her through the adjacent flaps. Her presence was immediately noticed by some warriors but not by others. A sudden feeling of exposure overtook her.

With her shoulders straightened, she placed the trays on the first table she reached. In order to collect more, Star turned back. She exhaled a sigh of relief until she saw all the food trays stacked up on the table inside the *tepay*.

"Are you planning to tell her where to put them?" Illasay asked.

"If she can't figure out to start with meats and bread rolls, followed by the *sok*, then pudding, there's truly no hope for her."

After grabbing more meat, Star assumed the orange stuff was *sok*. As the *fhalah*'s spoke of the lovely pudding, they pulled out a black jelly-like substance, which smelled so sweet that it filled the *tepay*.

Even though the orange liquid looked nice, it smelled bitter, with notes of wood and fruit. That meant the black sticky sweet substance must be pudding, she assumed.

Star didn't know, but she would serve it. Grabbing two more trays overflowing with meat, she glanced discreetly at the sixteen trays left, then at the twenty bowls of liquid and jelly. Even if she worked fast, she would have to take the liquid bowls out one by one. They would be heavy. While she carried it, the warriors would have to wait.

Unfortunately, it was impossible for her to convey that since she wasn't allowed to speak. In spite of seeing how irritated the warriors were becoming, the *fhalah*s did nothing to help.

After Star spread the liquid on the tables, the warriors appeared to unwind and become more bold. While holding a black pudding over a table, a hand explored slits in the silk as if they had the right. She couldn't put the plate on the table because she had frozen.

"Ghertun said she had legs like the dead, but I beg to differ." As he squeezed down on her tender skin, he said, "They feel warm enough to me." Laughter broke out around her, and she knew she would bruise.

"*Avayak* seems fascinated by her," observed someone further down.

"*Nen*, he threw her out so she's in to her own *tepay* this morning," he said as another arm snaked out, catching her waist and pulling her across his legs. He reached for the hem of her dress as she squeaked and batted at his hands. As he laughed, he said, "She doesn't understand Zandian? I want to give her an understanding of Zandian." To punctuate the point, he thrust his hips up, and she felt the blood drain from her face.

The sound of a swish. Suddenly, a sword appeared at her attacker's throat. Then he stopped moving, rolled his eyes, and saw Nasan holding the sword. Nasan's eyes were filled with cold fury. It had been a long time since Star had seen anyone that angry. "Let the *Immani* go now," he ordered. She shivered at his deadly tone.

Keeping his hands up, the warrior looked at her and smiled, "You want her *Ryss* all to yourself? You could share with me."

Nasan's gaze focused on her as she straightened the stained dress and put the pudding down because despite everything, she had kept her grip on it.

Despite the temptation to drop it on his head, she avoided doing so for fear of being hit. When Nasan watched her set it down casually like everything was fine, he grunted and sat down.

He stopped her when he noticed there were no *fhalah's* about. A sharp sound came from him.

Ghertun emerged. After a few tense moments, the *fhalah's* who had been watching Star come and go with sweat rolling down her temple now appeared like magic. Their arms were full of *sok* and pudding.

The momentary relief Star felt was tempered when she saw the hate in their eyes. Star's relief was masked. Once Nasan had been served, she made sure the tables had been cleared. A quick job with everyone working together.

Inside the *tepay,* the *fhalah's* left, making it very clear she had to wash the platters.

Her shoulders ached, and her arms trembled. Her muscles were screaming, and clearly not appreciating the abuse since she had never used them like that before.

Even in defeat, Star walked back to the *tepay* with a high head. She trudged through the dark paths with her head hanging and arms flopping limply, but at least she looked decent, she thought sarcastically, as she glanced at her silk dress with stains.

When she went inside and saw the light, she almost wished she didn't have one since it was illuminating the dust and dirt. Her rumbly stomach reminded her how hungry she was.

In addition to being exhausted, she was filthy as well. Those two furs in the corner looked so inviting, and that was a depressing thought because they weren't much.

It was impossible for her to fill the tub bucket by bucket, even if she wanted to. She didn't have a bucket or know where the water was. Only one option. Keeping the spark close to her, she blew out the light.

She longed for a weapon of some kind. As she gazed at the loose flap, she finally took off the stool and dragged it over to herself. Her weapon could be used to strike anyone who attempted to enter, consequences notwithstanding. Wind would have loosened the flap anyway, the stool couldn't hold it down.

As she shivered in the furs, she lay back in them tentatively and pulled one over her head. Howling noises were made by the wind, ripping through the opening.

The sound was like someone yelling at her. It made her head ache. While shivering, she felt as if her fingers were ice blocks, the cold biting at them. They had long since lost their sense of feeling due to the cold. When she squeezed them together, she felt a spike of icy cold.

Despite knowing what had to be done, she yanked the fur she was lying on off the floor and doubled the fur up on top of her.

The cold, hard floor was now directly beneath her, and she pulled both blankets over her. Her shivering didn't stop, but it warmed up a little. While tucking her hands by her mouth and shoving her head under the furs, she tried to breathe warmth into them.

She was strong. It was getting harder for her to hear her mother's voice as she repeated the words to herself. Her thoughts were instead consumed by the laughter of the *fhalah*s, chipping away at her.

All night, her teeth clacked together in the dark. After hearing people moving about in the morning and seeing the sun break through the clouds and warm her toes, exhaustion finally got the best of her. She fell asleep with her hips and shoulders pressed into the hard ground and her face buried under the fur.

Chapter 6

After a day of gruelling work, she tripped over a bowl of pink mush and slushed it all over Illasay. After slamming her lids in dismay, Star opened them and peered at her furious expression.

Illasay's lips were drawn into a sharp line. Her eyes twitched, and a drop of pink mush slipped off her and onto the floor with a 'plop.'

In anticipation of the bloodshed about to take place, the *fhalah* either stared in anticipation or turned their cheeks to avoid drawing attention to themselves. As Illasay glared at Star, her usually pretty face looked unattractive. "Get out!" she screeched.

Getting out of there as quickly as possible seemed wise, and it saved her doing the pots tonight. When she stumbled out of the flap, she was surprised to find a large body waiting for her.

"Where's the rush?" Hadak glanced beyond her, but the flaps had already closed. Instead of answering, she shrugged and started walking back to the *tepay*. Pulling her arm, he raised his eyebrows.

"What?" she asked. She was worried Illasay would come after her, and God knows what she would do if she did. Her impression was that Illasay was a different kind of person than she was used to dealing with. If it meant never knowing people like that, she would rather stay ignorant of Zandar.

With a firm frown on his face, he said seriously, "You haven't greeted me."

"You're serious?"

"Deadly," he answered.

A short bob followed the incline of her head. As she gritted her teeth and bent her aching legs, she wondered how disrespectful it would be to give him the finger. If she found out, her *Mathar* would thrash her. She was always so mild-mannered until she heard them swearing or doing something silly. The thought made her think of home.

73

Probably because it wasn't graceful, he didn't seem impressed when she got up again. She felt herself wobbling.

Her tired eyes searched over his stiff stance, his fisted hands. The thoughts that flickered behind his eyes, whatever was going through his head, she was too tired to figure out.

Gritting her teeth, she asked, "How long will I have to stay with the Horde?" She was anxious about how she would cope with the cold season and whether her *Tepay* would be able to endure it.

With his arms folded across his chest, he clicked his tongue as he shifted his weight.

As she waited, she bit her lip. Did he even know when she was going home if it took him this long to think about it?

Although it was probably not high on his list of priorities, Star couldn't wait to get back to her family after all the nights spent sleeping in the cold *tepay*. Even though she wasn't expecting it to be a holiday, she didn't anticipate living in these conditions.

"As long as is necessary," he answered, a strange light in his eyes.

As her eyes widened, she gasped. "That's it- as long as is necessary. You don't have a better timeframe than that." He stared at her until she realised what she had just said and quickly said, "*Kussa.*" Gods, was she determined to keep getting it wrong with him? It was wrong not to greet him properly and to yell at him.

A smile spread across his face. "*Kussa*? It's a little late for that, *Immani.*" He didn't look irritated. That had to be good, right? As he leaned in, his breath fell on her ear, the heat of his body caressing her. A blend of sweat, warm wood, and tangy citrus surrounded him. "A little disrespectful thing aren't you?" he whispered.

Her breath came out in a stutter. As she breathed in, she caught more of his scent. His eyes devoured her heaving chest. Was he teasing her? She was about to ask Hadak when Ulla appeared.

From the opposite direction, she strolled around the corner. She raised her eyebrows and swept her gaze over the three of them. Respectfully, she lowered her head.

Fire filled Hadak's eyes as he grunted in acknowledgement. Upon lifting his lids, it had disappeared. Hadak glanced at her once more before leaving with Furan at his side.

"Well, what did *Avayak* want from you?" she asked with a playful gleam.

"Nothing." A smile spread across Star's face as she shrugged her shoulders and shook her head at Ulla in amusement. Ulla regarded her with humour and speculation. Using one of her many throbbing sore fingers, she pointed at Ulla, "No, just no."

"Why? Despite Ulla's low voice and cajoling, her eyebrows wiggled as she replied, "He's handsome, strong, a leader and defender who cares for his family and the Horde."

"Ulla *nen*, I have enough problems with the *fhalah's* in the food *tepay*."

Seeing Illasay's head poking out of the flap, they both glanced at her, but she ducked back away. How much had she seen? Star didn't know, but she seemed a bit sour.

Ulla pulled a face, hissing in annoyance. "They are all after him. They want to become his mate, his *bryd*," Ulla said.

"Really?" She wasn't sure why she was surprised as it was the same in the human colony. There was a desire among the women for someone of influence and in a higher position.

Walking along the path, Ulla laughed at her with twinkles in her eyes. "*Seya*, of course. If they can convince a Horde king to join them, then they will no longer be bound to serve the Horde. They only want to become his *bryd* to hold it over the others."

"Hold what other them?"

"Some of them compete for whose warrior has the highest ranking, and *Avayak* is obviously 'the' highest ranking, coveted by all, and also hot." Ulla fanned her face dramatically. Star laughed at Ulla's antics, as she intended. Her voice was serious as she said, "Everyone wants him."

"Oh," Star replied quietly as they passed her *tepay* on the way to Ulla's.

"*Seya,* it's not pretty," she said, holding back the flap to her *tepay*. "Not all the *fhalah's* in the Horde are like that. It's unkind of me to generalise, but Illasay is the worst." Ulla grimaced, and Star wrinkled her nose in agreement.

Typical, she had ended up working with a group of females in the Horde who were all threatened by other females. There was competition in the colony, competition between some of the females and the males. Not many mated for love.

Once a year, there was a rush to find a partner. In the spring, the colony held a dance to see who had joined, then the games began. Games that showcase the best of males and females.

Ulla's mother waved her over, and she blinked when she saw her smile. She had lighter skin than some of the Horde and was the oldest Zandian she had seen. From the temples down, her dark brown hair looked lighter, as if it were fading out, not in a few white streaks, but all at once.

Ulla's mother seemed hesitant in her steps as if she wasn't quite sure of herself. That's when Star noticed Nasan hovering near Ulla's mother, watching her walk and standing nearby. She turned with a frown, and he took a huge step back and looked around innocently as if he hadn't just been standing guard and worried about her falling.

"Star, welcome. My Ulla and Furan told me all about you," Ulla's mother said.

Star shot Ulla a worried glance. Ulla shrugged, her eyes on her *Brathar*. Of course, he was her brother. She could see the resemblance now that she was looking at him.

"Do you all live together?" she asked, smiling warmly. It brought back memories of home for her.

"*Seya*, offspring remain in the family unit until they become warriors or *bryd*. If they get a place within the Horde, then they get their own *tepay*," Ulla's mother said, looking up at her curiously.

Due to the fact that she wasn't treating her like a bug, she didn't find it offensive.

The Horde worked much the same as at home. Families kept their children until they found a partner or job that enabled them to live independently.

"Could you please give us a minute, *Brathar*?" Ulla asked. In response to his nonplussed look, she huffed. "Time on our own, *Brathar*."

"Ah!" His eyes slid quickly to Star before darting away. Giving her a wide birth, he stepped out through the flaps.

She frowned at his odd behaviour. It was like he wouldn't look at her. "Is he okay?" she asked, her eyes still on the flap.

"My offspring is tongue-tied," Ulla's *Mathar* said. "You can call me Iylla."

"Hello. Thank you for your time. I hope I am not intruding."

"Absolutely not. Ulla told me you didn't know anyone except for the warriors and *Avayak*, and those lot don't chat up a storm." She pulled Star into a chair. "Sit, sit, we'll get you something to eat before you go to your *tepay*." Ulla grinned as she piled food onto a plate. "You are welcome to visit me at any time."

"*Mathar* thinks he should be more forward, but he's not the type," Ulla explained, gesturing where her *Brathar* had disappeared.

Iylla harrumphed and poured drinks for everyone.

"If he doesn't say what he wants, he won't get anywhere. I have one offspring who doesn't wish to have a warrior of her own and the other who doesn't go after what he does want," she sighed, shaking her head in exaggeration at Star. "I can't hold the next generation if these two things don't change."

She laughed out loud. Iylla looked at Star with a raised eyebrow. "You sound like my mother," Star explained.

"Ah," she took Star's hand gently, eyes full of kindness. "You must miss her."

"*Seya*, I do." She sighed heavily as Ulla sat to her right, proud that her voice only wobbled a little. "I'm glad *Fathar* is okay, that's all that matters," she said.

Iylla told her, "You are a good daughter to do what you did."

She blinked desperately to stop her eyes from watering. "How do you know about that?"

"Uh," Ulla said, flinging her feet up on the bar under the table. Iylla frowned at her and pointed her bony finger at the floor as she tapped Ulla's shin. As Ulla rolled her eyes, she popped her feet back on the floor again. "Nasan was one of the warriors who found you on the plains."

"Oh!" She never even realised. When she realised that a Horde king had come for her, she hadn't paid much attention to the other warriors. He hadn't come for her, but for...she didn't know.

"That's okay, Star, I know it was traumatic for you," she said kindly.

"Well, I suppose so," she replied.

The rest of the evening was spent in pleasant conversation. When she found herself with a silent escort to her *tepay*, one she knew was following her, she didn't call out. Nasan was evidently trying to keep his presence quiet. She didn't want to embarrass him by bringing attention to the fact that she knew he was there and he had failed at being stealthy.

Honestly, he wasn't trying all that hard. She wasn't judging, she was the least stealthy person. Ever.

It was sweet that he was making sure she got to her *tepay* alright. Having been smacked the last time she walked around with an escort, this gave her some peace of mind.

As she rounded the last bend, she saw Hadak fighting.

The air was filled with the clash of swords and grunts of pain. For a moment, her heart stopped. As she watched his back muscles bunch and shift, and the sweat gleamed on his body in the fading light, her mouth dried up.

A sudden image of him between her thighs made her face flame up. An errant thought of what it would be like to finish what he intended that night quickly swept through her mind.

As if he could feel her eyes on him, his head rose.

The pace of her walk slowed. The warrior sparring with him tried to exploit the split-second lapse in attention, but Hadak twisted.

A breath of awe and fear filled her lungs as he swung his sword down, catching the warrior's sword. There was an echo of sound as the swords clashed. With a dark frown on his face, he returned his gaze to hers.

Her life was in limbo while she was there, so maybe she shouldn't have appreciated just how handsome he was, but it was nearly impossible not to when all she could see was his broad shoulders between her thighs.

His only acknowledgement was a barely perceptible nod, and she hurried towards her *tepay*.

When she ducked under the flaps and stared around the cold, dark space, she shuddered at the thought of how long she might have to stay.

As she pushed away the negative thoughts in her head, she started digging up a spot that could serve as a fire pit. Scooping out dust, dirt, and tiny stones, she pushed until her hands ached. Her hands were on fire but not yet bloody.

Thinking of the next day's work, she decided it was wise to stop before she couldn't work. There was no doubt she would be accused of being lazy or some other nonsense by the *fhalah's* if she was unable to work.

Huffing when she noticed a few spots on her fingers that were open and weeping. If she had a fire, she could dry them out. She pushed away bitter, wishful thoughts.

Flicking off her boots - there was no use poking holes through her only pair - she pushed the dust out with the sides of her feet. Although it was long and exhausting, at least she wouldn't have to sleep while inhaling everything.

Her eyes were fixed on the place where she planned to dig out. If she lit a fire without a pit, it would spit on her or her furs during the night. Her already shivering body agreed that she needed to finish it before the cold set in.

As her exhausted, shivering body collapsed into the furs, her arms wrapped around her middle, the lonely room was oppressive, dark, and too quiet.

Having to sleep alone in a strange place with people she didn't know had her hair standing on end and her eyes widening. It was exhausting.

As a matter of fact, she had slept better in Hadak's arms than on her own. There was something about him that should have scared her: he was big, male, and attractive in a rough, wild, and sexy way. The thought of him made her hands clench as she clamped down on the fur.

In the days spent on the plains, he confused her, but he made her feel things for the first time. It was not in her nature to be sensual. Unlike the girls in the colony, she had never felt that overwhelming desire for someone. The males she flirted with were more of an experiment to see if she would ever want to kiss someone like they were her last breath of life. She didn't until Hadak.

The monotony or boredom of her life seemed so overwhelming. When she wasn't playing strings for others' amusement, she served her parents faithfully. Never had she strayed, and never had she slipped away with a boy behind the house for a quick kiss. When Hadak threatened her with punishment and ordered her to come along, did she bat an eye? No.

Okay, she batted an eye, she wondered what might happen, but she hardly fought. She had spent her life not fighting and doing what any good girl would do because that was who she was. An eternal optimist. Usually, she tries to look on the bright side, but as she collapsed in her furs, she wondered if there were any positives to look forward to.

After three hours of thoughts spinning in her head, she eventually dozed off.

A sigh of pleasure filled her as she woke up under the fur, breathed hot air into her hand, and buried her nose in it.

Getting ready didn't take her long. Glancing at the stains on her dress, she slipped it on. It took her even less time to walk to the food *tepay*.

There was a frosty reception, but she wasn't expecting anything different; even so, it still chafed a bit to have them make things difficult. Illasay appeared to take her presence personally, going so far as to bump into her with a tray of hot drinks. Star cursed, and Illasay offered an insincere, "*Kussa*."

"No problem," Star murmured in the common tongue, still pretending ignorance.

"It's so *sako*," she laughed, then pouted at Star, faking concern as she checked Star over.

Oh good, she just loved being called it as much as she loved being called stupid.

"Leave the *Immani* to her pots and pans," Ghertun ordered with a smirk.

With a nasty smile on her face, Illasay said, "Have fun." Didn't she know her face would freeze that way?

She was glad they had left. She didn't have to watch her back while washing, nor did she have to flinch whenever someone passed behind her.

Gritting her teeth, she rubbed her sore arms and longed for a bath. Before leaving, she washed her hands and face with leftover warm water. The process didn't take long, and when she left, she was surprised to see Hadak waiting for her.

When he saw her leave on her own, he shifted. "You are later than the others," he observed, checking behind her as well.

Mind on her furs, she shrugged her shoulders and noticed he was holding something. "What's that?"

His eyebrows furrowed. "I see you have forgotten to greet me again."

She could tell he wasn't interested in going through the formality of greeting because he was already pulling his hands out from behind him, and when she saw what he was holding, she gasped.

"Is it for me?" she asked with excitement.

"Who else would it be for? I'm here waiting for you, aren't I?" He asked, giving her the most beautiful strings she had ever seen. "Will you play for me, *Immani* Star?"

Her hands shook as they touched the bronze, precious metal strings. Her hands clenched around it like she was holding a part of her home. The soreness in her hands protested against the thought of playing. While sniffing, she tucked the strings under her arm, trying to think of an excuse.

"*Kussa*, it upsets you." There was a visible sense of concern in his voice.

Holding out his hand, he escorted her to her *tepay*. "I should have thought it would remind you of home." The reddening of his face was accompanied by a grimace as he wiped a hand across the back of his neck into his hair. "How are you settling in?" It was obvious that checking on someone's well-being was a new experience for him. It was clear that he wanted to know what was wrong, but he seemed hesitant to ask as if it wasn't something he was used to doing.

"It's fine," she answered, since there was nothing else she could say. She couldn't exactly bite out, 'Considering the conditions I live in, I am likely to die in the hovel you built for me. And oh yes, the *fhalah's* in your Horde, except for a few, are horrible creatures.'

Hmm, yeah, she wasn't telling him that.

When they reached the end of the row where her *tepay* was, she was about to go in when he moved.

After shifting, he opened his mouth as if to say something before closing it and reaching out. She swallowed as his fingers traced her cheekbones. His black eyes followed.

She felt her heart pound as his hand clenched around her cheek. He looked as if he was about to say something when Furan called out to him. His frustration was evident as he glanced over his shoulder and then let go and walked away, leaving her confused.

At least, she didn't have to play the string. She sighed in relief.

Chapter 7

She was vastly mistaken if she thought the next day would be better. She had to be woken up by someone. In the cold light of the day, with almost no sleep, the vile words of the *fhalah* only seemed more horrifying.

In addition to her cold skin, she had dark circles under her eyes.

It seemed that Nasan was a permanent fixture at any time food was being served. When the warriors came for food, he stopped her from doing everything. However, once the warriors left, it was evident that the *fhalah's* wouldn't do anything heavy. Illasay took it to a whole new level of cruelty with the permission of Ghertun.

Bringing in big pans of water, lifting meat, and even cleaning the metal shoots that let out smoke and prevented fires, all fell to her. Ideally, it should be a two-person job.

There were several comments about how her thin legs couldn't hold a warrior to her during mating, unlike Zandian's muscles. She had to work hard to keep her blush at bay. The whole thing was obviously aimed at boosting Illasay's ego and tearing down Star.

The way they addressed her made it clear that they were talking negatively about her, even though they didn't know she could understand them. They talked about her as if she wasn't there.

No one in the colony would behave like this. There was something jarring about their hatred.

At the back, two *fhalah*s didn't get involved. They didn't comment, nor did they get involved in giving her their tasks.

The warriors stared at Star even though she made no attempt to speak with them. Intuk sat at the table and glared at her, despite Star's lack of engagement. Her presence seemed like a personal insult.

There was only one time she spoke in front of him, and she definitely learned her lesson. Ulla said it was an old-fashioned view that most warriors wouldn't object to now, but some still adhered to the old ways, like Intuk.

She flinched on the third day when she heard how much 'it' smelled, meaning her, especially when they started to wonder loudly if she was actually an animal. Star had just about had it at this point.

It had barely been a week since she began working with the vile *fhalah's*, and she was already finding it hard to keep her mouth shut.

Every day that passed without seeing her family made her miss them more and more. Concerned about how the Jutin had entered the colony, she racked her brain for answers. Her absence and the lack of news from home probably contributed to her wondering about it. It was unlikely that she would get any answers.

She was worried about everything now. Jutin, the Horde, everything. At night, while lying in her furs, she stared into the darkness while warriors laughed as they passed by her *tepay*. It was the echo of laughter that brought her back to life outside her *tepay* and made her forget about the horrors that she experienced in the food *tepay*.

Her fatigue prevented her from visiting Ulla's. It was a blessing that she still walked with Star. She finally found the courage to ask Ulla why Hadak wasn't present at meals; she explained that the *fhalah's* in the food *tepay* were bringing the meals to his *tepay*. The only time he joined them was at feasts. Most of the time, he ate with his first.

He had become this presence she had never seen but always heard about. The *fhalah's* hoped to catch his attention. It seemed particularly clear that Illasay thought she stood a chance. She boasted about Hadak watching her while she served him, his gaze straying to her arse. As Star frowned, she wondered if she felt jealous. A small amount was present, but it was mostly hidden under her feeling of fatigue and hopelessness.

Her teeth gritted in fury as she replayed the conversation she had heard earlier.

"For now, I'll keep him happy, just in case *Avayak* doesn't want me," Illasay scoffed like that was impossible, and she didn't believe it.

Star continued scrubbing, a bit more vigorously this time, as she considered the rest of what she had said.

"My favourite thing to do is sneak out with the warrior. He kisses me in all the right places," Illasay giggled, and her friends joined in gushing and fawning.

"What if he tells someone?"

"Ha! I told him that I had the *Avayak's* interest. He won't tell anyone in case *Avayak* takes me as his *bryd*. He's worried *Avayak* will punish me or him," she giggled again. It sounded obnoxious to Star. "It made him jealous, and the love making was violently grand, but I have no fear, he'll keep it quiet. We'll just keep meeting by the river," Illasay continued.

A river? She thought it sounded great, and her aching muscles agreed.

"What's it doing?" Ghertun asked, pointing at Star with a bony finger.

"Cleaning the bottom of the fire pit," Illasay replied.

"We never clean that."

"Exactly, might as well have her do it instead of standing doing nothing," Illasay said with an air of authority.

She heard the patter of feet before dirt was kicked over the spot she had just cleaned, to the laughter of the *fhalah*s standing with Illasay. In order to calm herself, she promised herself that she would wash in the river. All she had to do was hold it together.

"You can try to make her talk to the warriors. If we manage to punish her, we might be able to put an end to Nasan's disapproving stares and Ulla's *Mathar* telling my *Mathar* about the abuse," her audible disgust made Star's mouth twitch.

It was at least good to know that she had some friends. Nasan, Ulla's brother, hovered over her like she was somebody to be cared for. The protective nature of an older *Brathar* towards his sister's friend. Star used to do the same with her *Brathar*'s friends.

In an attempt to get her to speak in front of the warriors, the *fhalah's* tried to trip and pinch her. It was obvious they wanted her punished for speaking, but Star refused to utter a word.

Today was terrible.

Another comment about how she smelled, and she might throw a platter at them. When she had finished cleaning the last platter, she blew out the lights. After closing the flaps, she returned to her *tepay*. She was mocked by the empty tub and dusty floor.

She would take a bath in the stream, but only if she cleaned the furs and floor of dust. Sure, it'd be back in a day after blowing in all night, but if she was getting clean, she wanted a fresh *tepay*. She beat the fur with her hands, causing her red raw palms to tighten and ache.

As soon as she had finished dusting the furs, she laid them over the bathtub. Using her hands, she pushed the dust out of the *tepay*. It was a good thing no one was watching her because now she felt like the animal the *fhalah*s kept calling her.

It was dark by the time she finished; the second sun had just set behind the horizon.

Horde warriors around the Horde's edges had one blind spot, according to Illasay. Not everyone stuck to the rules of not speaking to males if you weren't a *bryd*. Illasay laughed when she recalled meeting her warrior on the rocks by the stream, which was a favourite place for them. Other *fhalah's* tittered, asking her where.

Her directions gave Star a general direction to the river, so she was quietly grateful.

The dried guts on her dress, along with other fluids she tried not to think about were weeks old and disgusting. Not to mention she could smell herself.

It was Illasay who had unintentionally provided her with a way to get clean. The tub wasn't an option yet, but she'd get there eventually, one day.

Her hands were slow to form the pit she was digging. She might be able to have a fire in a couple of weeks. The constant cold and hot in the food *tepay* was jarring. She was hyperaware of slight changes in wind direction, sudden temperature drops, and the heat of the fire.

Using her feet, she moved the mud, dust, and dirt as far from her *tepay*s flaps as possible, but it wouldn't make much of a difference. The wind would blow it back into the room.

Finished, she shut the flaps and began walking. She kept her head down while sneaking through the *tepay*s.

As she wondered whether she should ask about her dress with the cape, she hesitated. It wasn't pretty, but it was warmer than the silk one. In the food *tepay*, she would probably sweat more than she did right now, but she didn't want to sleep cold anymore.

Warriors were paces apart, and a flat edge of a *tepay* backed up to a rock. She ran behind the rock, waiting for a cry to go up to say she'd been caught and exhaling when there was none.

She sighed in relief as she made her way to the sound of water. Suddenly, her heart pounded faster because she desperately wanted to be clean. Was it risky? Yes, of course! Groaning, she just hoped it wasn't too deep. She could stand in the river up to her knees and clean without worrying or flinching.

She exhaled with pleasure when she saw the water.

Grasping the hem of her dress, she grimaced at the sticky feel of juices and other substances. Then she whipped it off and scrubbed it in the river, trying to remove the stains and marks. Cool river water made her hands freeze.

The river appealed to her. An overhanging branch was the perfect place for her dress to hang.

She waded in, bracing herself against the cold. Maybe she was just numb, but the first touch wasn't as shocking as she had expected.

To ensure something was underneath her, she took care to put her foot out first. After reaching waist height, she picked up handfuls of grit from the bottom and rubbed it all over. It must have been cold for her body to tremble, but she didn't feel it.

Just being clean made her happy.

As she walked back, her dress would probably cling to her body. There was no one around, so it was a good thing.

As she ducked down for the sixth time to wash her hair, a strong whoosh of water caught her and pulled her under.

A short and garbled exclamation escaped her lips as her head slipped under. Trying to grab something or find purchase with her feet, she flailed her arms and legs in a blind panic.

She was dragged along by the river and thrown around like a doll. A particularly sharp rock struck her shin. After she surfaced, her head was dragged under again before she could catch her breath.

In the midst of doing cartwheels underwater, she realised that she might die. She panicked when she realised it was all too real. She felt her lungs burning and her eyes popping out of her head.

The journey down the river felt short. Hopefully, someone would find her body and return it to her family.

In spite of the spinning, when she pushed her feet down, all she found was more water, no seabed. In an attempt to figure out swimming's mechanics, she kept pinwheeling her arms. Although swimming didn't appear difficult, she was unable to make any progress.

She heard crashing, stirring in the water, then felt an arm around her waist dragging her up. Her arms were floating, and her eyes were just closing when she heard a muffled voice.

When she was pulled out, she collapsed onto the chest of a warrior, taking desperate gasping breaths that were pain-filled while she coughed and sputtered. The tightness in her chest was accompanied by burning in her throat as she breathed in. Her body trembling, she felt furs being laid over her by whoever pulled her out.

Upon looking up, she saw Nasan frowning deeply at her. "What did you think you were doing?" he asked, throwing on his fur.

This was the first time he had spoken to her, and she wasn't sure what the protocol was, but she was too tired and scared to hesitate. She coughed out in a reasonable tone, "I need a bath."

He raised his eyebrows, and she thought that until then, he hadn't released he'd spoken to her. What happened to the tub? Why didn't you fill it up?" A wrinkle in his brow, he continued, "I thought you were waiting for a free day to bathe."

The fur he lent her was a small one he threw over his shoulder, so it didn't cover much of her nakedness. He clenched his jaw as his eyes fell on her.

Was he disgusted? It was hard to tell.

Being naked as the day she was born and shivering like a lost young *Guyipe* was embarrassing. "How could I fill the tub?" she stuttered, struggling to get the words out.

When understanding filled his eyes, he groaned, nodding and running a hand down his face. "What happened to your dress?"

"Back where I was, it was hanging over a tree. I'll get it."

As she began to stand, he stopped her, his fingers curling before he touched her. "No, stay there. I know where you went in."

She rubbed her arms as he marched on to the other side of the river, thanking the god, Satur, that Nasan had found her. If he hadn't done what he did, she might have died.

Her body dripped cold water, but it was worth it. Afterwards, when she was all wrapped up in her furs, all clean and a little warm, she was certain she would appreciate it.

Nasan suddenly crashed through the tree and dust, holding up her dripping dress. "Were you planning on walking back in this?" He glanced at her and rumpled the dress in his fist as he spoke.

"I don't have anything else to wear. Someone took my dress away from me," she stated, tears welling up in her eyes. While shivering, she reached out her hands, but when he looked at them, he shook his head in disapproval. "Well, I can't go back naked."

Inhaling deeply and pinching his nose, he closed his eyes before taking a deep breath. He said, "Turn around."

After hearing his sharp tone, she turned at once. A few moments later, she felt the weight of his fur as he laid it upon her. Her cheeks burned as she realised he had given her the rest of his fur. He was standing naked beside her, and out of sheer curiosity, she was tempted to take a peek. Although he was handsome, he was not right for her.

There had only been one Zandian she really wanted to look at, but as days passed with more of the same misery to deal with, that one was evaporating fast.

As resolutely as she could, she kept her eyes open in front of her. "*Behku*," she whispered in thanks, and he twitched his eyes in response.

He bunched her dress in his hand while she wrapped the fur around herself properly. In the midst of the coughing fit, his eyebrows dipped low, and the sharp edges drew inward, giving him a look of concern. "Let's go."

"But you've got nothing on!"

"I'll survive," he deadpanned.

Her eyes closed as he pulled her alongside him. She found his bare skin to be warmer than she anticipated after he had jumped into the river to save her.

"Come on."

With purpose, he pulled her through the *tepay*s, his arm curling around her, tucking her close to him. After dodging into a space, he crouched over her, blocking her from being seen as two warriors passed by. The two of them looked over at him and laughed, assuming he had a Zandian *fhalah* pinned to the side of his cart.

In order to cover her head, he crouched further over her, tucking her head under his chin. Embarrassed and hoping that they would pass, she closed her eyes in mortification.

"*Radac huysis ryss*," said one with a dirty laugh. *

"*T'e fhalah traeas t'uh thlana*." **

Nasan grunted and made hip movements imitating something she didn't want to think about. A faint feeling hit Star, and he whispered, "*Kussa*."

Nodding, she hoped they'd leave. Her cheeks were red, her ears burned, and the mortification she felt doubled when he grunted again, making mating sounds. She'd never wanted to melt into a puddle more than she did then, to disappear into nothingness. He had a weird look on his face as he moved his hips, and his eyes were on her, filled with something she couldn't put a name on.

After seeing nothing but Nasan's backside for a while, the warriors grumbled about not getting a show. Nasan shuddered, leaning forward. Her face was pressed into his chest for a minute. He inhaled deeply, then abruptly pushed away from her.

"Come on," he gruffly said, breathing hard. He held his hand out for her. It was such an unexpected gesture, she took it without thinking.

After slipping into a *tepay* and pulling her inside, she recognised his sword and braces. He had bought her to his *tepay*. She didn't know why, but she assumed he lived with his *Mathar*. She didn't know if that was allowed, but she wasn't going to argue. She felt safe with Ulla's brother; with Nasan.

Letting go of his hand, she walked to the edge of the fire pit, sat down on a bench, hands out, face close to the flames, sighing with satisfaction. A rock could be falling out of the sky headed right for her, and she didn't think she could move.

"You should move your face away from the flames," he urged, his voice vibrating.

Finally, her hands were warm. Her fingers tingled, and her eyes closed. She heard him moving around but couldn't move because it felt like a heavy weight had fallen on her. Although she knew she should, and she tried to tell herself to get up, her head fell back, and her body listed sleepily to one side.

She felt hands on her arms. She jolted, but he shushed her and laid her down by the fire, placing a fur under her and another on top. Her voice shook as she whispered, "*Behku.*"

"*H'ay tasar bas seya,*" he said as he sat beside her, and she finally drifted off to sleep. ***

As she had become accustomed to being alone during the night, when he shuddered, she was startled and peeled her eyes open. He was still in front of her, but the breaths that she was taking were falling on his neck. At some point, he must have laid beside her. As she breathed out, he shuddered, and she tucked her head back in and fell back asleep.

She was woken up by a rough hand. "Morning," she tossed her head and ducked it back under the fur. It's so warm. Another shake.

Her voice was hoarse as she croaked, "*Seya.*" She felt relaxed and rejuvenated for the first time in days. Stretching, her body protested, wanting to soak up the warmth a little more and not get out. Please don't let it be morning yet.

"Wake up," a rough voice said, and she immediately recognised the tone. Her eyes flew open to find Hadak standing by the opening, his shoulders stiff, eyes on her.

She cleared her throat and pushed up to her elbows. Hadak's eyes stayed on her as she stood. Star spotted Nasan by the fire pit with no expression, black eyes straight ahead, hands behind his back.

As he looked at her in Nasan's furs, Hadak's lips curled. He clenched his fist at his side, and a tick appeared under his eye.

"Kanek and Dassay saw you with a *fhalah*. They described her as small." Hadak's questioning tone was irritated, and Star looked at Nasan uncomfortably.

There was really no way she could explain this without sounding whiny. She didn't want to seem ungrateful. It could be worse. That was obvious to her.

It might feel bad now, but the city regularly whipped humans for punishment. They put them on hard labour for six years before reviewing the case. Therefore, there was no way she could complain.

Nasan's lips curled, and he turned to her, but she shook her head. He could make things worse if he complained for her. When no response came, Hadak opened the flaps.

As she licked her lips, she asked Nasan, "My dress?"

He didn't flinch, just extended his hand toward the fire pit, grinning at Hadak. What motivated him to do that? Now Hadak was murderous. When she wrinkled her nose, she pulled it quickly down, then dropped the furs around her. She handed the bundle back to Nasan, but he refused to take it.

"For your *tepay*," he hissed, eyes on his *Avayak*.

Hadak's eyebrows shot downward. She was almost propelled through the flaps by his arm. His presence cast a dark and looming shadow behind her. Furan looked up from *Guyipe's* pen with a frown and a look of concern when he saw Hadak with her.

His much bigger legs covered more distance than hers, despite her efforts to keep up. The moment he reached his *tepay*, he threw back the flaps violently, almost shaking with anger. He pushed her in and then left quickly.

He left her there. After spending all day pacing, she finally sat by the fire and waited. The anticipation was unbearable. Why did he leave her here? What was he so angry about?

When he returned, his anger had subsided. There was a relaxed look on his face, and his eyes seemed curious.

She twisted her hands as she waited, assuming she had done something really wrong to cause him that much anger. She finally caved and asked him. "What's wrong?"

"*Immani*, you let him touch you after I explained our ways to you," he hissed, cutting his hand through the air between them, making her jump.

Her eyes rolled as she told him, "I didn't have much choice, you know," she said, shrugging her shoulders.

"He took you by force." His eyes blazed with uncontrollable fury and the need for retribution.

"No, not really. It was nice to be warm."

"Warmth?" he questioned darkly, a deadly glean in his eye.

"From his fire pit, it's been cold at night," she said, which confused him.

He pinched the bridge of his nose in frustration. "Did he take you, *Immani*?"

"He had to," she told him.

"Had to?"

"Yes, I was soaking wet and shivering."

He gave her a look before gripping her throat tightly but not choking. "You let him touch you?"

Frowning in confusion, she was sure they weren't talking about the same thing. She tried shaking her head, but she was stopped by the pressure of his hand. "He pulled me out of the river when I went under, took me back to his *tepay*, kept an eye on me," she explained in a choked rush.

As he froze, his hand trembled. He clicked his tongue sharply, "Why were you in the river?"

"Bathing," she answered. He believed Nasan had mated with her. *Fhok*, no wonder he looked furious.

"In the river," he scoffed. "*Sako Immani.*"

Despite knowing he wasn't saying it maliciously like the *fhalah's*, she didn't want to hear it right now. Being dragged down all day by those bitches was too much. They were bitches to her.

She let out a frustrated growl.

He dragged her close by the throat and onto her tiptoes.

"You'll drive me mad," he hissed, eyes on his hand with satisfaction, his thumb stroking her throat lovingly.

"Why?"

"My mind wonders to you even when I order it not to," he told her with seriousness, whispering it against her lips as he bent down.

As he tried to kiss her, she turned her head and shook her head. "No, I won't do anything with you. The last time you threw me out, you were harsh," she said.

"You make me weak, *Immani*," he whispered to her. It nearly caused her to weaken when she heard those words. His nose drew a line along her neck, making her breath shaky.

"How do I weaken you?" Was it the same feeling she felt around him? As if there was an awareness of him all the time, like a hum of reassurance and comfort just below the surface. Perhaps, comfort wasn't the right word. It was more like safety and comfort combined. There was also a buzz of attraction. Added to that was a flare of need.

"Because I didn't know what was happening to you, it was a feeling I hadn't had before," he replied. "I am *Avayak*. You were in my care and the Hordes' care, and you almost died." He shook his head against her neck. His lips settled at the bottom of her ear as he whispered to her. "I never expected to lose you. Zandians don't get fevers."

"You weren't sure how to handle it?"

"*Nen*," he breathed against her. Goosebumps broke out on my arms. "It would have been impossible for me to have you here when I returned. My state of mind was too tense when I left the *tepay*. I was afraid that if you stayed, I might hurt you," he explained.

"Afraid you'd hurt me?"

"My need for you is frightening, it's almost single-minded, and I'm much stronger than you. When I thought Nasan touched you," he stepped away, shaking his head, struggling to contain his emotions. "*Nen*, it's almost illogical how I feel for you."

"How do you feel?"

"Like there's something I must explore. I never ignore a sign from the gods." Eyes on her face, checking to see how she would react. Star was mostly confused. Days had passed with him ignoring her.

"I thought you'd decided on my punishment and wanted nothing else to do with me," she told him, shrugging.

His eyes grew hooded. "I wanted to lick your *ryss*," he whispered, moving, stalking her now with a hungry gleam in his eye. "Still do."

"But you stopped!"

"Because your eyes rolled in your head, and you choked," he said, looking at her exposed skin.

"I did?" Well, that sounded horrible.

"Yes, you did."

He suddenly said, "I want you, *Immani*." It made her squirm because she always felt the same, but she had never been with a male before. After spending a night with the *Avayak*, she felt her expectations would be changed.

She always pictured a quiet man working in the fields, maybe with a small home where she and her husband could raise their children. It seemed fanciful, and her brother and father scared off the few men she was interested in. Over time, it became one of those things she didn't think about.

"How was I supposed to know you..." she choked on her next words, aware that anything she did could extend her stay.

"Speak freely," he told her as he pulled her down onto the cushions in front of his fire pit.

Her envious gaze devoured his plush fabrics, but his fire pit was what she craved most. If she could build something like that, she would never move from it.

The last time she was here, she hadn't appreciated simple things, like the firepit and seating area. Mostly, she had been thinking about how little he had in his *tepay* compared to hers, but now, his was a palace.

Some of the *tepay*s she had seen since overflowed with furniture, fabrics, books, and things they had picked up at markets or had taken from the human colony. Occasionally, if something appealed to them, they took it.

Since her voice was hoarse from the river, she said, "I don't know what you want from me." He reached for a cup and handed it to her, an orange liquid that smelled just like the stuff the *fhalah's* had in the food *tepay*. "What are you looking for from any human?"

Humans were so thankful to be given somewhere to stay when they would have died in space, they never questioned their rules. Many humans in the colony, including her *Mathar* - she made beautiful covers by hand - placed anything they thought the Hordes would like on the main path. It was always their hope that if they saw something they liked, they would allow them to move freely about the planet and gather more resources.

After taking a sip of the drink, her eyes widened at the sweet and sharp flavours. When she swallowed the rest, she felt a pleasant burn followed by his eyebrows going up and his mouth quirking. After filling it, he handed it back to her.

"What would you like?" he asked, surprising her.

Before answering, she took a sip of the *sok* and thought about it. She no longer had dreams, at least not very interesting dreams, as she used to have.

"I don't know."

There was a hissing sound, perhaps a confused exclamation. He filled her cup as she drained the last drop. She was fascinated by the flashes of orange and yellow as she watched them dance.

"You don't know what you want?"

"Not anymore," she replied, looking at him in the firelight. The play of light and shadow on him was just as captivating as the fire. In some ways, Zandians were barbarians, but watching them this week, she noticed they looked after the Horde and dealt with any threats to it in blood. "Simple things, maybe."

"Simple things, *Immani*?" he asked. "No family of your own."

His probing tone made her cheeks flame, and why was she blushing so much?

She admitted, "Maybe once."

"What do you do apart from playing strings?" He stared at her intently, almost as if he wanted to see inside her. Hands clasped loosely behind his head, his eyes held hers.

I helped my *Mathar* deliver babies. I always liked seeing tiny, squalling infants with button noses and screaming." She laughed and shook her head. "I thought it would be peaceful and beautiful, but it wasn't."

His eyes glowed with interest, he drank *sok*, and she mirrored him. There was a heavy feeling in her limbs. When he smiled like that, his lips looked delightfully kissable. As if about to laugh, one side of his face was pulled up. His eyebrows rose and tilted to the side as she cleared her throat.

"Oh, it was beautiful, but it was my first time attending a birth. The woman let out an unholy shriek." He laughed at her as she grimaced. "From that moment on, it was all shrieks, shouting, and cursing. At one point, I was convinced I would never have children. Ever," she said, her face soft, her eyes dreamy.

"You don't have children then? Did it scare you away from the idea? Is this why you don't have a warrior?"

Letting out her breath in a slow exhale, she took a drink while thinking about her future. "No, it didn't put me off. When the baby was delivered, the mother's face told me she thought it was all worth it, and when she fell again within three months. I realised she truly thought the effort was worthwhile." Star grinned at him, her nose wrinkled. "Even after all the cursing of her partner, she thought it was worth it and loved him still."

"Is there a reason why you don't have a warrior of your own?"

A little confused, she evaded, "We don't have warriors." It was clear from his nod that he understood her point. "They are simply called men."

"What do you look for in these men?" His eyes glinted with jealousy.

"Me?"

"*Seya*," he rasped.

It would be nice to come home to a friendly, quiet man who brings a smile to my face. A home with three rooms. Our family had a small one when we were growing up, then two when we started working."

His eyes flitted over her face as she talked about her home, taking in every expression, every glance. When she talked about men, his mouth pulled down.

"I suppose I wanted someone like my *Fathar*. To share the love he and my *Mathar* have. There was always whispering, laughing, and talking between them. It was the first thing we woke up to and the last thing we heard at night." Her lips twitched with a smile as she remembered.

"Wanted?" he asked, filling up the cup again, his eyes on her.

She struggled to lift her eyelids and remain focused on him. Taking a midnight dip in the river left her more tired than she expected. Her response was, "Hmm."

He stood pushing the wood over the fire. When he sat, it was closer to her this time. His exposed shoulders and flexing muscles on his rock-hard abs caught her eye when he relaxed back.

"Not anymore, then. What are you looking for in a warrior now?" he asked.

"I don't know," she answered honestly.

"A Horde warrior?" he asked, his fists clenching.

"Hmm, I hadn't really thought about it."

There are no warriors you want." His whole focus was on her, desperate for an answer.

"*Nen.*"

"Maybe you need an *Avayak.*"

"*Nen,*" she answered, sure of that. There was a strong attraction between the two, but would her personality be able to stand up to his?

His eyes danced as he leaned into her. "This is why you need an *Avayak*, someone more stubborn who can take that *nen* and change it into a *seya,*" he whispered, the air heavy with meaning between them.

Sweet gods!

*Ride her cunt

**The female looks too small

***You deserve better

Chapter 8

She shook her head at his temerity and was surprised when the room tilted. "Have you noticed your *tepay* is at an angle?"

His laughter hit her neck, and he grabbed her chin while looking into her eyes. He smiled, and she poked at his lips, intrigued by this small quirk. She squealed as he bit the tips of her fingers. As soon as he had taken it in his big hand, he placed her hand firmly on the cushion. The soft fabric slid between her fingers as she flexed a few times, gripped, and enjoyed the feeling.

Taking the cup from her reluctant hands, he said, "I think you've had enough *sok.*"

As Star tugged on the cup, he simply smirked, kissing the fingers curled around it. As a result of her surprise, she dropped the cup from her hands and her mouth fell open.

"Why?" she breathed out, trying to steady the room by blinking rapidly in an attempt to stabilise it. As it tilted, her head tilted as well.

His palm placed on her cheek righted her head, allowing her to look at the *tepay* tilting again. A contemplative look entered his eyes as he touched her lips and his thumb rubbed across them.

After becoming aware of how drunk she was, she asked, "It's alcoholic." She felt just like the drunk men who stumbled out of the taverns late at night. "Was it a deliberate attempt to get me drunk?" It was a valid question since he had been plying her with drink and pestering her with questions all night long.

Laughing loudly, his body shook with laughter. He pulled her head onto his shoulder and cradled it against his chest. She struggled to pull away from his hands, but he tugged her closer to him, his shoulders still shaking with mirth.

Putting her head on his shoulder, he stretched her limp body across his body as she rested her head on his shoulder.

She shuddered at his heat.

"I didn't need to get you drunk, *Immani* Star. You would have given me what I wanted," he told her, the last traces of laughter leaving his lips as he looked into her eyes.

"Hmm, what do you want?"

"It will wait until you get up."

"Wake up," she murmured.

"Hmm," he grumbled. He stroked her hair back. A flutter of her eyes caught her attention, and she was certain she could hear him say, "No more Nasan, *Immani* Star. At least not if you want him to breathe for a long time to come."

After her battle with the river and the numbing effects of alcohol, she fell asleep in no time.

She had shattered dreams of drowning and being stuck at the bottom of the river, watching life go by as the river froze and people moved around above her. In the cold water, her body would stay stuck, floating and drifting, watching the world go by.

She woke up to the warmth of a body. Could it have been a dream? Her hands curled into her chest when she hit a hard body. The way he cradled her in his arms stuttered her breath.

"*Immani*, you'll feel better if you get up and eat."

Her eyes popped open when she felt a tug on her foot. When the light pierced her eyes like a needle, she groaned. Shutting her eyes again, she groaned and licked her lips. Again, she felt a tug on her foot.

"Up," he commanded. In that voice, she recognised the Horde king's command.

She sat up, blinking her eyes open and placing a hand over them. She should have been surprised that he put her in a black dress, but she wasn't. It was Illasay standing just inside the flaps with a tight pinch to her mouth as she saw her in *Avayak*'s bed that surprised her.

His fur covered her, and she knew that her dishevelled state led Illasay to draw conclusions Star wouldn't want her to. Any hope she had of leaving the *tepay* without anyone knowing had just gone down the river. No doubt, Illasay would make her life hard if her fury was any indication.

She couldn't even explain because she hadn't yet told them she understood them. It's not like she should have to. From the moment she arrived, the *fhalah's* had been mean-spirited. Honestly, she didn't think she needed to explain herself, but she thought it would be easier since she worked in the food *tepay* with her.

"Sorry, should I have been in the food house?" she said in her common tongue before Hadak could spill any secrets.

Hadak's eyebrows disappeared under his braids. He paused while getting a drink from the platter for Star. When Star swung her legs out of the furs, his eyes were full of confusion. His eyes stayed on her bare thighs until she shook the dress down to just above her knees.

As Illasay's mouth tightened, the hatred she already felt spiralled before Star's very eyes. Illasay would kill her if she could.

Hadak instructed Illasay to place the platter on a low table he had acquired. Hadak turned to look at her but missed Illasay's expression.

Illasay's gaze was closed, her facial expression. Star's eyebrows twitched, finding Illasay's hatred of her scary. Having never experienced hatred like this, she didn't know what to expect. Hatred for someone you don't know and have no reason to dislike baffled her. The only hate she experienced was for Jutin, but even that was filled with fear.

Taking the platter, Hadak followed Star's gaze to Illasay's, and his eyes darkened. "How's the *Immani* doing?" he asked Illasay in Zandian. In common tongue, he said to her, shocking Illasay, "You have three days now to recover."

Most Zandian's learn the common tongue, but not all. That's why they had been so determined to learn Zandian, even though it had been so hard to find. Because they didn't have a traditional alphabet, their language was written in symbols, making it tough to learn. Nearly impossible. It took them almost a century to piece it together.

Zandian wasn't spoken by everyone in the colony since they didn't interact with the Zandians much. It was only spoken by people who travelled to the market or traders like her father. When she and her brother were young, he taught it to them, and her mom picked up the basics from him.

"It's..." Illasay paused suddenly, a titter of sound escaping her mouth. Hadak clenched his hand on the cup as he handed it to Star. With burning eyes, he stared at Star, furious she hadn't told him, but she wouldn't say anything. Illasay couldn't see his expression, so she kept talking. "...I'm sorry, I mean she..." Illasay emphasised, "Does her best."

After he handed her the cup, his lips formed a firm line, and he stroked his finger over hers in apology.

"Hmm, there's something wrong with what she does?" he asked Illasay. After pointing at the cushion, he picked Star up, sitting her beside the low table. "Sit, eat," he said in heavily accented common tongue.

"She is slow, lazy, and clumsy. In this case, it's a light punishment since she does nothing she doesn't have to do. Lazing around while we finish jobs, then taking over." When he nodded, she seemed emboldened. "She also shows off her skin to the males, trying to tempt them."

The clicking sound he made was taken as praise by her, and she became excited about Star getting into trouble.

"She has a look in her eyes. She does it intentionally," Illasay said emphatically. He jerked at that, seeming confused.

Was he actually believing what she said? She didn't think so.

She watched his stiff neck muscles tighten even more with each word Illasay spoke. "Trying to find a warrior to protect her or get out of punishment. You know Nasan is enthralled with her," Illasay stated in a sly tone.

Star knew he wouldn't like hearing that. He hadn't been impressed to find her in Nasan's *tepay*.

"Do you think she needs more punishment?" He asked, and Illasay's chest expanded, thrusting out her hips and pushing her shoulders back because he had asked her opinion. She looked like she had just been handed the world.

"She should be sent to the city to work hard labour. It will teach it to behave better," she said, licking her lips lewdly.

Astonished by the absolutely scathing image she had just painted of her, Star shook her head. As Hadak bent down in front of her, her eyes caught his. He watched her with steady eyes.

After briefly wondering if he'd send her away, she noticed something in his eyes she hadn't expected. Compassion. He knew she could hear every word. He Probably figured out why she wasn't talking. His lips lifted in a smile, and her heart skipped a beat.

"*Avayak*, you can see it in her eyes," she said with satisfaction. Her hateful tone was tinged with glee at the thought of Star going away. "It..." Whatever Illasay was about to say was cut off by a gasp of shock.

He gripped Star's chin and quickly angled her head taking her mouth in a blistering kiss. He tangled his tongue with hers, and her shocked eyes took in the fierce look on his face as he kissed her and moved his hand along her jaw. It was as if he was trying to breathe her in.

When he finally softened the kiss, Star's heart raced. As his hand circled her throat, Illasay gasped again.

He pulled away, his eyes burning with desire. Her eyes were filled with astonishment as she stared into his black eyes. The idea that he would kiss her in public was something that Star had never expected. She had no idea what it meant.

Illasay's face had changed from its hateful expression to one filled with fear now as she looked at Star. Her eyes seemed fixed on Hadak's hand on Star's neck, a look of devastation on her face.

Star licked her lips. It was the male taste of him that lingered, warm, fresh, and tempting at the same time.

His expression of satisfaction gave way to one of coldness toward Illasay as he stood up and turned to look at Illasay. "Do I make myself clear with that kiss?" he asked Illasay. Taking a deep breath and looking down, Illasay gave a frantic nod as she swallowed hard. "Good, I do not want to lose you from the Horde."

Gasping, Illasay bobbed down. "*Avayak*, I'll just keep my mouth shut."

She fled when he pointed at the flaps, probably before she said anything else that would make him notice her. After flinching, she left, almost running.

"They haven't been kind to you?" he asked her when he finally turned to look at her.

Star shrugged and ate what he put in front of her. As he sat across from her, he tugged her foot onto his lap, examining the damage there. "Your hands," he demanded. Having finished the piece of fruit, licking her fingers to remove the juice, she offered her hand to him. As he stared at her mouth, his eyes flared with heat.

His attention was drawn to the raw areas on her hands and to the sores. "They work you hard, don't they?"

"I thought that was the point," she replied carefully. His eyes darted to hers in distress.

"There is no point in hurting you; they behave like beasts."

She shrugged, not knowing what to say to him. This was the first time she had seen women act in such a way.

"What about the warriors?" Do they treat you badly?"

As she shook her head, she said, *"Nen."* His eyes dimmed, and he was about to argue, but she kept her cool and said, "Nasan's presence stopped them." His jaw began to tick as she continued. "He made sure the warriors knew how much he cared for me. After that, they stopped trying to touch me."

"Which ones?" The deadly question ended in a long hiss.

"There were only one or two. I don't know their names or even what they look like, and most ignore me. It was just a matter of keeping my head down and getting on with it," she told him.

He let out a growl. "It's time for me to join my warriors if they think they can touch what belongs to me. I made it perfectly clear; you were mine to care for." He cracked his knuckles and rolled his shoulders.

No way was Star touching the 'mine' statement. While she ate, he stood up and paced about, his muscles tense. "I don't want you to get into fights because of me," she murmured while picking at the food.

Fighting because of her was the last thing she wanted. They would only blame her if he did. He couldn't protect her all day long. It was better to let these things go.

A grunt escaped his lips as he placed himself across from her. To help her up, he extended his hand. She stood with a frown on her face. "What is it?"

As he ran his fingers gently over his hands, he said, "I don't like these marks on your hands. We'll go to the healers after you dress."

She creased her forehead in confusion. "The only one I have is the one I wore at Nasan's. The other I arrived in hasn't been returned yet. There was no one to tell me where it ended up."

Suddenly, he froze, and he stormed over to his chest. Taking the lid off, he looked inside, slamming it down with a curse. His gaze shifted to the flap, and he whistled, and like magic, Furan appeared. Was he just loitering outside Hadak's *tepay* until he was called?

He hissed and yelled sharply at Furan as he blasted questions at him. Furan frowned and gestured to the flaps, moving his hands up and down. In spite of whatever they were discussing, Hadak's furious expression remained the same.

As Furan turned toward her, he asked, "What's in your *tepay*?"

"Nothing," she replied, worried that they would accuse her of stealing.

"Did you get clothes to change into?"

She frowned and wondered if there was something she was missing. Putting her tongue against her lip, she said, *"Nen,* I left here in furs, but I found a dress in my *tepay*." She sighed, "It was one of the reasons I walked to the river. Since my other dress wasn't returned, I was forced to wash it."

"What were you wearing while you were in the river?" Hadak asked suddenly. As he vibrated with energy, she felt a shiver of apprehension. As Furan's eyes flitted between them, he became increasingly concerned.

While clearing her throat, she turned to Furan and asked, "Why are you asking?"

Furan grimaced as he said, "We left some things in your *tepay* so you could be comfortable."

"They were supposed to be delivered by the *fhalah's*?" she inquired. Looking at Hadak, she saw a glare in his eyes. Star honestly wasn't surprised they hadn't delivered them. Hadak looked more than disappointed.

She was relieved that he wasn't the monster she believed he was. Star smiled slightly at Hadak. Exhaling hard, he glanced away.

"Yes, along with some other things." Furan glanced at Hadak when he didn't elaborate. Furan explained, "We never thought they wouldn't give them to you, they have never done this before. Those who disobey the *Avayak* risk being expelled from the Horde."

She coughed and shook her head. "I don't want that."

"They'll need to be stripped of their belongings for a week, and she'll need to toughen up if she wants to survive," Furan explained to Hadak as if she weren't even present.

Hadak's gritted teeth, and intense gaze indicated that he was still thinking about her naked dip in the river and how Nasan had seen her.

"What should I do for three days?" she asked in an attempt to distract him.

A huff of breath escaped Hadak's lips.

"I'll find something for you to do," he muttered as he rubbed his sharp jawbone with his hand. The smile on Furan's face was hidden behind his hand. She choked back a sound of dismay, and her flaming cheeks couldn't be hidden.

"Leave it with me, *Avayak*. I'll handle the *fhalah's*," Furan replied. In response, Hadak gripped Furan's forearm, and Furan left.

Taking out a roll of cotton, Hadak shoved it into her arms. After shaking it out, she found a simple but nice dress. There was something niggling at her, though, mostly why he had the dresses and who owned them.

As she walked behind the flaps in the *tepay* with the bathing tub, she began to change. Although she knew he couldn't see her, she felt his eyes searing through the flaps. Though he had seen everything more than once and had changed her, that didn't mean she was ready to strip off in front of him.

Upon coming out from behind the flaps, his face hovered behind them. She stopped dead in her tracks; he practically devoured her with his black eyes. Waiting for him to do something, anything, she bit her lip. His grip on her arm was achingly gentle, more so than usual since he usually grabbed her tightly.

"Let's see the healers. I want to ensure your hands are fine," he waited until he saw her other foot.

Their exit from the *tepay* was together, and she walked with her head down most of the time.

Even though she wished she could show the healer how damaged her feet were without Hadak seeing and getting angry, she didn't think that was going to happen somehow. She would have sorted it out in the *tepay* but didn't even have basic healing supplies.

"It would be easier for me if you told me where it is," she suggested. "I'll be fine, I'm sure you have things to do."

She assumed she could talk to him since he started the conversation. When they first came through the Horde with her on his *Guyipe*, he wouldn't let her talk. Now he was making conversation with ease. Still, she wasn't going to speak to anyone else.

"*Nen, Immani* Star, I'll see how you are hurt."

Her eyes moved up to his face to see him looking forward resolutely. Whenever a Horde member stared too long, he had a frightening look on his face.

"Why am I able to speak to you?" She knew the rules about not talking to males unless you had a contract.

A wave of surprise passed through his eyes as he stiffened and exhaled. "Because I'm *Avayak*," he said simply.

Her eyes rolled as she told him, "That's not an answer."

"The Horde won't question me. Unless a warrior challenges me, no one is allowed to tell me how to run the Horde." He shrugged. "I'm the strongest here. None defeated me in training."

"Hmm, modest too!"

"*Immani* Star, it's nothing but the truth," he smiled wickedly. Her knees weakened. "Modesty won't get me anywhere." His eyebrows danced, and his tone was warm.

A smile spread across her face as she told him, "Okay, I'll take your word for it."

"It's good you trust me," he said as he squeezed her hand.

"It is?" Why did she feel they were talking about something different? He was having one conversation, and she was having another.

They came across a *tepay* with a red stripe showing that it was the healer's *tepay*. She waited with him outside, wondering why they were just standing outside. After a few moments, the flaps opened and a warrior emerged with a salve.

In order to indicate that the healer's *tepay* was not occupied, the warrior moved the material hanging on the side to the stool. Hadak hung it back up when they approached.

The smile he gave her was encouraging as he tugged at her arm, his touch gentle around her hands. Stepping under, she saw an older *fhalah* and immediately stopped, wanting to escape before she could scold or, otherwise, verbally tear her apart.

The healers' *tepay* was smaller than she expected, with two benches and a long table full of bottles and salves. It was nothing fancy or elaborate. The colony's healer liked to get fancy things for his room, but this was nice as well. Herbs and spices from whatever ingredients she mixed perfumed the air.

As she looked at Star, she was intrigued.

There was a growl from Hadak. "Be kind to the *Immani*, the *fhalah's* she has met have not been kind to her."

"Those are young *fhalah's* with youthful desires." She made a point of looking at his body which made him grin and scoff. "Old Ghertun was hoping for a better position. She decides who delivers your food. There will be plenty of benefits to her if it's someone she helped become your *bryd*."

As the thought of food crossed Star's mind, her stomach began to growl. In the past couple of weeks, she had been eating sporadically, eating any leftovers and whatever Ulla had been kind enough to share with her.

Hadak glanced down at her stomach and gently pulled her forward as he frowned at it. "Not anymore," he whispered, looking at her with a grim look on his face. While she was trembling, Star was greeted by the healer with a smile, and she offered a tentative smile in return.

"There is something so striking about her that I have never seen before in an *Immani*. The golden highlights are amazing. I have never seen a colour such as that." He shrugged, and the healer bopped him on the head with her mixing spoon. Star choked back a laugh while he rubbed his head. "It is important that you tell the *fhalah's* about these things because you cannot get a *bryd* just by bedding. A few sweet words would be welcome."

It was for a different reason that Star's breath rushed out, and his smile made her heart pound so hard that she could hardly breathe. It was obvious that she didn't know that Star was able to speak Zandian. "It is not my intention to be his *bryd*," she replied in her Zandian.

A raised eyebrow appeared on the healer's face.

Again, Hadak's hand strayed to her neck.

In the blink of an eye, the expression of disbelief on the healer's face faded into a knowing glance, leaving her wondering what it was she was missing out on. "Who can say *nen* to such a handsome *Avayak*?"

Sputtering a little because there was no right or wrong way to answer that without possibly offending him, the healer stood up and pointed the spoon at Star once again. "There you see," she said to him. "She knows who would be good for her."

"But I... I never..." Words failed her as Hadak urged her slack body into the chair.

"*Seya*, she knows who would be a worthy warrior for her. You made the right choice." The healer patted Star's hand and talked to Hadak about her injuries while Star floundered.

"My feet," she blurted out inelegantly, still obsessed with the *bryd* thing and that Hadak had not yet denied it.

"What's wrong with your feet, *Immani*?"

"The blisters might be infected. I soaked them in the river," she explained as she became furious.

As the healer bent over, she pulled off her boot. As she examined Star's foot, she brought it up to the shaft of light. Before tutting, the healer gently manipulated her skin with concentration.

"You didn't get this from walking around all day long, did you?" the healer asked.

"*Nen*," she replied but didn't elaborate on how she obtained them because that wasn't the question. It was obvious to her that it would only annoy Hadak.

"What happened?" he growled.

Shifting uncomfortably and swallowing hard, she debated how much to say to the healer as he bathed her foot in the stinging mixture. She thought he didn't offer her a broom, but now she knew it was the *fhalah's*.

"I had a flap in my *tepay* that wasn't pinned down properly," she said. Hadak closed his eyes, his expression pained. "I had no tools or anything to peg it down with, and it was heavy," she paused, hesitating. When Hadak opened his eyes again, he nodded for her to keep going. "There was dust everywhere, and I had to sweep it out by hand since there was no broom. The boots." She gestured down at her old, sturdy boots. "It's all I've got for my feet. Because I didn't want to ruin them or damage my hands too much, I moved the piles outside with my bare feet."

Hadak was like a statue in the corner as the healer stared at him. He was looking at her, but he wasn't seeing her. However, the healer nodded and rubbed her arm. "Amazing, resourceful *Immani*, with so little."

After so much negativity, she felt uncomfortable with the praise.

"You don't have a tub?" asked the healer, her thoughts turning to Star's dip in the river.

Hadak interjected, "She does."

"Hush," she said to him, then nodded at her.

"I didn't, but my friend had one," she told her. She was at least glad she had Ulla and Nasan, who were friendly.

"Swimming in the river is dangerous. Why not bathe inside?" the healer asked.

"Believe me, I know, I can't swim." She shuddered.

"Yet you went anyway?" She wasn't judgmental, just curious and kind, which is why she kept talking. Hadak was so still in the corner that she almost forgot he was there.

"I sunk up to my waist, but I was pulled under. I was fortunate that a friend was passing."

"I don't understand why you went in?"

"I needed to wash myself and my dress after shifting dust and dirt with my hands and feet."

"The tub?"

"Not an option. It's been freezing at night, and I've been trying to stay warm. All my energy was poured into washing myself and working. If I brought water from the river, I had nowhere to boil it, and it would be a wasted effort."

"You don't have a fire?" she asked, casting a sideways glance at Hadak, who looked to be eating something sour, his hands twitching.

Slowly, she replied, "No."

"Resourceful, strong, and determined." A grin spread across her face as she told her, "I like you."

When Star heard the flap hitting the *tepay*, she lifted his head to see Hadak's angry form exit.

Sighing, she said, "I made him angry again."

"Hm, *bryds* do that to their warriors."

It was pointless to try to convince her otherwise. By the stubborn glint in her eye, Star knew she would only hear what she wanted to hear.

"Where do you think he has gone?" Star asked, watching her apply a thick gloopy salve to her foot and protect it with a bandage.

"To sort out a few wrongs, I suspect," she muttered.

"I don't suppose you've ever treated a human before to know how long it will take for the salve to work. By tomorrow, the floor will probably need to be cleaned."

The healer laughed loudly, her black eyes sparkling. Startled, Star wondered what was so funny. She grinned at her.

"I don't think you need to worry, *Immani*," she told her, amused.

"My name is Star," she said.

"Bhutun, cousin of Ghertun, but don't hold that against me." She smiled, her eyes lifting in delight.

Now that she was looking closely, she could see some similarities around the mouth and eyes. "It's a pleasure to meet you, Bhutun." Star extended her hand. Star shook it in greeting, and she did the same while using too much force. Star winced a little, and Bhutun softened it.

"He worries that his strength will hurt you," Bhutun said.

"There have been a few hints that he doesn't like my frailty, but I am not sure why it's so important to him. I'll be going home once I have done my punishment."

Suddenly, Bhutun's eyes widened, and she stared at her in astonishment. "You're going back?"

Star nodded her head with a frown as she was confused. "I wasn't picked to come here to learn or stay with the Horde. It isn't a holiday.

Nen, I came here because I was caught outside the colony trying to find my *Fathar*."

"What happened to him?" she asked while soaking Star's hands and putting salve and a bandage on her other foot.

"He was taken by the Jutin. They only take from the outskirts of the colony, but now, they are bolder than ever." Yes, she had to get home. "All of us live close together now, but that night, they came into town and took him away. As soon as I heard the noise, I followed."

Bhuntun nodded. "Of course, you did."

Outraged, Star said, "I couldn't leave him."

"Nen?"

"Nen," she snapped sharply. "He's older and slower now, *seya*, but I love him." Her voice was filled with the same fury and fear as before as she declared, "He's my *Fathar*." Her eyes sparkled as she spoke. "There was a trail I could follow, so I did. I took a *Guyipe* and rode as hard as I could. Seeing the Horde warriors approaching and realising the *Avayak* was with them, I began to think of how I could save him."

"Did you try to hide?" she asked curiously, her gaze flickering up at Star as she rubbed at her sore.

"Nen, I got down from my *Guyipe* and waited for them. In the best case scenario, they might be able to help me, but in the worst case scenario, they might take me back and explain that I'm being held for my crimes, in which case I would be able to request that someone find *Fathar*."

"Do you have no fear at all, Star?"

"Are you kidding? Of course, I do. Half the time, I never knew if I was going to be beaten or if the warriors would use me." She winced and apologized, *"Kussa*, I didn't know the warriors then."

"Even so, you haven't seen our most attractive characteristics yet either," Bhutun said fairly.

"*Nen*, but I've met a few decent Horde members. I imagine it must be difficult for some when they perceive me as different, as unwelcome."

Her tutting was sharp. "If *Avayak* says you are welcome, then they listen. If they don't, then they are not welcome. It is an insult to mock his promise of safety for you." Her tone was harsh, and her voice was filled with disgust. To soften her anger, Star smiled at her.

As the saying went, "It could be worse."

"How?" Bhutun scoffed with a dark laugh.

"I could be a body under the river or working hard in the city; there's always worse," she told her.

Her nose wrinkled adorably, and she huffed. "*Seya, seya*, I think you should expect better from now on."

"I should?"

"*Avayak* will take care of you," she assured Star earnestly, sipping her drink and offering Star a cup, which she accepted, wetting her parched throat.

"It's not his job to do that. He's given me a *tepay*, and I have started work on a firepit. It should be easier in a week or two."

"You dug your own fire pit?"

"Well," she replied sheepishly, kicking one foot back and forth and lifting a shoulder. "I started, that's why I couldn't finish the floor by hand, but I managed to dig a small hole in the middle. If I dig deep enough, I will try to build a bench. Right now, all I need is a deep enough hole to burn a fire in."

"How do you stay warm?"

"By pulling the two furs over my head and shivering all night," she said dryly with a grin, and the healer laughed.

When she laughed, the flaps rose, and Hadak regarded her with an eyebrow raised. His body seemed less tense, and he seemed more relaxed. He nodded and leaned back against the chair when he saw that Bhutun was almost finished tending to her hands. His eyes inspected her feet as if he could see through the boots to her bandages.

A delighted smile spread across Bhutun's face as she told Hadak, "Her, I approve of."

As she looked at her, Star shook her head. The corners of her mouth twitched, and her eyes positively danced. She did not expect to like her when they entered the *tepay*.

"What have you been telling her, *Mathar*?"

Oh damn!

Chapter 9

"You should have told me that she was your *Mathar*," she remarked with only a hint of disapproval in her voice.

He replied, "If I had done so, then you wouldn't have spoken freely to her." Yes, he was a sneaky male. He was probably going to question his *Mathar* about her later. After noticing that her boot was on the ground, he grabbed it and examined her foot carefully. A frown appeared on his face as he turned her foot to inspect it, seeming upset by the extent of the bandages.

"How is she, *Mathar*?" he asked, ignoring Star's curious stare. She poked him gently in the shoulder with her toe. Grasping her toes, he gazed at her in astonishment at her playful side.

When his fingers brushed the bandage, her eyes widened, and she tried to understand his expression and what he was thinking. His eyes were filled with concern and something else that left her speechless. Taking care of her wounds, he slowly placed her boot on her foot.

"She will do better than most would expect," she answered. In agreement, Hadak nodded his head.

As Star frowned, she wondered if they were discussing her being his bed partner again. "I hope this isn't about..."

"As far as the injuries are concerned, they are not severe. Keep her off her feet as much as possible, as well as being careful not to get her hands constantly wet, and she should heal nicely," Bhutun advised Hadak as she wrote down something on a piece of parchment and interrupted Star.

Star watched them both in amazement. "Am I even here?" she asked of the room.

Hadak glanced up at her, his black eyes shining and mirth dancing around his lips. He stroked her foot, eyes heavy and daring, and slipped on her other boot.

Bhutun shifted, drawing their attention. She looked at them knowingly, making Star swallow at the expectation she saw in his eyes. She didn't want to look too closely at the expectation.

"You can be sure she will take things easy for a while," he promised.

"And what are you going to do?" Bhutun asked as her gaze slid to Star beneath the fall of her hair.

As he shifted his gaze to Star, he wore a thoughtful expression on his face. As he stood, he brushed her hair back from her face. Inhaling rapidly, Star paused. Her eyes were drawn to his *Mathar*, who was watching with sharpness as his hand moved toward her neck.

Bhutun hid behind a tuft of dark hair and bent over her desk. The relief and happiness she felt were more difficult to conceal.

Star's eyes moved to Hadak.

Except for a tight smile, he did not look away from Star's neck. He then assisted her in getting up from the chair. Star, confused, stretched out her legs and carefully placed her weight on them. It was immediately apparent that she no longer had sore feet. The salve numbed them, and her feet were cushioned by the bandages.

As she shuffled forward, she let out a sigh of relief. "*Behku*," Star thanked her.

He helped her out of the *tepay*, and they walked in silence for a little while, him watching her steps anxiously. During the short walk back to her *tepay*, he stopped her with a shake of his head just as she was about to enter hers.

"What? But your *Mathar* told me to stay off my feet."

He agreed saying, "*Seya*, come."

"But I want to get off my feet and relax for a bit while I can," she said. Soon enough, Illasay and Ghertun's group would be running her into the ground again.

She shrieked with embarrassment when she was suddenly lifted into his arms as he carried her and started walking. She clenched her hands around his neck, holding on tight.

She looked around at the eyes on them. "You could have warned me, and will you put me down?" she hissed quickly.

His tone rang with finality as he replied, *"Nen."*

"Seya, now," she said in a hushed tone.

"Nen."

Blowing a frustrated breath and seeing shocked faces and whispers, she avoided looking at anyone.

"Have you always been this stubborn?" she asked through gritted teeth.

He answered, "I'm *Avayak.*" As if that was answer enough.

"And that explains why you're stubborn?"

His eyes were serious, but she could see a gleam of amusement in them. He was getting easier to read. He made short work of the distance to his *tepay.* When she realised he wanted to put her back in his fur, she cringed. As she looked over his shoulder, she saw that everyone was watching them.

There's no doubt that every *Avayak* needs a streak of stubbornness.

"You do?" Seemed an odd thing to claim they needed.

His lips pursed as he nodded. *"Seya,* so when we meet little *Immani's* with no respect, we can teach it to them," he teased.

"And you have got to be stubborn for that?" she asked, confounded.

"Hmm, *seya,* because *Immani's* are stubborn and don't know what's best for them," he replied easily.

"Ha!" she exclaimed. "I know what's best for me."

"That's something we have to disagree on. You don't take care of yourself very well. I'll be keeping a close eye on you," he told her, making her feel like she was a misbehaving child.

"I'm not a pet."

"*Nen?*"

A smile spread across her face as she uttered, "Oh, haha. Since I met you, I've had more cuts, scrapes, and illnesses than I've ever had in my life."

Unconvinced, he hummed and ducked under his *tepay* flap, still holding Star right under the nose of the curious warrior. He placed her down on a cushion and slowly adjusted her limbs.

"I'm serious! My head is spinning. I don't know what's going on."

"*Seya*, I know. I should explain this..." he began, grimaced, and trailed off. Leaving her on the cushions to stew in her thoughts, he moved over to the fireplace and placed a branch on the fire. Poking the flames higher, he stared, lost in thought, eyes unfocused.

"Getting me to greet you, what was that all about?" Star asked instead, remembering his insistence on her greeting him.

He took a moment to gather his thoughts before responding. "You need to do what the Horde does. That's what I told myself. It was important to me that you not be accused of disrespect. The situation is bad enough with you being..." He gestured at Star, who frowned and prepared to be insulted. "*Immani*, I am fond of you, but not everyone will be enticed by you."

Well, that was a bit better than what she thought he was going to say. "What have you told yourself?"

"Hmm, I didn't want you to do it. I don't want you to do anything like the Horde. It's my responsibility to take care of them. I have to look after them. They give me the respect due as *Avayak*. The *fhalah's* want me for my position and want to enjoy the position as my *bryd*, but they don't want Hadak; not like you do. You're attracted to me, and I want to see that look in your eyes always." His hot eyes devoured hers as an uncomfortable heat swept over her.

There was no doubt in her mind that she knew exactly the look he was talking about when she whispered, "What look?" She held her breath as he stepped closer, filled with excitement and anticipation as he approached.

Taking her ankle by the ankle, he whispered to her, "You know the one, the look you had that night." Resting his body over her legs, his face was level with her breastbone.

She was struck by the look in his eyes because she understood what it was like to have someone look at her in such a manner. It is undeniably sexy and filthy at the same time. He made her feel like the most beautiful person on Zandar.

The intensity of his attention was almost unbearable. "I enjoy caring for you. Free of restrictions. Not by the Horde's rules," he said, placing a warm kiss on her collarbone. As she held her breath, her heart raced.

"Was there a reason why you were there that particular day? It was as if you knew. I had just gotten my *Guyipe* outside when I noticed you riding toward me. You and the warriors. Like a bell being rung," Star asked. As his hands left her legs, they trailed over her arms, circling her wrists before returning to her neck.

"We discovered the trail of the Jutin; however, we did not expect it to lead to the *Immani* colony. My eyes were drawn to your *Guyipe* first." He curled his fingers around her neck.

With the pressure of his fingertips, he gently controlled her head with his hand, encouraging her to tilt her head back. Her eyes found the highest point of the *tepay*, his breath fell on her neck, and her eyes fluttered.

He briefly touched her neck with his lips. "Then I saw you," he said as he moved his lips towards the junction of her shoulder and neck. He nibbled his teeth along her skin. She shivered at the threat of his teeth, but not out of dread. "You were next to the *Guyipe*." One hand reached for hers, slowly lifting it above her head as she leaned back on the bench.

As the flames danced across his face, it lit up his fierce desire for her. A desire that was eating him alive. It was impossible for her to contain the sensual need in her eyes.

He whispered, "Like a *wicch*," against her collarbone. The witch was charismatic and tempting, a healer of sorts, mystical and seductive, rarely seen, not what she ever imagined herself to be.

She whispered, "You're blind," to his chuckle. She tried to touch him with her hand, but he held it tightly, bringing up her other hand to join it. He clasped her wrists above her head. It pushed her breasts upward and outward like an offering. According to the look in his eyes, this was an offering that he appreciated.

"You were in a white dress. In the middle of the plains, it was a flag to me and mine." Without warning, his lips circled her nipples over her dress. She cried out softly as he rubbed his tongue around it.

A flick of his tongue touched her nipple, and his eyes rolled up as he observed her reaction. As he set his teeth in gently, she bit her lip. He lifted his head and said, "Keep your hands where they are."

As his hands released her, she gripped the edge of the bench, holding on for her dear life. His hands circled her waist as he licked her other nipple and tilted her hips.

His actions were followed by the removal of her dress before she could think. As he kissed her deeply and thrust his hips against the area between her legs, she gasped. Her laughter brushed her face.

One hand disappeared below. His fingers found her folds and parted them as he thrust over her once more. The sensitive bundle of nerves pulsed, and her gasping breaths changed as he located the button between her legs. His eyes were captivated by the exposed skin on show. He watched her pant as she moved her hips and threw her head back.

"*Fhok*, your *ryss* is hot and wet for me." His words were followed by a finger entering her, causing her legs to uncurl.

The feeling that followed was unlike anything she had ever experienced before.

Even though Star had tried touching herself, she had never found it as pleasurable as this, like being wound tighter and tighter. His chuckle was as filthy as his words as he worked another finger inside her. As she was tight and unaccustomed to being stretched, the sensation was strange and confusing to her.

"You need my cock, don't you?" He licked her skin between biting kisses. He asked, "Don't you, Star?" After his question, he thrust again, first his fingers, then his cock over the sensitive bundle of nerves. Her eyes rolled, and he gripped her neck again, a groan coming from him.

When she opened her eyes, she noticed how intensely he was staring at her neck. His hand was wrapped tightly around her neck while he thrust against her. She vaguely thought she would have to ask Ulla about it before he distracted her with a thrust. A smile spread across his face when he noticed she was watching him. "*Fhok*, you need it as much as I do."

She didn't disagree with him, not that she even would have. She made a sound of disappointment when he removed his finger. "Don't worry *maye Immani,* I'll make it better."

His cock circled her entrance, causing her eyes to widen. The fur around his hips had bunched up, so he ripped it off. As she gazed at his thick cock, her breath caught.

She was slightly fearful by its length, thickness, and the dark, angry veins running down it. The three ridges were hard and bulging. When he noticed where her eyes were, he laughed again, bringing his weight over her. Before placing himself at her entrance, he drew her hips up to his and rubbed against them in teasing circles.

A gasp of anticipation accompanied every breath. As his breath rasped across her body, her skin began to tingle.

There was something about his body that called to her; the heat, the feel. There was only one thing that made sense at this moment, which was touching and being close to him. Before he got to her, she should have fumbled with someone. His width was the only reason she thought that. With apprehension, she watched it between her legs.

She really should tell him, she really should. He thrust into her mouth before she could open it.

As he broke through her barrier, Star cried out in pain. Hadak stilled, sweat dripping from his forehead, and his black eyes widened as they searched her eyes. "You had no one before me?" he asked, holding himself away from her, his voice harsh and fast.

She shook her head. As she waited for him to move again, hoping the pain would fade, he disappointed her by not moving.

Instead, he dropped his head down to rest on her forehead. His eyes flashed with strong emotions so quickly that she barely caught it. As he grasped her throat again, his fingers relaxed, and he stroked her thumb up and down. Up and down. There was something soothing and reassuring about the motion.

"You should have told me," he whispered.

The hand Hadak wasn't using to circle her neck dipped down to that deliciously sensitive nerve bundle to massage it again.

While she was doubtful he would be able to make her want to move again with his width throbbing inside her, his hand was like magic. She was gently moving before she even realised it.

She was soon thrusting her hips into his hand and impaling herself on his cock, but it didn't hurt. If anything, it felt better like this.

"That's it, *maye Immani*. Take your pleasure." He held her head down, his fingers still encircling her throat. The experience became even more erotic as he felt every raspy inhalation and every hasty swallow as the moisture in her mouth dried. As pleasure spiralled in low circles, he watched her face melt into rapture.

A flash of possession lit up his eyes as he declared, "You are mine."

The intensity of his words was shocking because she could tell he meant them. Her hips met him almost violently as he thrust again. In a trance, he pounded into her. Spurred on by her moans, his eyes aflame with deep need.

When he seemed to lose track of where he was, she gently called out, "Hadak." The call seemed to shock him out of his trance. He ceased thrusting. He stilled his hips.

He looked distraught, but she quickly reassured him that she had not been injured by adjusting their movements to something less punishing. "It's okay. I'm okay," she whispered, her breath trembling.

Looking into her eyes once more, he picked up the pace, but this time he appeared to be able to control the punishing need.

She was concentrating on the sensation he was giving her because she had never truly understood the reckless impulse to run behind buildings and mate like an animal. Suddenly, she was able to see the side of it that the girls enjoyed laughing and giggling about. The side that made you want to disobey everything in order to experience it again.

As he thrust back into her, swivelling his hips, Star bit her lip.

"*H'ayer ryss's ryns,*" he said roughly. *

Moaning at his claim, she writhed beneath him as he picked up his pace. He stared into her eyes, refusing to let her look away. As her body was rocked by the pounding motions, he let out a low groan when her muscles tightened around him.

He gripped her neck tighter, not enough to form a bruise, but enough for her to know he was still holding her. She could only watch in awe as he groaned at the sight, closing his eyes in ecstasy. "*Fhok,*" he breathed.

As he hit a particular spot that heightened her pleasure, her breathing became laboured and raspy. With a loud scream, she reached her climax, and her inner muscles clamped down on him.

She moaned loudly, and he growled in response. It was inevitable that the sound would be heard, but she didn't give a damn who heard her, and he didn't care either, because he said with a satisfied grunt, "That's it, *maye Immani*, let everyone know whose *ryss* this is."

A deep chuckle turned into a groan as he thrust to the hilt, filling her, and then shouted as he found his release. Warmth splashed inside her as his release hit her, and he shuddered.

He placed a chaste kiss on her shoulder as his head rested there.

Finally, he released her throat from his grasp. He placed his hand on her hip before standing with her in his arms. A yelp erupted from her. Carrying her was becoming a thing for him. After walking over to the furs, he gently placed her on them.

After disappearing, he returned with a cold cloth and cleaned between her thighs. The tenderness in his eyes was unlike anything she had ever seen before.

Having caught the trail of blood, he gently wiped it off. She was surprised when he finished, he kissed both of her thighs.

As he cuddled up behind her, she felt the warmth of his presence. His fingers traced up and down her shoulders and neck. The thought of saying something occurred to her, but when he drew her closer and tucked his arm around her, suddenly, she no longer felt the need to speak.

There was no discomfort in the silence. She felt extremely comfortable in his arms.

She shouldn't be having any tender feelings for Hadak. There was a chance that they might be able to come to an agreement in the short term - not that Star thought he would want to. The point was moot anyway because, as a Horde king, he couldn't take her as anything permanent, only as a temporary lover.

Regardless of the outcome, she could see herself being heartbroken as the Horde moved on to the next plain when all was over, and she was back home.

As she had spent the last couple of nights alone, it should keep her awake to have someone in the same room, wrapped around her. There should be something strange about having someone there. She was obviously missing that closeness, however, she slept like a baby as soon as her eyes closed.

When she felt a kiss on her head, she awoke and found herself being pulled from the furs. There are clothes on the bench and food waiting for you when you wake up. Just shout when you need someone," he whispered in her ear.

A shiver ran down her spine, and it took a minute to get her brain working again. It was those dark eyes that mesmerised her. "There is a gold necklace," he exhaled deeply, tucking a piece of hair behind her ear. "Wear it," he ordered. Then added in the common tongue, "Please."

Her eyes blinked. Was that the Horde king speaking or an imposter? Nope, that autocratic tone was familiar as he commanded her to wear the necklace.

When she saw him picking things up and leaving, she noticed the muscles in his back shifting, confidently striding forward. Star's mouth dried as she recalled his firm backside moving rhythmically.

After swallowing hard, she closed her eyes. Was it a bad idea to be his lover? Probably. But if something felt right, and she hadn't had a lot of that, surely she should enjoy it for now.

As far as the Horde was concerned, he didn't seem concerned. She would try to be less worried.

She lifted her head, saw the clothes, and walked over to them. Pulling on the dress and boots, she found a thick gold necklace. It was more like a choker than a necklace. The line began several inches below her chin, making it impossible for her to tilt her head down.

As it approached the little dip at the bottom of her neck, it came to a point.

A hesitant voice called out, "Star."

"*Seya*, come in."

A question was on Ulla's lips as she stepped through the flaps, eyes wide. Aware of the warrior behind Ulla, Star shook her head at her. After closing the flaps, she waved Ulla over and connected the collar at the back with three links. Ulla sucked in a breath of shock when Star turned around.

"What's wrong?" Could she tell what they did? Was it so easy to see?

Lifting her finger, she gestured towards Star's neck.

"Does it look terrible?" Frowning, Star tucked her neck to see what it looked like. "*Avayak* asked me to wear it. More like ordered," she grimaced, then touched the necklace. There was something strange and foreign about the feeling of cold metal on her neck. Ulla's eyes were still fixed on her neck. Star finally huffed and asked. "What is it?"

"*Avayak* gave you that?"

"Yes, why?"

"It's...He!" Ulla's mouth flapped, and Star began to worry about her.

"Ulla!" She gestured with her hand before letting it fall to her side. "God, what is it?"

"You...accepted...you accepted the choker?"

"He asked me to wear it, so *seya*," Star didn't quite understand what the fuss was about.

"It's what warriors give their *bryd*s. It must have caught your attention that the Horde warrior *bryd*s wore them," Ulla observed, her eyes glued to the sparkle thrown off of it as it caught a stray flash of firelight.

She nodded her head dumbly, her mind whirring with plenty of questions. Yes, she had noticed, but nothing quite as extravagant as the one she was wearing.

Ulla said, "He wouldn't give this to you by accident."

"Why?"

Ulla raised an eyebrow. The question was loaded. Star didn't expect her to have answers, however, Ulla's poor brain was having difficulty processing this information. "Why? His desire to have you as a *bryd* explains this. *Avayak* mated with an *Immani*." She shook her head, closing her eyes before refocusing on the subject with sympathy. "Wait until I tell *Mathar*." Her expression became sad as she realised what was happening.

"What now?" she asked worriedly.

"*Nen*, nothing. There'll be a few horde warriors who will be disappointed when they see that."

Star laughed at her. "You're joking, right?" No one's even shown any interest."

As Ulla shook her head in disbelief, her eyes twinkled. Star wondered if she had in mind a specific individual.

"He can't mean it," Star stated to herself as much as to Ulla. "I'm just *Immani*. The Horde won't accept me as his *bryd*. Even if they did, I wouldn't be able to do so. I have a family to take care of." Outraged, her voice rose as she became aware of what he was attempting to accomplish with the simple piece of jewellery. In the event that the Horde were to see it, they would be aware of its significance. "I'm not going to do it."

She tugged the choker off and was reminded of the look in his eyes last night as he held her neck, which now made sense to her. She couldn't figure out why he thought this was a good idea. "Is it significant if a Horde warrior grips your neck?" Star asked.

A lighter shade of tan appeared on Ulla's cheeks, Zandar's version of a blush. "It's a declaration of ownership when they hold your neck in public. Any warrior who disagrees with them may challenge them. They fight to put chokers around your neck."

"If a *fhalah* doesn't want the warrior?"

There was choking from Ulla. "You can refuse. Once a warrior declares his intent, no other warrior will stand with you unless that warrior challenges the warrior who first claimed you."

Star shrugged and shook her head. "That's okay, I won't be here for long."

Star could imagine Illasay's face and how messed up her life would be if she walked into the food *tepay* with the choker around her neck as if to say, "Hey, look at me, sleeping with the male you want," while the others watched her humiliation.

Star rubbed it in her face. No. She shuddered at the thought. No way! And for what? There would be a brief dalliance, and then Star would be gone.

It was embarrassing for both him and Star that he gave it to her in the first place.

She told him she wasn't sure what she wanted. He just decided for her after what she said. Star wished to have children, of course, but a family now? No.

He knew her concept of what type of male she wanted. In fact, the only male she had pictured since joining the Horde was Hadak.

What had gone wrong this morning? Oh yeah, because Hadak took it upon himself to make Star his life partner.

Taking a deep breath, she was rubbing her eyes because it was just too hard to figure out.

When he got back, the two of them needed to talk about it. It was right up there when she got to go home. She knew herself pretty well, so leaving those questions hanging was unlikely. Eventually, her impatience would get the best of her, and she'd be rude.

Star shook her head to get rid of the thoughts and focused on Ulla, who was sitting on the bench staring at Star in disbelief.

"Will you stop?" It was seriously making her squirm.

Ulla threw her hands up, then something tickled her because she melted into a smile. A suppressed chuckle shook her shoulders. She laughed when Star gave her a questioning glance. "Wait until Illasay finds out."

"I'm glad you're finding humour in this," she poked at her before laughing herself because it was so absurd. It was funny, ridiculous, and unbelievable. At this point, it was laugh or cry.

Putting a fresh bandage on her hands, Ulla hovered over her while she did it. With curiosity and interest, she watched every move Star made. "It's not healed yet?"

It wasn't within Star's capabilities to explain the differences in their physiology, so she settled for, "There's a big difference in how we heal." Star knew Horde members wouldn't even have a scratch left. It would probably be scabbed over by now if she was Zandian, maybe even healed.

After unclasping the necklace's catch, she gently laid it on the chest. She had no problem appreciating how pretty it was. It wasn't cheap fake gold from the market; it was beautifully made. His *bryd*'s neck was clearly in mind when it was commissioned.

"Why would he have this?" It's not like the warrior would know how big the *bryd*'s neck would be.

This started a series of weird looks before Ulla tentatively reached for the choker. When Star passed it over, she saw Ulla holding it, and she got a weird feeling. As she pushed it down, Ulla's hands gently manipulated the clasps. As she adjusted them, they slid along. Ulla swallowed as she put it on Star's neck and pulled it in.

Star now noticed how wrong it felt when she tried it on before. Now it was like a glove, fitting her skin like a long-lost love. Rather than feeling like a weight, it felt like a protective layer.

"He'll adjust it each morning," Ulla said reverently as she emerged from behind Star. "You know, it's a thing between lovers."

"What is *Avayak*'s *bryd* called?"

As if she wasn't sure if Star would find the next thing she said humorous or infuriating, she squirmed, tilting her head to the side. "*Avae.*"

"*Avae,*" she repeated. The words felt soft on her tongue, not as harsh as some of their words, almost loving. Not that she had plans to be called that.

Ulla stared at Star's face before breathing out warily. "It means Horde." Ulla's eyes flickered to the choker. "This word has a wealth of meanings, but it's reserved for the *Avayak*'s *bryd*. Basically, it means she's claimed by the Horde - the Horde king and the Horde warriors. It means Horde queen - his queen and the Horde's. It means putting the Horde first. The only time the title is given is when the *Avayak* finds someone worthy of all this."

Her mouth was dry, and her hands were sweating, so she asked with a bite, "Do they usually have a choice?" Did he plan on telling her anything about this and what accepting the bloody choker entailed? There was just as much beauty behind its symbolism as there was horror.

She was getting hot just thinking about him putting it around her neck every day, an intimate thing between them.

After taking it off, she carefully laid it down again and left with Ulla, intending to ask him all those questions later.

The first day, she didn't get disgusted side eyes or a tongue lashing - as if she didn't understand. Of course, Star ignored them most of the time. There was no need today.

There was a sense of new beginnings with the Horde. They glanced over at her with furtive looks and kind eyes. She couldn't say if any of them had looked kindly on her before, but after so many days of Illasay's group pulling her down, she had ducked her head as she walked through the Horde.

She felt confident enough to check out *tepays'* offerings for the first time. For trade, they were painted purple.

Despite the *bryds'* hard work, Star shook her head when one attempted to press a soft covering into her arms. In spite of the fact that she had nothing to trade with, Ulla took hers with a soft smile and a few words of thanks. "*Behku, Behku.* I will make sure she takes it back with her."

As she tucked the cover into a bag, Star whispered to her out of the corner of her mouth, "What are you doing?"

"Better to take it. It'll be worse if you don't take it. Your night at *Avayak's tepay* has been mentioned to her. It would be bad for her trade to dismiss her without even offering compliments or feeling the fabric."

While Star considered a pair of hard-soled boots for her *Mathar*, she mulled over that thought. A grin spread across her face when she thought of her *Mathar*.

"Hordes trade within each other and with other Hordes when they meet at markets and in cities."

"If I refuse, it can't be that bad, can it?"

"Refusing isn't the issue. It's about being able to refuse in a proper manner. When you ignore her without looking at her things or showing any interest, others of the Horde will assume there's been bad business and avoid her."

"It can't be that bad." The women in the colony were sometimes known to bitch about one another, but if they didn't want something, they could say no without offending each other. It might have been because they traded coins.

As Ulla nodded emphatically, she grimaced. "Oh, it can be. A trade here can be destroyed by it."

"God!" Fearful of approaching anyone, Star tucked herself behind Ulla, who laughed. A gentle poke from Star reprimanded her. Ulla collapsed into laughter, holding her sides. "Very funny, this hasn't eased my nerves at all."

"It won't take you long to get the hang of it. Just wait, you have the other *Avayak*'s to meet yet."

A frown spread across Star's face as she pulled on her arm. "Hey, who said I was staying? My glorious presence here isn't a dead certainty."

Ulla giggled happily. "There is no way *Avayak* will let you go without a fight. Horde kings are unknown to you. He's fierce, and he'll keep you with him," she said, ignoring Star's weak protests.

She stared straight ahead with her eyes. In spite of the *tepay*s teaming with eager, *Mathar*s and their offspring hanging behind them, she chose not to take a closer look at any of the offerings.

Ulla pulled Star to his *tepay* with joy and humour after getting this well of strength. Despite Star's protests to return to her own *tepay*, it was late by the time, so they just reached his. His *tepay* was surrounded by warriors who grinned as they passed.

As Ulla eyed one warrior with interest, a daft smile appeared on her face. It was Star's turn to pull her along, rolling her eyes, which shocked one of them, his black eyes widening and becoming darker.

It dawned on Star that her eyes rolling was shocking for Zandians who had never seen humans before - he was obviously one of them.

Ulla's final act was to pull out a few things, lay them on the bench, then leave before Hadak returned. The soft fur covering a persistent Horde *bryd* that Ulla accepted ran through her fingers like silk. It was hard to resist the impulse to rub the soft fur over her face. Instead, she rubbed it between her fingers to satisfy herself.

"If you'd like, I'll give you something else to stroke like that. Although I can't guarantee it will feel the same," Hadak said in a deep, heated voice.

A smile spread across Star's face as she dropped the fur. Even though she was new to this, the easy way he joked with her kept her relaxed. It might not be a joke, she thought, as she caught an expectant gleam in his eye.

"*Kussa* for the mess, Ulla helped me pick things up," she said, pointing behind her at the pile. "I'm afraid she went a bit overboard."

As he stripped off his harness for his short sword, he shrugged unconcerned. One by one, he took the rest of his blades. It was impossible to ignore the glisten of sweat on his muscles as he disarmed, the line of his body as he disarmed, and how he was incredibly attractive for some reason. She licked her lips before trying to calm herself. Putting her newly awakened carnal appetite aside, she knew she had to speak to him.

"Hadak about the..."

"Where's the necklace?" he asked, raising an eyebrow as he stepped out of his boots, eyeing her with predatory intent.

"Er...you see, Ulla explained..."

His mouth was pulled down as he stalked her. "Oh, did she?" She backed up as he rounded the bench, his mouth twitching. Taking a step back for each step forward, he lunged, pulling her into him suddenly. Hadak's hands were behind her head, his eyes focused on the fire she had forgotten. "Be careful," he muttered.

Before she could say anything else, he pulled her on top of him and onto the bed. She straddled his lap with her legs. The first thing she thought was that he wanted to do more of what they did last night, but he surprised her by grabbing her hands and inspecting the damage. Taking care not to injure her sensitive skin, he kissed only the parts of her palm that were not red.

"They don't look any better." He turned them this way and that, as if changing the angle of the light would speed up healing. There was a softening in Star's heart. His care for everyone was genuine.

Did that make her the lecherous partner in this pairing? Maybe considering her thoughts were far from pure since he walked into the *tepay*.

"They are healing," she answered and avoided any humour, giving him only the truth, careful of his furious response to her being hurt.

And in this, she could see he was tender.

It was his duty to look after the Horde, he had told her. All the Horde kings were there because of their strength of character, will, and just plain strength. He had a vulnerable look in his dark eyes when he said he wanted to look after her.

"Okay, good," he grunted, shifting her from his lap and moving to bathe.

As he crossed the *tepay*, Star's eyes followed him. His abrupt shift was confusing, to say the least. Without a word, he got into the tub. When Star and Ulla arrived, the water had just been brought in and was still steaming. He scrubbed his skin viciously, rough enough to hurt.

As she thought about her hands, she reflected on how much better they looked.

Now that the open wounds had dried out, she could get them wet. Besides acting as a barrier, the paste that *Mathar* gave her also had an antibacterial effect. It would be okay to wash them as long as she didn't soak or overdo them.

The roughness of his scrubbing increased. After a few minutes of this, she'd had enough. It was time to see if her personality would stand up to his or if she would crumble under his shadow, like a plant deprived of sunlight.

*Your cunts mine.

Chapter 10

"Give it to me."

She grabbed the cloth from his hands without waiting for a reply. Although she was trying to look confident, she felt a slight tremble in her limbs. She'd only ever touched one naked man before, well, two if she counted Nasan pulling her from the river, but she didn't.

She dipped his cloth into the bath water, the heat shy of blistering. Her black eyes strayed to her face with a question in them. Putting his hands on the tub's sides, he leaned back and let her rub his skin.

Though his body remained tense, his eyes closed. Trying to put some distance between them. She felt it. Her prodding got him to lean forward, and she asked, "What's going on?"

She felt his shoulders move under her hands as he took a harsh breath. He tutted, speaking in quick Zandee.

Despite the fact that he might not see her, she lifted her eyebrows and pulled a piece of his hair. "Don't avoid the question."

"You didn't wear the choker; I don't understand what you want from me."

When she was scrubbing his lower back, she paused for a moment to bite her lip and take a breath. Trying to scrub away the stubborn specks of blood on his back, she began rubbing all over his back carefully and took her time to reply.

There was no end to the questions and sour accusations that she could throw at him. However, he seemed so peaceful with his head bent forward, his muscles finally relaxing under her touch as he leaned over his legs to look sideways at her.

She didn't want to start an argument with him when she didn't know what he meant to do with her, so she asked instead. "What would it mean to you if I wore it?"

There was a harsh exhalation from him. Under her care, his body remained relaxed. She watched his muscles tense for a moment before relaxing again as she dipped the cloth just above the curve of his cheeks. When she pushed him back so she could wash his front, he surprised her by allowing her to manoeuvre him.

There was a slight parting of his lips, and his long jet black lashes swept down as his eyes were closed. He trusted her completely.

At that moment, she thought she felt her heart race and a flare of heat run through her. The strokes she made over his chest changed from broad and circular to shorter and lingering.

She was working her way over his pecs, where his pebbled nipples fascinated her. She must have stared for too long because he coughed for her to continue working.

"It would be..." He hesitated. Her hand rested above his belly button.

She made an educated guess. "It's a statement that I'm yours?"

With his head tilted back, he frowned, his eyes twitching. "No, not just that, nothing so simple."

Her hand skipped down; her breathing was stuttering as she walked around his impressive length. She moved quickly to his feet, working her way up to touching him in such an intimate place. He didn't comment on her skipping his cock. Her thoughts turned as she imagined them both touching him.

"What does it mean?" Her breath sounded raspy, even sensual to her. She ignored the fact that her breasts were heaving. Suddenly, his eyes were open wide, but there was no sign of tenderness. Like her, it was a violent desire and a stabbing need. Determined, she moved over the muscles in his calf.

Though she wasn't sure if what she was doing was correct, it felt right to her.

"It's not a statement," he replied, bringing her back to her original question regarding whether or not the choker was a statement. "It's not a symbol of ownership either, just in case you were concerned," he explained. He shifted his leg so she could work on the skin above his knee. "It's a long tradition among the Horde, ancient."

"Yes, I heard," she replied. Over his raised leg, he peered at her. Then she moved on to the other one, starting at the ankle again. "It is beautiful," she remarked.

He closed his eyes and sighed. "I am not interested in using you. For a time, a lover or even a passing fancy is a plaything. That is not what I would like between us. I need to be able to call you mine in truth." His fierce declaration was followed by Star ceasing all motion and holding her breath as her heart thumped wildly.

"Why?" she gasped in confusion.

"The moment I saw you across the plain, I knew you were mine, and I have always been certain of that since the moment I saw you." Shaking his head when she opened her mouth to ask him a question. "Don't ask me why I feel that way. I don't understand it, but it is something that I have deep inside of me. For the Horde to know who you are to me, I wanted you to wear the necklace today."

"But I wasn't told; you didn't tell me. You left me blind and dumb, which is what I have been since I first arrived here," said the woman, her frustration leaking through her words.

"You are not dumb," he snapped, circling his fingers around her wrist. Using his other hand, he cupped her face.

She enjoyed the feel of his strong, possessive hands, just for a moment, as she leaned into his touch. "It is not your place to make decisions for me. You know, I would never have worn it if I had known what it was, and I don't want what we have to be casual either; there is something about you that tells me you won't be easy to give up." Her smile was strained. Deep down, she knew it would happen one day. A whispered reminder returned to her, causing her to pull back. "I have a family."

"I thought about that, but I would like you to choose me first." He settled back into the water, reminding her of the task she had given herself. "To choose Hadak A'tay," he rumbled, eyes closed, a satisfied smile on his lips.

Even though she was startled by his full name, she still smiled at the little bit of information he provided about himself. "Will you consider asking me first and giving me some time?" As she moved toward her inevitable destination, her practical head was screwed on, but her sensible thoughts were becoming a stream of desires. She was about to place her hand on a place that she had never imagined she would be able to touch. In almost every way, the anticipation was overwhelming.

"*Seya,*" he said.

A small exclamation of joy burst from her when she thought about what he had asked. The decision was a major one, one she had to make when she was not overwhelmed by her attraction to him

A tiny voice in the back of her mind asked, was this a wise idea? Having made up her mind that she would think about it, she banished those thoughts by focusing on the present.

He hissed as she cupped him in her hand, almost dropping him as she had become lost in her thoughts. Now she was able to feel the full warmth and throbbing length of his cock, her cheeks turned bright red.

The weight of his sack in the water was greater than she had anticipated. As she ran the cloth over it carefully, she took her time to feel every inch of him. There was a boldness within her that she had not experienced before. Almost as if his silent urging gave her the courage to explore this with him freely.

She felt free to touch him without judgement or expectation. As her other hand dipped below the water, the splash caused him to open his eyes wide.

A blazing fire burned within his black eyes as they met her own. While gently cradling him below, she stroked the length of his cock. Her fingertips gently stroked his sac, just a reminder that they were still present. As his gaze remained fixed on her, he clenched his hands on the tub's sides.

"*Maye Star*. More," His encouraging tone made her take a firm hold of him and manipulate his flesh to the point where he was almost leaping out of the tub. While her throat burned and small wings took up residence in her stomach, her excitement at seeing him come apart was a strange, heady feeling that she welcomed.

It was satisfying in its own way to give pleasure, to know that she had control over this release at that moment, making her throat tighten with emotion. Whether to deny him or give in to the crash of pleasure just waiting out of reach. The hard work that led to the point where the strain of waiting for an orgasm was almost painful made her feel like she was close to bursting. As if she could feel it all as much as he could.

"Hadak," she whispered in awe of him, in awe of his power. The whisper almost made him crazed as he raised a hand to touch her neck. The move was undeniably assertive, but he was unaware of it. His focus was on what she was doing to him.

When her fingers brushed the silken ridges on his cock, her hand tightened. She moved up to the tip and then down again, marvelling at the contrast between the hard and the soft feel of him.

Grunts indicated that he was close, and his body guided her toward what he liked. Having been dared by his gaze, she licked her lips as she unleashed a wicked smile, sensual in every sense of the word. Feeling desirable and wanted was a powerful feeling. All it took was her hands and a look to finish him off.

The muscles in his neck became rigid, and his shout echoed throughout the *tepay*.

She smiled as she sat back, pleased with herself. In response to her satisfied expression, he chuckled darkly. As she stared at him in confusion, he stood up, still fully erect and impressively so; clearly, she had only taken the edge off.

Taking a deep breath, he said, *"Seya,* now it's your turn." He stepped out, the water still soaking him and running down the firm surface of his stomach in rivulets.

With a swift move, he picked her up and threw her to the furs. A burst of air escaped her, and she made a soft noise of surprise.

"My turn," she breathed, anticipation rising as he eyed her.

As he watched her bite her lip, his eyes were fixed on her. His thumb was on her plump bottom lip, and his lips followed it. He kissed the sting of her teeth away. She closed her eyes just as he nipped her lips. Her eyes opened to see his head disappearing.

At his insistence, her legs fell open.

He moved her legs apart with his hands. She was expecting him to tease and drag out the pleasure, but her lids slammed shut when his mouth moved immediately between her legs and started moving sensually.

There was no doubt he was in control; he knew exactly what to do. He snaked his tongue over her with practiced ease, making her eyes roll. He found her entrance, and her hands clenched on the furs. His chuckle reverberated against Star's skin as she tried to stifle her moan.

There were sounds coming from her that sounded a lot like animalistic groans. There was no doubt in her mind that she could easily be heard. It didn't matter to Star, though, as he put pressure on her sweet spot, rubbing it. She didn't care who could hear her, and she didn't care what they thought.

The sensation he was drawing out of her was too intense and pleasurable.

As she looked between her legs, she saw his head tilted upward as if he sensed her attention. She was seared by the look in his eyes. She had to ask herself if it was okay to be possessive of him.

She moaned in delight when his tongue rubbed over her again. When she was a writhing mass of pleasure on the fur, he finally managed to push her over the edge with a precise movement of his fingers and a sucking pressure that had her eyes widening.

Lost in him and the pleasure he created, she cried out. As the waves of ecstasy seemed to rush away all too quickly, she was gasping for air, and her heavy breathing filled the *tepay*.

"It'll be a fire between us, Star. A fire," he whispered to her as he kissed her delicately with small butterfly kisses as he worked his way up her body.

Star was high on the feel of him. She felt sated and as if the pleasure was too much for her to handle.

In a whisper, she turned to see his face by her and said, "Then let's burn." as she claimed his mouth.

He tangled his tongue with hers, and the kiss turned into a war as he took control of her mouth. The Horde king was unwilling to give in. Hadak was the same, but she was willing to let Hadak have her. Star was his. There was only one thing she had to decide; whether or not she would give in to the Horde king.

It was a frightening prospect. Her decision to leave her family and give him control of her life was a big decision for her. In her mind, that was all that it could be seen as. To be his *Avae* was all she would ever be.

As far as Star was concerned, she didn't have lofty dreams or unattainable goals. It had always been said of her that she was meek, or so she had been told. Compared to other females of her age, she was a quiet individual. Generally, she adhered to the rules.

Being his, completely his, would require her to adhere to the rules without fail for the rest of her life. It would mean obeying the

Horde king, not just Hadak, and in so doing, she might lose a very important part of herself.

The other side of her said she just proved she could ask for what she wanted, and he gave it to her. He gave her time.

Could he have given her time if she had asked mere days ago? No. He didn't know about her trials or even a sliver of her personality. She thought he probably would have taken whatever he wanted as his right or as he thought it was his right.

He gave her what she wanted today without a doubt because he knew what she was feeling. He knew she needed to be sure they'd be equals.

She let him control the kiss. The harsh rasp of her breathing filled the air as he backed away with a frown, obviously feeling her shifting thoughts.

Using her fingers, she stroked his eyebrow. There was a hard ridge of bone in that area that was different.

Grabbing hold of his hip, she drew him against her, making sure he understood in no uncertain terms not to stop.

It was only his feral grin and hard grasp on her hip that served as a warning before he slid home. The grip he had on her throat was firm.

She let out a whimper when he began to move. Taking a moment to check on her, he paused. "Just give me a minute?" he asked.

She nodded and reached between them, flicking the sensitive button between her legs. Within a few minutes, she had melted around him. Her body was shaking, and her hips were beginning to jerk.

Hadak began to chuckle as she moaned, "More." He thrust his hips into her, making her see stars as they snapped back and forth.

He pounded into her as she gasped and felt her breathing stutter as pleasure overwhelmed her. Hadak focused on his hand, which was on her neck, with single-mindedness.

The only time he glanced away from her neck was to watch her face change as she tightened around his cock, those ridges giving her indescribable pleasure.

Her cry and his roar mixed.

Later, when they lay side by side, she wondered what plans he had for her. He didn't look willing to give her up and allow her to make a choice. As much as her heart might break if she were to leave him, it might also break if she were to leave her family. The thought of leaving her family completely would be enough to shatter her into a million pieces.

It was a fitful night. The only saving grace was his warm body encircling and protecting her.

When his fingers tickled her ribs, and he trailed them down her body, she awoke laughing. "Stop that!"

She pouted, and he kissed her hard and fast before standing gloriously naked. Seeing his perfectly formed buns on display, she was tempted to take a bite and see what he would do. It was as if he was able to sense what she was thinking as he shot her a look.

Innocently grinning at him, she began to settle back into the furs. Before her back could hit them, he tugged at her. "Up, we must be moving by afternoon."

"What? Why?"

"The king has asked us to meet, so we will meet," he shrugged before striding through to the bath, picking up a cloth he washed with cold water. When he ran it along the length of his cock she swallowed hard.

Even though her mouth dried up, she still asked. "You want me there?"

During the process of drying off, he grimaced and hurriedly moved. "*Nen*, but I don't want to leave you here either."

"Who else will be there?"

"From our Horde, my first Furan and his first warriors, then a few second warriors. The rest of the second warriors we'll leave behind with the Horde."

"Second?" she asked, having never heard of the term before.

"Furan has warriors trained in different things from politics to stealth to spying to pure strength. They have specialised skills that make them stand out, and they are called the first. The second warriors are our second line of defence and are skilled with blades."

She nodded. Observing her washing up, he pulled his fur over his hips. She pulled a dress over her head. It was thicker and warmer, and it was soft like cotton.

"The warriors will never be led by anyone other than *Avayak* during a battle; he will always defend his Horde, while the firsts and seconds follow closely behind."

"Are there many battles?"

"Hmm." He sat, pulling her with him. He pulled her close and fed her a piece of succulent fruit. Star's mouth watered as he traced his fingers over her lips. "Not every *Avayak* is worthy," he whispered while licking the juice off her lips.

She could have sworn he muttered, "Some of them are rotten," when he pulled back to grab a round fruit for himself.

"You're leaving for a while, in your absence, who will be in charge?"

"The *fhalah's* have more influence than you know, so if anyone attempts to step out of line while the *Avayak's* are not with the Horde, they'll punish them severely." He chuckled, "My ears were pinched red when I tried to get up to mischief while the *Avayak* was visiting a market."

"So, it is the females who will control the situation?" she inquired with a cheeky grin. "It's not surprising that females actually run things." Shooting her a look, he hooked his fingers and tickled her.

"*Seya*." Taking a piece of meat between his fingers, he popped the grisly portion in his mouth and gave her the tender portion. Chewing on it, she felt her heart clench in her chest. "I won't say otherwise; I am smarter than that," he grinned with delight. "I leave some of my seconds behind, and the rest of the warriors will follow them into battle."

"Nothing will happen, though, right?"

"*Nen*, there's no warring right now. The kings, all of the *Avayak's*, have united to combat the Jutin threat.

"I don't understand."

"The king in the east is only king by appointment by the Horde kings. Ultimately, if he fails in his duty to oversee the static city or the Hordes, we can replace him if sufficient numbers of us outvote him."

"And this is what you will be considering?"

"*Nen*, not today, but it's on the cards. There is no doubt that we have long ignored the threat presented by the Jutin, and I am not the only one who is tired of the ignorance toward the human colony."

"Wait, are you telling me that you can replace him?" The shock had her speaking in the common tongue.

His eyes were fixed on her as he nodded. "We're planning to, *seya*. The king in the east is a Horde king – or is supposed to be – the city is only static because the first Horde king grew old, and his Horde did not wish to lose him. They stopped moving the Horde, settled in the east, and the next Horde king stayed, as he liked the area. Soon, the city was being built around them, making it impossible for them to move.

"So he's not really your king, then?"

"*Nen*, it's a respect we give to the city since many wise *Avayak's* have watched over it throughout the ages. Through the Hordes, it became a place to exchange information, then a place to trade, and now, it's a place where *Avayak's* meet without bloodshed. As long as most Horde kings agree, the king sits in place and governs."

"You meet there because it's neutral and not a travelling Horde?"

"*Seya*, it is now a crucial spot for the Horde, so the city stands, and the *Avayak* king will always have his seat in the east."

Nodding, she sipped her drink and pondered the question that had been niggling at her, so she asked, "My punishment?"

She lightly slapped him on the stomach as he chuckled. "Star, *maye* Star."

His star.

Leaving her heart undamaged would be impossible if he kept being like this.

"What about your punishment?" he asked, sliding his feet into his boots. Then he gently pushed her boots on, kissing the arch of her feet before he did so, making her heart melt.

Mostly thinking about avoiding Illasay, she asked, "How long will I have to work in food *tepay* before my punishment is finished?" He chuckled. Her hands fell to her hips. "I don't think it's funny."

"*Maye Immani* Star, you misunderstood if you thought that was punishment. Basically, it was keeping you out of trouble and giving you something to do. Punishment is harsh, it's not meant for you."

His answer hit her like a punch in the gut. Why was she there? "You're not punishing me?" Did he take her from her family just because he wanted her? Even after she told him how much they meant to her, he still hadn't let her go.

Her head tilted, and her eyes were fixed on him as he spoke. "My warriors saw you. Even if they hadn't seen you, I couldn't avoid punishing you. The *Immani* can't get it into their heads that they won't be punished for infractions."

Her shuttered expression caught his attention, and he breathed deeply, wariness in his eyes. "I should have punished your father, too," he grumbled and shook his head. "He had a deep enough cut

I could pass off as an injury. But you..." His eyes were filled with regret, and he winced. "It was impossible for me to leave you behind. Imagine if humans were exploring and came across the wrong Horde. The punishment would be severe, and if the Jutin got them, we both know what would happen."

After holding her face for a moment, she breathed roughly and nodded a small *"Seya,"* to him.

"The Horde sees how you are punished. It might seem like a light punishment, but they won't question me."

"When is it going to end?"

For a moment, he traced the skin on the side of her neck with his fingers. Furan came through the flaps...panting...before he could reply.

"Furan," he growled, letting go of her.

"*Kussa* - there was no time to waste. There was a message sent ahead by the *Avayak's*. They heard that the Jutin were gathering in numbers near the human colony, and they wanted to meet nearby. Tenek's message was the first to arrive. He has taken his warriors and begun the journey."

In the instant that Hadak rose to his feet, she grabbed his arm and wobbled. Her voice was filled with fear as she whispered, "My family," as she gripped his arm tightly.

A harsh glare from him dared Furan to say anything else. Hadak turned his attention to her, framing her face with his hands. "It's not necessary for you to be concerned if Tenek is making his way there. He's a fierce *Avayak*. A terrible beast in battle."

She almost laughed when she heard that. He was trying to comfort her – only his version was to tell her how bloodthirsty his fellow Horde king was.

Her whole body shook; she realised that all her procrastinating about whether she should stay didn't matter at all. All she wanted was to get home and make sure that her family was doing well. Find that her *Brathar*, who was still young and headstrong, was flirting with the bartender at the tavern. "I'm going," she said firmly.

He did not disagree but gave her a strangely intense look before speaking. "I always intended for you to be there. I want you to get ready and join me by the *Guyipe*."

An astonished "What?" escaped her lips. She had assumed that with the threat of battle, he would make her stay.

"*Seya*, I want you with me."

She nodded, moving her hands to tie her boots with shaky hands. After missing the loop on her third attempt, Hadak stilled her hands. His forefinger stroked the back of her calf as he laced up her boots.

"We will leave in an hour, so make sure everyone is ready," he instructed Furan, his gaze fixed on hers.

Furan nodded, his lingering gaze catching her attention. After looking between them in confusion, he strode out of the *tepay*.

"Get your things and pack them up. We will move lightly," he said, kissing the top of her head. "The lighter we are, the faster we move," he reassured her.

While she sorted through the pile of tunics and leathers that Ulla had brought for her, her hands trembled. "Ulla?"

His head shook in response. "If she comes with us, I cannot spare warriors to protect. I need everyone on alert."

"Why?"

"Because I want eyes to be on you at all times."

When she shook her head at him, she thought he was joking until he grabbed her tightly and glared at her.

"You're serious, aren't you?"

"*Seya* Star, deadly."

She held her tongue, not wanting him to change his mind. She hardly thought he needed every warrior to keep an eye on her.

A wave of his hand prompted her to move. "Right, I'm getting my stuff together."

Muttering, he grabbed a few things, then left. She contemplated stopping by Ulla's house, but there was no time. She was sure that once Ulla heard what had occurred, she would understand Star's need to leave.

She was as close to her mother as Star was to hers, so yeah, she would be able to understand. Furthermore, it gave her some time away from Illasay, so at least, she didn't have to confront her immediately.

Tears filled her eyes as she considered what might happen to her family if they failed to arrive in time.

Jutin had no mercy; they were vile *Immani* who had no regard for the people or the planet itself. They were conquerors who had not yet conquered this planet.

They must have been driven mad by the situation because they kept trying.

Star's pack was ready, and when she stepped outside, she was met by two warriors. They straightened when they saw her and followed behind her as she strode toward the *Guyipe* pen.

"Star..." She heard a voice calling from her right. Ulla walked between the warriors and reached Star. She held something tightly wrapped in her hands and passed it over. Star glanced at her with confusion. "It's like bread; it will keep for the journey. We heard you were traveling. *Mathar* wouldn't allow you to leave without it."

"*Behku*. It is greatly appreciated."

"It's nothing. Just be careful."

Nodding, Star embraced Ulla in a hug, an experience Ulla wasn't accustomed to, given her loose arms.

She couldn't remember ever seeing a Zandian hug before. Touches, clasps of the arm, that sort of thing, but never a full-on hug; perhaps it was just a human tendency.

Her voice was small and hesitant as Ulla said, "Come back." Star realized that her concern wasn't just that she might get hurt but that she might decide to stay.

A frown formed on Star's face as she opened her mouth to say, "Yes," but it stuck.

How could she say with certainty that she would be coming back? Even if there wasn't a fight, Star wasn't sure she would leave her family again. It was difficult enough the first time around to see the tears in her *Brathar's* eyes. Her parents' silent, heavy, and sad acceptance must have hurt them, knowing they could do nothing.

A warrior to her left cleared his throat, saving her the trouble of answering. It's time for us to leave. We can't hold up any longer."

"*Seya*, I'm coming."

It took her a few minutes to strap the pack to *Guyipe*. She watched warrior after warrior arrive until she couldn't see behind them anymore. When Hadak broke through the crowd, he grabbed her waist and threw her onto *Guyipe's* back.

"Let's ride."

Just like that, they departed from the Horde. Their destination lay ahead of them on the rocky and dusty plains

.

Chapter 11

Her attention was caught by a familiar face in the crowd of warriors during the journey.

She was sitting in silence while Hadak talked to Furan, so she moved her *Guyipe* over to Nasan with a ready smile on her face. It was a relief to see someone she knew. "I didn't realise you were a first or second warrior?"

The sound of her voice startled him, and he tightened his grip on the *Guyipe*. He glanced at the front of the Horde warriors before looking at her with slanted black eyes. Rather than answering her, he seemed to struggle for a moment.

"Is everything okay?" she asked.

"*Seya.*"

That was it, nothing else?

"I thought we might be able to ride together. Apart from Hadak and Furan, you're the only face I know. They seem too busy right now, so I don't want to bother them."

They had been in a deep conversation for the majority of their journey so far. Whether they were talking about strategies, theories, or just mindless gossip, she had no idea, although she seriously doubted it was gossip.

The snipe she made about mindless gossip was harsh. He wouldn't waste time on that. It was probably just a matter of her being unnerved and taking it out on the only person she knew.

Nasan shrugged his shoulders, his facial features tightening.

Her forehead wrinkled in confusion. "Was there something I did that offended you?"

Hadak yelled, "*Avae.*" She felt her stomach drop as a few warriors grunted in shock, twitching in their seats. For a moment, she closed her eyes because there was only one person there he could mean, and she couldn't believe he had said it out loud.

When hands closed over hers on the *Guyipe* reins, she opened her eyes to find Hadak steering them away from everyone, far enough to talk without being overheard.

"That was uncalled for," she hissed, her temper flared.

"*Nen*, I will not keep what I want from you a secret. Do you think that my Horde are not aware of this?" He asked through gritted teeth, his words hissing out of his lips.

"It doesn't give you the right to claim me as your property."

"That's how you think I treat you, like property," he spat. With a harsh breath and clenched fist, he rode away, giving her or himself space.

Infuriating warriors!

She was ignored by one, Nasan, for reasons unknown, while she was claimed by the other, Hadak. Yes. Warriors were infuriating.

She muttered under her breath. Music had been her only source of happiness and calmness in life so far. She kept her strings in her pack because they were her favourite instrument and a gift from Hadak.

As soon as Hadak found an outcropping of rocks, he signalled, and everyone settled down. The *Guyipe's* weaved around boulders and small rocks.

To calm her nerves, she decided to play. While she disappeared into her own world, the warriors heated some water.

Watching the horizon in the direction they would be heading, Hadak climbed onto a boulder and crossed his arms over his chest. As if he knew something, Furan glanced between Hadak and her. Despite her anger, Nasan didn't look away from her. It was disconcerting to see him change after being a trusted friend.

As she closed her eyes to block out all distractions, the strings hummed under her fingers. It wasn't long before she found herself playing a familiar tune. As she listened to the music, a smile spread across her lips. She sang quietly, drifting into her music as she put her heart and soul into the song.

Too soon, the song was finished. At the end, she drifted into a melancholy string, then brought it back with an uplifting beat. That's when she realised how quiet the camp was.

Upon opening her eyes, she found everyone staring at her. Clearing her throat, she tucked the strings behind her. The song was vibrant and alive. Suddenly, she wondered if bringing the strings was a bad idea. She had brought them along with the tiny picture she had kept curled up in her fur; the one of her and her family.

A slight shift in her heart, a shadow of doubt. If they weren't able to reach the colony in time, what would happen?

Wincing, she apologised, "*Kussa*." Possibly they weren't fond of the melody, or perhaps happy songs were not their cup of tea.

"Can you play again?" asked a warrior with much shorter hair.

Checking to ensure there were no negative comments or head shakes and seeing more than one eager face, she smiled shakily. Pulling up the strings, she played a few of her favourites.

A tentative smile touched her face for the first time since being told her family was in danger. When she discovered her talent and love for strings, she didn't intend it to be her whole life. Playing used to be a pleasure, but then it became a duty. Because of Hadak, she was able to enjoy the pleasure of playing once again.

As a result of her worry, she had been bitter and harsh. His expression implied that he was eager to hear more of her playing, and Hadak seemed to truly care about her. A small smile could be seen on his face as his eyes remained on the horizon.

Eventually, he sat back and relaxed as she played.

She had to make things right. There was no clear choice for her. She had been leaning towards Hadak but could not abandon her family with this fresh worry.

It was Hadak who saved her father, who saved her from a worse punishment. It was Hadak who gave her strings, and yes, there was the *tepay* mix-up, but even that wasn't his fault. Immediately after discovering the mix-up, he took steps to fix it, even getting her feet and hands cleaned and creamed so she could heal.

It was obvious he cared, and that struck her.

Star tried so hard not to let him take her heart, but it felt like he reached in and took a tiny piece of it for himself. The place he filled felt as if that part had always been missing. There was no way she could leave her family.

He could never understand how tempting it was to explore her planet for a lifetime. The human colony would always be her home first because that was where her family lived. They were trapped and terrorized by the Jutin.

She couldn't have left them like that with a callous 'Good luck, I'm okay?'

Her attention was drawn to something hanging around the camp's edges.

She was surprised to see Intuk. How could Hadak invite him?

In the aftermath of her song, they applauded, and she grinned widely, but her mind was buzzing with questions. She knew she wouldn't get answers from Hadak tonight.

She ate the food offered and sat down around the fire afterwards. Having expected to sleep alone, she was surprised when an arm came around her and squeezed hers. As soon as she smelled the warrior behind her and felt his muscular body, she relaxed. Hadak.

Then, in a low tone, he said, "Sleep," squeezing her arm once more. She closed her eyes just as she had moments before, staring into the fire.

Her worry finally surfaced in the morning, and she approached him about it. "What's Intuk doing here?" she whispered the next morning as they packed up. His eyebrows rose as he looked over at

Intuk. "Well, don't stare at him," she said quietly. She was appalled and checked to make sure Intuk wasn't looking their way.

"*Immani Star*, I won't be hiding my gaze from my people. Intuk was one of my firsts, he's now a second, still a good fighter." Hadak tugged her hair playfully.

Her insides almost froze when Intuk glared at her. She still had a bad feeling.

When they were up on the *Guyipe* and travelling, something he said bothered her. "What do you mean he was a first?"

"He touched something of mine," Hadak growled, his body stiff with rage. His slitted eyes lit upon her cheek, and as much as she pretended she didn't understand, she knew instantly that he was talking about when Intuk slapped her. "If he messes up again, he loses his place in the Horde."

"I thought I was in the wrong."

"It doesn't matter. The fact that you were with Furan and *Immani*, he should have known better. There are some of my people who still adhere to the old ways. Others not so much, and he could break your bones if he hit you hard enough," he scowled. "I have seen you get a fever from a cut. I don't want to see you die from a hit from one of my warriors."

Her eyes widened at the unexpected sentiment. It would have been funny if he hadn't looked so serious and had a sliver of fear in his eyes, as if he couldn't bear the thought of her not being there; Alive by his side.

After dragging her eyes away, she focused on the horizon for any sign of familiarity.

The first signs of life were seen two days later. As soon as they spotted the trees she recognized, they rode hard. She was sweaty, exhausted, and worried.

She sat tall and straight on the *Guyipe* as she watched the warriors in the distance. There were so many new faces in front of her that her eyes struggled to keep up. They didn't look any different from Hadak's Horde. Their hair was braided intricately, some had beads on it, and they all had dark skin.

"This is Tenek's Horde. He's crazy," Hadak said humorously, a big grin stretching across his face.

First, they were greeted by a scary warrior she took to be Tenek. Her mind was blown by the fact that Tenek was much larger than Hadak, which she had never thought possible. Hadak's hands slapped into his with comfortable ease - they were friends then.

Tenek smiled as his black eyes moved toward Star. He had a line of white running through the black of his left eye. It ran parallel to a scar bisecting his eyebrow and ending with a small scar on his cheek. It appeared that his eye was still working since it moved about in its socket. It looked like an old injury. It was hard not to stare at the unusual eye amongst pure black eyes surrounding her.

Tenek's full lips tilted up, pulling his high cheekbones up sharply. "You must be the *Immani* I have heard so much about." Tenek's expression changed. His lips twitched as he noticed Hadak hovering over her.

Her gaze drifted to Hadak, and he nodded that she could speak. "*Seya*, I'm from the colony. How did you find out about me?"

After hearing her speak Zandian, he clapped and shook her arm vigorously in greeting. She was on top of her *Guyipe,* so she wobbled a little. "An *Immani* with a brain as well. There's been talk." Tenek turned to Hadak, who was sliding off his *Guyipe.* "Tell me, Hadak, are they good between the furs?"

A frown crossed Hadak's face. "How do you feel about living suddenly on the edge of death?" Hadak wondered. "Have you lost your will to live? You are asking me to take your head off."

She slid off her *Guyipe* and handed it over to the waiting warrior. For a moment, Tenek's white teeth flashed at them.

"*Nen*, I wonder if I should go to the trouble of collecting one for myself." His grin was full of mischief but also had something dark and hidden beneath.

Hadak shrugged as they stride through a group of warriors, a clearing ahead with a stone displaying a map.

"Always a warrior of too many words," Tenek laughed and pulled at his ears mockingly. "*Nen, nen*, stop talking, else my ears will surely fall off."

A sudden laugh erupted from Star. A few warriors nearby were stopped in their tracks by the loud and joyful sound.

The smile on Tenek's face was unabashed. "It might be worth it, you know."

Laughing, Hadak scoffed, "You'll end up with your balls inside your stomach." Star smiled.

Hadak's arm wrapped around her neck, then he gripped her hips. His touch was casual, but it was also full of meaning.

"You needn't worry; I have no intention of stealing your *Avae*."

In response, she crossed her arms. She frowned at Hadak, expecting him to correct the error. He glanced around the camp, looking anywhere but at her. Everyone knew she was off limits because of that stupid neck hold. She knew it.

Star should be furious, but in her mind, the only person she would ever belong to was him. She accused him of treating her like a possession which wasn't true. She felt as though she had given herself over to him, so maybe it was partly in her mind.

It didn't feel wrong. It felt exciting, new, and different.

Refusing to let their talk of Star being Hadak's anything get in the way of her questions, she waited until they were far enough from the others to ask him, "The human colony?" Her fingers clutched her sides tightly as she waited for news.

"Unharmed," Tenek reported softly.

Thank God. Her hands were freely shaking as she trembled in relief. Taking a deep breath, she sank back onto a large stone that protruded from the ground.

"The Jutin will die by my blade like all others who came against me," Tenek snarled as his enchanting eyes danced. With a smile, she shook her head at the boast.

"He is mad," Hadak loudly declared, laughing. "He's never come against me. I'm better in every way than him. He would die a bloody death by my sword."

"A bloody death, *nen*, you would be dead before you reach me," Tenek paused, then pointed at his eyes with a laugh. "By a look alone."

Hadak said, "You would be dead before I even saw you because you would be afraid of facing me."

"Ha! When I'm done with you, you'll be a puddle on the ground, with no parts of you recognisable," Tenek replied. As they bantered, her head whipped back and forth.

"A puddle?" Hadak asked, his lips twitching. Tenek shrugged before they both began to laugh.

'Children!' She huffed silently. It was amusing to see this side of Hadak- Carefree and not *Avayak*.

In greeting, Hadak slapped Tenek on the back. He grabbed cups for them and filled them. "It's good to see you, my friend," he said, passing her a drink. She swallowed it all down immediately. There was a dryness in her throat. Frowning, he refilled and gave her another drink which she sipped. "What news do you have from the Hordes?"

Tenek's lips tightened in displeasure. "*Avayak* A'pak. That *Fhok* is on his way," he spat onto the ground, his disgust evident. Tenek grinned at her as her eyes widened. "That pile of steaming *hak* can go rot. He's not a good *Avayak*, not like me, *Immani*." His suggestive wink got him a punch in the gut from Hadak. Unrepentant, Tenek extended his hand in a gesture of what can be done. "What! I'm a very good *Avayak*, all of my Horde know it."

There was something cute about this boastful Horde king with the hard glint in his eyes. He was a kind-natured, easy-going warrior who was easy to warm up to. Even joking around, she could see the appeal of the *Avayak* for his Horde. The sheer size of him was intimidating. She was already overwhelmed by Hadak's sheer maleness, not to mention his size. Whoever took on Tenek should have stone lady balls.

She chuckled at the thought. Both Horde kings turned to look at her simultaneously, mirroring each other. That set her off into giggles that had Hadak's mouth twitching.

"A'pak, is that his name?" It sounded very similar to Hadak's last name.

"*Nen*. It belongs to the Horde. *Avayak* takes the name of the Horde. We have family names, but we use them only for our families. When we come of age and decide to join a Horde, we introduce ourselves under the name of the Horde we choose."

"Oh, okay, so this A'pak isn't very pleasant to be around?"

Hadak replied, "*Seya*, although not very pleasant, doesn't quite touch it." Hadak grabbed the empty cup from her and pulled her across the log and between his legs, sitting on a patch of fur across from Tenek.

Tenek folded his arms and leaned against the tree, watching them intently.

She found comfort in the warm weight of his body against her back, and after days of traveling hard and worrying, her body was exhausted. It was natural for her to relax against him, so she allowed him to take her weight.

"What is your Hordes name?" she asked Tenek, who was eyeing Hadak's hand that trailed up and down her arm.

"A'shay, my horde is the most coveted, don't you know?" His eyes twinkled as he teased Hadak, who grumbled behind him.

"Who else comes?" Hadak asked.

"Kadak A'rey has the potential to defeat Paken here, I hope."

"Hmm," Hadak said, feeding her a piece of fruit she had not previously tried. His eyes heated and focused on her mouth as she licked the juices from her lips. "It is true that Kadak is capable of calming him, but from what I have heard, it has gone beyond even friendly warnings. The last time I saw Kadak, he told me he had cut ties with him."

"Well, let's hope we get this done before Paken arrives."

While they were discussing the Hordes, she felt her eyes grow heavy, and her hands slid down to rest on his thighs. Her eyes were closed. Pushing her head back to get comfortable, he grunted and shifted her.

"You are lucky, my friend," Tenek said.

"Why?" Hadak spoke with the rumbling of his voice vibrating against her cheek.

"You found your *Avae*, I'm still looking."

"You haven't found what you want because you're too fussy, hopping from bed to bed."

Tenek chuckled. "I don't mind enjoying what's on offer, but it's becoming a bit sour leaving the fur as soon as the pleasure is over," he grumbled. Then there was a rustling sound as if he'd shifted. "There is something that doesn't seem right about taking any of the waiting *fhalah's*. It's too easy. I want passion."

"You think you can find what you're looking for in an *Immani*?" Hadak stroked her hair back, his touch warm and gentle.

"Maybe I want that look you shared. I've never had that look before. Fumbles that were mutually beneficial. You know me, I've never been greedy." His voice was filled with laughter.

"I remember you, *seya*. You had no shame when your furs overflowed with *fhalah's*. That was before you became a Horde king." With one hand on her face and the other around her waist, Hadak held her tightly in place.

"The *fhalah's* all love me, what can I say?" Tenek chuckled, but it tapered off. "But I'm becoming greedy. I want one person that's mine; I want my *Avae*."

"There's no guarantee you'll find it in an *Immani*."

Tenek said, *"Nen*, but I like the idea of trying." His laugh split the air, followed by heavy footsteps taking him away.

When he lifted her, Star groaned. She felt as though she could sleep for days on end.

"Shh, sleep, *maye* Star."

It was a surprise to her to find Hadak already up when she woke. He was usually wrapped around her at the beginning of the day, and now he wasn't.

Sitting up, she blinked. While they slept, she noticed he had laid them down slightly away from Tenek's warriors. She was surrounding with Hadak's warriors as if he wanted to keep her safe with only his trusted people.

She stood up, the fur stuck to her, and she grimaced. While pushing aside the thought of how sleep-ruffled she must appear, she began to walk towards the stream. There was at least some familiarity here, since the water that ran into the colony originated here. Taking handfuls of water, she washed as thoroughly as she could, dipping her toes in the water for a few moments.

As a voice said, "You look beautiful," she jumped and screamed in terror.

"Don't scare me like that." She slapped him firmly for frightening her and grinned because it was the first time he had complimented her appearance. Her expression must have conveyed some of her thoughts because he frowned. She was pleased to hear that he thought of her as beautiful. "It is silly, but your women are different," she told him.

"So are your males." Realising he might have the same doubts as she did, she kissed him on the chin, rubbing her thumb over his sharp cheekbone.

Her expression was thoughtful as she told him. "I have never been in a relationship with anyone else, so you can be sure I find you attractive." Her grin widened with his chuckle.

There was a serious look on his face. His hand slipped around her neck as he firmly grasped her chin. "I miss the feeling of you clasping me tightly last night," he whispered, lowering his head to lick at her neck, kissing the areas not covered by his hand.

She moaned, and his hand tightened a fraction before he let out a sigh of disappointment and took a step backwards. "We have no time. A party of Jutin is approaching. Tenek and I have a strategy."

Her face fell. She grabbed her boots and pulled them on as soon as she had dried her feet. "Let's go." She grabbed his arm and stopped. Hold on, do the humans know what is happening?"

"*Nen*," he replied, his body stiff as he spoke.

"We should inform them."

He started walking away again, saying, "*Nen*."

"What, why not?" Surely, it was a good idea to be prepared.

After touching his arm again to stop him, he suddenly became rigid.

"The king in the east has no tolerance for *Immani*. Telling them about the troubles of the land is forbidden."

She parted her lips and rubbed her arms. "That's absurd. They could arm themselves and stick together. Who's to say the Jutin won't take them if they don't know and walk about on their own? You saw what happened to my *Fathar*. He was taken from our home."

"I know, Star," he gritted his teeth. "I need to talk to Tenek about our plan of attack." He ripped his arm from her hands and started walking.

Furious at his dismissal, she snapped at him. "Don't ignore the danger. Even if you weren't sleeping with me, would you help?"

"*Seya*, I'll never ignore the danger to my planet."

"You wouldn't do that, but you'll leave my family vulnerable. If they don't know, they can't defend themselves."

He snarled, "It's not up to me."

"You said he was only king by your vote, so surely you can warn the humans. Let them arm themselves. You know now that the Jutin have been picking us off," her voice wobbled as she pleaded in her native language. "Please, Hadak, they need to know."

"Your family," he said, clenching his fists.

"Yes, *Teyae*," she pleaded. "Tell them, let them know they need to get ready."

"I can't," he snapped, pulling away from her. Fear gripped her as she watched him walk away. What went wrong?

She thought he cared about her, and she thought he would protect her family. Because of how protective he had become of her, she had been drawn in. For a moment, she forgot that he was *Avayak* with duties to his Horde and the king first. It was impossible for her to become his *Avae* as long as her needs and family were put last.

She let him meet with Tenek alone. Her heart hurt. She looked at the horizon, where the human colony was located. It was half a day ride by *Guyipe*. If he didn't tell them the Jutin were coming, then she would.

It was about time she firmly planted herself in reality. Her reality was that the people she loved were trapped in a walled-in colony, unaware of the dangers. Star didn't want to leave him - it was almost painful to think of leaving him. Her family needed to be taken care of. He knew that; he always had.

There was never a doubt in her mind that she was going back to the colony, to her family, and she never told him otherwise. He might want her to stand by his side, but he didn't know her well. Hell, he didn't even know her last name.

All she had to do was find the perfect moment to leave him.

Despite the whisper inside her that it could be simple, that they could love each other, she rubbed her sternum and ignored it.

There was no love at first sight. On the plains, he first touched her without regard to the warriors around them. He didn't strip her, but he might as well have. In her mind, what he did wasn't okay. However, he was very careful where he touched her in front of people after that.

He always gripped her neck as if he knew and planned to have her. A softer romantic side of her swooned at the idea. There was no point in listening to all those thoughts running through her mind.

"Star," a deep voice called, and she turned around to see Nasan, his face filled with concern.

"*Seya*," she answered, wondering how long he had been standing there.

"I've been distant, but I see that you need a warrior in your corner," Nasan glanced over to Hadak's retreating back and grimaced when he realised he had heard.

"Maybe, but I don't think it will help. Either I can be his equal and work with him, or I can be a prize *bryd* - there only for one reason." If her words weren't clear, her disgusting tone implied it. That she was there for what was between her legs.

"Hmm, I understand where he's coming from. Before disobeying the rules, he must consult with the other *Avayak's*. It could cost him his life and position if someone wanted to challenge him."

"What?" Her voice was high-pitched with shock.

Nasan lifted his shoulder. "If any Horde king works autonomously without the majority of the others or the agreement of another king, then they can be killed or overthrown. It's like a shared throne, a juggling game, delicately balanced, but it works."

"Why didn't he say that?"

"I don't know."

"Thank you for telling me." She didn't need to run off just yet, but she wasn't ruling out the possibility. She would be leaving if no word was sent to the human colony.

Her thanks made Nasan squirm as she stood behind the rocks. "Is something wrong?" she finally asked him.

"Nen" Although he said no, his eyes twitched, his arms flexed, and his fingers clenched in disagreement. "Okay."

Leaving him at the stream, she found herself by Hadak's side, waiting for a hurtful comment. When he saw her approaching him and standing beside him, his eyes filled with relief. After kissing her knuckles in apology, he tucked her hand into his own and held it tightly.

Tenek stood by the rough map and huffed at it as if he was daring it to keep secrets from him. "These are the trees you found the first Jutin in?"

"Seya, they took an *Immani* man." Hadak rubbed her hand.

"There have been reports of flares in the skies, and the Jutin are gathering in groups."

"Hold on, are those flares in the sky the Jutin's landing?"

Tenek replied, rubbing the hard ridge on his eyebrow and passing her a drink as he said, *"Seya,* the Drak system has other habitable planets. We know this, but the Jutin are the only ones who come to us with their flying ships."

"Don't you want to go exploring?" The thought of seeing another planet intrigued her.

Hadak grumbled, *"Nen,* look what happens when you do that. There is a human colony here because no one wanted to help you, and the Jutin want to conquer the system," Hadak said.

"Ah, okay, you have a point there."

With confidence, Tenek said, "The Jutin will attack in numbers. That's why we're gathering here. Up until now, it has been small attacks meant to weaken our numbers."

Star jerked in surprise as Hadak said, "We must warn the humans." Her hand clenched tightly on his. Thank God he did what she asked. It made her heart melt even more. She was both exhilarated and terrified at the thought of this big warrior taking care of her. It would be easy for Star to live like this.

"I agree," Tenek said carefully, his eyes flickering as a thunderous sound began. "Paken comes."

As she followed his gaze, another Horde appeared, their *Guyipe's* heading towards them. An *Avayak* jumping off a *Guyipe* in one movement was clearly an act of theatrical performance.

Following this, Tenek's eyelids began to flicker, and Hadak's hand began to tighten around hers. Hadak passed her something he pulled from his fur. As she grasped the gold choker, it bit into her hand.

Hadak said, "Put it on, it will give you some protection against him." Tenek nodded in agreement.

The foul smirk on the other Horde king's face as he lumbered toward them made her immediately clasp it to her neck. Hadak was seemingly able to find the clasps instantly and put them on without looking.

"What is this?" the new Horde king asked Star, staring at her with no regard until he reached the choker and scoffed. "Disgusting," he spat.

"Be careful," Hadak warned.

His voice boomed, "I thought you were smarter than this."

"Who are you to question me? She's my *Avae*. What I do with my horde is my business."

"Maybe, but do you think the king will be happy? The king will not be happy, and rightfully so, since this is an abomination."

Before she could blink, Hadak grabbed his neck. It was the most raw fury she had ever seen on his face. There was still a killing haze in his eyes, and Paken shoved his arm off with visible effort.

"The king will hear about this."

"The king," scoffed Hadak. "I won't let another Horde tell me who I take for my own." He tucked her behind him, and Tenek stood beside him, silently supporting his choice. While Paken's lips lifted in a sneer, his warriors seemed almost embarrassed, though they were doing their best to maintain a blank expression.

"You don't respect Zandar by taking an *Immani* for a mate," he spat. She changed her mind if she ever hated the way Hadak called her *Immani* because the way Pakan had spoken in a disgusted tone frightened her. Even when Hadak hadn't known her, he never said *Immani* the same way Paken just did.

"We are here to save the *Immani* and our planet. If you wish to leave, feel free." Hadak threw his arm out of the way; he had just come with a huge smile, daring him to do so.

"I won't abandon my people." His glare shot Star's way and made it clear that she was not one of their people and Hadak was letting the planet down by standing with her.

There were doubts in her mind. Hadak must also have them, but this stranger's dislike was as vile as that of Illasay and Ghertun. Considering how long they had been on the planet and how established their colony was, she would have thought they would have had a better repertoire of skills or at least some mutual respect by now.

Most of the time, they adhered to their rules.

While keeping her head down and trying not to draw attention to herself, she began to step back and move away from him. When she bumped into a body, she was prevented from retreating. Looking up past the angry line of the body, she saw Nasan's gaze fixed on Paken.

"We are working on the problem now. I am taking *maye Immani* home so we can warn the humans," Hadak spoke.

"Those *sakos*, what can they do?" Hadak ignored the sharp retort as he turned to face her. Star's gaze caught his, and a moment of satisfaction flared when he noticed her choker. He gave her a gentle kiss on the lips. This was a slow tease, one that was barely noticeable but that set fire to her in a way that deeper kisses had not done. *

"We go," he said in the intimate space between them. Her eyes popped fully open.

Tenek looked hungry for what they had. Paken looked like he wanted to vomit, and Hadak flicked sharp glances at Nasan. He considered him for a moment, then announced, "You come with us."

Nasan, whose body was still too close to hers for comfort, especially with the heat of Hadak pressing against her, jerked in response to the command. In quick succession, Paken began issuing orders as if he wished to make sure everyone understood that he was in charge. She felt he was trying too hard, but she would never express that opinion.

As Nasan collected the *Guyipe's*, Hadak whispered to Tenek before returning to Star.

"The rest of my warriors will remain here. If the Jutin are able to get past them, it will not matter who is in the colony."

She nodded in agreement. It was just after she had finished gathering her belongings that she asked him, "Why Nasan?"

"Who better to protect you than someone who loves you?"

She paused in the act of putting her pack on, and her heart remained still. The look on Nasan's *Mathar's* face when he refused to speak to her, the caution he showed after the river, and Ulla's exasperation all hint at something deeper. But love!

"It's not real, he only thinks he loves me. I don't know if it's true or not."

Hadak shook his head and rested a hand on her cheek as he shook his head. "I don't think you should tell him that. He's a warrior with a fierce heart who would protect those he loves even to death if need be." When she made a negative sound, he shushed her quietly. "Don't deny him his feelings because they make you uncomfortable."

"How can you be okay with this?"

It was obvious from the shifting of his tense jaw and the flicker of his eyes that he wasn't. "It doesn't matter; your heart is mine." That arrogant statement should have made her want to slap him, but instead, she found herself smiling with a silly grin across her lips. With a shaking of his head, he ran his thumb over her smile as he looked at it.

His head dipping swiftly, he grabbed her up in his arms and pushed her against the rock with both arms. A moan fell from her lips as he kissed her. The kiss was hot enough to melt ice. His hands were all over the place, and her own were clenched in his hair. She held his braids, holding him to her.

In a whisper, she said, "God, I want you."

"*Seya*, I can see that," said another voice making her jerk and blush. Tenek stood behind Hadak with his bright eyes and lecherous grin. He also had an expression of amusement on his face. "And that's what I want," he said to Hadak.

Hadak tightened his grip on her before letting her slide down. Hadak arched an eyebrow at him. "You have terrible timing and find your own." The two started walking, picking up their packs and throwing them over their shoulders.

In the clearing, Tenek dared kissing her cheek goodbye. Hadak permitted it, but when Tenek cheekily reached for her mouth, Hadak smoothly shoved him away. Holding his hands up in surrender, Tenek laughed.

"I would kill you if she didn't like you so much," Hadak stated. Star expected to see anything but laughter, but she should have realised the crazy Horde king played by his own rules. Tenek laughed loudly, catching the attention of the others. Star swung up onto her waiting *Guyipe*, ignoring the hard and disgusted look Paken threw her way.

Star still couldn't believe Hadak was taking them to the colony. As she gazed at him sitting proudly on the *Guyipe*, she was overcome with emotion. It choked her.

She looked forward with a smile, excited to see her family for the first time in what seemed like a very long time. She threw a cheeky grin at Hadak before turning her face back towards the sun. There was a smile on her lips as she said, "Race you."

She couldn't help but laugh as he chased after her, followed closely by Nasan. She was leaving the two Horde kings and a small army of warriors behind them a line of defence to protect them. They made their way to the human colony. Her home.

* Excrement

Chapter 12

"It's quiet," whispering made things worse than they already were. She clamped her lips together.

It was as if the town had died. At the top of the gate, there was no movement at all. There was a noxious smell in the air, something that wasn't pleasant to breathe.

There was an immediate warning that screamed out of her brain - To back away, to turn away from there and never come back. She had no choice, though, that was her home. Hadak's stiff form rode alongside her, and he nodded in response to her statement.

In a flash, Nasan took up a position on his left side, protecting her as he held his sword in his hand.

Something in her mind rejected the chilly barren landscape before her. Most of the time, there was a bustle as the colony carried on its daily activities. Evidently, even when people were scared of the Hordes and hid, there was more life than there was today. It was not uncommon for stragglers to wait on the sidelines hoping that the sale of their goods might result in some form of recognition or payment.

"There should be someone here," her hushed voice echoed through the hazy fog that shrouded the area in front of them. The fog wasn't so thick that she couldn't see through it. It did seem to have a heavy malevolent feel to it, or maybe it was her fearful mind that made it seem even more sinister than it was.

No, she thought as she saw Hadak draw his sword.

"Hello," she bravely shouted as she approached the gates of the building. She shrugged when Hadak glared at her with his black-as-night eyes.

If they didn't try, they would never know. Somewhere, something strong had risen in her, refusing to be quiet or a voice in the back. It all started with Hadak, and she desperately wanted it to end with him or them.

Hadak said, "There's nothing there," and he got in front of her and blocked her path. "You two stay here, I'll go ahead."

"My family!" she whispered with a great deal of fear in her voice, and it must have been apparent to him because he bent down and placed a kiss on her forehead in an attempt to reassure her.

"Let me check the colony first." He waited for her to nod and said, "We'll find your family."

Nasan swung his sword and nodded at *Avayak* as it flew through the air. The solemnity and readiness he showed during that moment were silent promises he made to Hadak to protect her. It was a struggle for her to keep her teeth from chattering. There was no way she was going to be able to do much to defend herself against someone who meant some harm to her. Therefore, accepting help was the only thing she could do.

There was no use in getting other people killed because she got in the way and didn't accept help when needed.

As the fog rolled over the city, she had no choice but to wait for news, which felt like one of the most agonising moments of her life. Not even blistering her hands and feet had been as painful. She was afraid when she remembered pursuing the Jutin all by herself, single-handedly, without any assistance, but not as terrified as she was now; this was more.

She bit her lip. There was something stubborn about her, wasn't there?

She quickly pushed that realisation to the side and focused on spotting any movement in one of the windows of the house and noticed that a sheet was twitching. She didn't want to get her hopes up, but the gasp that came from her caught Nasan's attention.

"What is it?" he asked, his eyes moving over everything in front of him.

"I think I saw a movement," she said, explaining what she had seen.

"Where? He looked in the direction she was pointing, his sword raised as he gazed at her. He nudged his *Guyipe* forward, then stopped.

"What?" she whispered, craning her neck.

"It's not safe for me to leave you unprotected to go over there."

She said rationally, "We should do this together."

There was a jerk in his head. When she came up beside him, he huffed. As they headed for the gates, their *Guyipe's* were nose to nose.

She began to dismount. She reached out her hand to the side. Nasan's hands suddenly curled around hers, stopping her from slipping off the *Guyipe*. "*Nen*, we don't dismount here until we know more. It is important that we can get away as quickly as possible."

Of course! Her stupidity made her want to slap herself.

Nodding in understanding, she almost fell back in horror when someone raced up the path. In the silence, the sound of thudding footsteps was eerie. A shroud of nothing choked her like a heavyweight.

It was Hadak!

Fearful of asking the questions on the tip of her tongue, she twisted her hands together. Normally, she could tell exactly what he was thinking and feeling from his face, but today, there were no clues, no emotions.

She felt the weight of her heart in her chest like a stone. The pain in her ribs made it difficult for her to breathe. After he stopped beside her, her stomach was in knots, and she felt lightheaded.

Her first inane thought as she gasped for air was that he wasn't on his *Guyipe*. Tears filled her eyes as she waited for the dreadful news he would soon utter.

She was on the verge of breaking. She could feel it. Behind him, a figure drew up as her skin felt like it was going to tear and rend. Due to tears welling up in her eyes, the figure was indistinct and blurry.

"*Sithar*," her brother's shattered voice brought her back to her senses as she fell off the *Guyipe* to reach him. Her legs trembled as Hadak steadied her, and she closed the distance between her and her brother.

She smothered him, smothering him, and then laughed with relief, petting his hair.

"Black!" she cried. Her eyes were drawn to Hadak's over his head. Hadak's eyes were filled with understanding, and possession burned within them. Star's hands tightened around him. Her relief was so great she almost crushed Black.

"Let...me breathe," he managed to wheeze after she squeezed too hard, and she laughed, letting him breathe. She kept her hand on his face. Her first step was to check for cuts and scrapes, anything that would give her a clue as to what was occurring.

"You're okay?" she asked. In a hungry gaze, she scanned every inch of exposed skin, ready to tear the hide of anyone who harmed him.

"*Seya*, I'm fine. *Sithar*, how are you? You don't appear to have been punished?" he asked in a quiet and wondering manner. He was well aware of the tall and broad stature of the Horde king at his back.

For a moment, Star's gaze flitted to Hadak. The heat behind his eyes made her swallow. "*Nen*, I've been treated well." Very well...and she wanted more.

"Are you back?" he asked, his voice hesitant. He wouldn't have asked a question like that before. While he may have pleaded with her to stay, it was in a boy's voice, but this had a hint of steel, and she realised that her brother was growing up.

Before she could formulate an answer, Hadak interrupted, "What happened here?"

Black hugged her tightly and shuddered. He acted like the boy he used to be. Holding him tightly, she smiled at the memories that flooded her mind. Hadak contemplated Star with a new kind of tenderness.

"Come." She gestured to Nasan, who was tying the *Guyipe's* next to Hadak's. "This is Nasan and Hadak. Nasan is a good friend of mine, and you've met *Avayak* before." Nasan stiffened at the description. Star frowned. Her mouth dried at the description, recalling Hadak's certainty that Nasan loved her.

They passed him some water, and her gaze swept over his cracked lips. He drank quickly, but her touch on his arm slowed him down. Then Nasan offered him a piece of bread. Star smiled at him in appreciation. He blinked and pulled a barrel over for them to sit on.

Black cringed as he looked into her eyes after setting aside the food and rubbing his stomach. A cold piercing feeling struck her chest, a premonition of sorts.

Licking her lips, she glanced up at Hadak, who stood above them, watching their conversation. "Tell us what happened?" Hadak ordered.

Black's lips trembled as he said, "I'm sorry, I didn't know how to get you. I couldn't leave because the Jutin came." The trembling and stuttering as he hastily offered titbits would have driven anyone insane. All it served to do was make her anxious. A terrible feeling in her gut.

"What happened?" she asked with a hardness that her brother understood she needed him to talk this time.

Black grasped her hand, and her fingers curled around him as he offered comfort. "The night you left...it was fine. *Fathar* was in good health, he patched himself up, and they sat together as usual, laughing and joking." Black's smile was sad, and there was a haunted look in his eyes.

Star didn't want to know.

"Stop," she whispered, and her pulse pounded as blood rushed past her ears in a thunderous echo. A scowl appeared on Hadak's face. Nasan shifted closer to her.

"I thought we would be fine; we all thought so. It was the first time the Horde king had defended us; they had never done that before," he shuddered and shrugged his thin shoulders. He was never a large individual, to begin with. The excitement of seeing him had faded, and she scanned Black's dark, drained eyes and noticed how thin and tired he looked.

Her hands twitched as she said, "Don't." She stood up.

His eyes were filled with tears as he looked at her. "The Jutin..." Black stammered, then found Hadak's eyes. It was as if it gave him strength because he spat out the rest of his words, "...they came the next day. They don't usually come during the day."

She clenched her hands in frustration when she thought she had left him behind because of Hadak. In the end, she left them all behind.

Black had tears falling from his eyes. She stepped backwards. "They found him again. In the middle of the night, the door splintered, and I woke up. By the time I had gotten my head around the door..." He shook his head, bowing for a moment. As he looked at her, he croaked, "They were gone."

Her mind blanked as she shivered. Her body began to shake. Her mind was like a thunderstorm. In what should have been a tremendous explosion, her heart exploded. Nothing but silence greeted her.

Boom, boom, boom. That might be the sound of her heart pounding or the sound of it breaking, shattering, splintering.

Star knew. As they approached the gates, she knew that something was amiss.

With her head spinning, Star heard shouts behind her but ignored them as her feet pounded faster, heading home. Her feet stopped at the threshold because she was unable to pass through the door.

It was no longer there. Just like her, the door was in pieces.

There was a mess on the floor. That horrible mess was how she felt. Star didn't know whether her brother or the Jutins had done anything with their bodies. Pulling her hair back, she gazed at the patch of dried red on the floor.

The dark splashes were an accusation.

How could she leave them? *Mathar's* fierce nature was so giving and kind, so protective of her children, who were young but seasoned. It was her father who was wise and quiet. He never said anything he didn't mean and only spoke when he needed to say something. The relationship between her mother and father was one that she had envisioned for herself as a child.

It never occurred to her that this would happen. She imagined them dying peacefully alongside each other, holding hands. Not like this. There was a stark contrast between her pale skin and the red that covered the floor as she hovered her finger above the patch. Despite the fact that it had been scrubbed, it stood out.

She was aware of the presence of others, but she didn't care about them. Her knees hit the floor, and she began to cry.

Hadak knelt beside her. Immediately, she recognized the smell of him. Despite the fact that she could feel him waiting for her eyes, she was unable to move her gaze away from the patch. A keening cry emanated from her lips. Then, arms as thin and pale as her own wrapped around her and rocked her.

Brathar.

That's when the Horde left them to grieve.

In front of their home, they stood guard.

It should have been safe to live in the colony. It would have been better if they had stayed an extra night. Why wasn't she strong enough to fight the Horde? What prompted her to let Hadak take her without protest?

The tears had long since dried when she rubbed her eyes. Seeing light piercing the fog, she lifted her head. Her body was stationary, the day moving from day to night, while the world continued to spin around her. How long had she been there?

"What time is it?" Her voice was hoarse and croaky, something beyond human comprehension. It sounded nothing like her.

During her raw grief, Black sat with her and had red-rimmed eyes. We have been here for some time now. *Avayak* and Nasan are outside. They have been speaking to some of the humans."

Her heart was cold, and her eyes were hard as she stood, feeling shattered and fragile under such a weighty tragic loss.

Her brother glanced at her and flinched. He had been alone, without anyone to offer him comfort. She touched his cheek, smiling sadly and promising not to leave him again.

Star opened the door with a silent promise ringing in her ears. In the process of opening the door, Nasan was leaning against it and almost fell inside. Hadak noticed her across the dusty path and left a human couple to walk over to her.

She was reminded of the last time he stood there. Her mother's eyes were filled with hatred. She hated Hadak for taking her away, only to die without knowing what had happened to her. Would her mother be disgusted that she gave him her innocence?

There was no doubt that some of her thoughts were evident on her face. He took care not to touch her, but that didn't mean he had left her alone. She could feel his gaze on her as she shuffled around the small kitchen area, offering people drinks because there wasn't much else to do. Her hand reached out to grasp her brother's arm at the memory of how alone he had been and perhaps struggling.

The shaky smile on his face was tinged with relief. He had been waiting for her to return for a long time, and now that she was there, she would never leave him again. If she had to fight every Horde king there, then she would.

"We have spoken with humans who do not fear us," Hadak began, stroking her fingers as she passed over a drink. She curled her fingers into her palm, away from the heat of his hands, his eyebrows furrowed. "The Jutin have been attacking in scattered patterns, taking some and killing others." His eyes were fixed on hers as he spoke.

She became increasingly enraged at their helplessness and lack of defence. It was her heart twisted into something harsh and angry as a result of her grief. She recognised it for what it was. So be it if that was what she needed to get through it. As far as anger was concerned, she could work with that.

"Our parents?" She turned to Black, whose hollow eyes in his skinny face rolled towards her.

"I buried them. My only option was to obtain weapons I could get to protect us." She pursed her lips and nodded in understanding. "I was only gone for a few minutes," he continued. "By the time I returned, they were carrying out the woman from the adjacent house." When I returned..."

The fact that he found them dead was obvious. He did not need to say so.

A tightening of her hand caused her to shuffle closer. In a similar manner to when he was a boy, he tucked into her side. Their age difference wasn't vast, but it was enough that, at times, their relationship resembled that of a mother and son. At that moment, he was in need of both.

As she hugged him tightly, a bitter laugh escaped her lips. As her laugh echoed in the quiet room, everyone jerked back as if something foreign and unwelcome had entered the room. "The purpose of our visit was to warn them!" Her words were filled with self-hatred as well as bitterness.

"We will protect everyone that is left," Hadak reassured.

"Everyone left," she said in a harsh tone that cut to the bone.

There was a change in Hadak's gaze over them. "You should take more time to grieve."

It was difficult for her hardened heart to find a rhythm in this new reality, so she agreed, *"Seya."* That didn't mean she had the luxury of time. As she shook off maudlin thoughts that wouldn't aid them in the coming fight, she found herself meeting him head-on. "My grief can wait. The Jutin won't."

"Nen, you can grieve. I will protect both of you."

There was something wild and raging about her laugh. It was Black who leaned away from her, watching her with concern. Star replied, *"Nen,"* as steel and frigid cold surrounded her words, transforming them into sharp barbs. "I will take care of my family while you go be with your Horde. Do what you need to."

He didn't flinch. He replied calmly, "I have come to assist the human colony, and that is what I intend to do."

A small surge of regret rose. She couldn't let it go though. "Really?" she barked back at him, fury igniting inside her.

"Seya, I am *Avayak,* and I am responsible for all under my care." The words 'including her' weren't said, but she could hear them. If Nasan and Black's widening eyes are any indications, so could they.

"It's a bit late for that," she spat venomously before standing, her eyes fixed on the faded stain left behind by her parents' deaths.

For a moment, he stood. She expected him to argue with her or shout at her, but instead, he gave her an icy glare and left the room.

The temporary door they had erected slammed shut. While glancing at him before he left, Nasan smiled sadly, closing the door quietly.

"Sithar," Black's concern made him sound young and fearful, like when they were children, and he got stuck in a tree.

A friend of his ran to find her, and when they reached her, his fearful shouts of "*Sithar*" drew her attention. When they reached the tree, they discovered a small ball of skin and bones. His thin, shaky arms were wrapped around a tree branch, holding on for dear life. He pleaded for her assistance with a terrified look in his eyes. As soon as she saw him, her teenage body climbed that tree after him. Having safely carried her *Brathar* on her back, he looked at her like a hero for the next week.

Seeing that same look now made her want to throw up because she hadn't protected him. Star may be meek when it comes to herself. However, when it comes to her *Brathar*, she would slay a Horde and conquer every mountain if he asked her to do so.

"Don't worry, we're going to be fine. Please let me know what's been happening. Give as much detail as you can."

Once he was finished, there wasn't much more he could add to what she already knew: people were taken, people were left behind dead, almost discarded. As if they had no purpose or value.

"Hang on, we know they breed like crazy for this never-ending army, don't we?"

"*Seya*," he said with eyebrows wrinkled in confusion.

"So why do they sometimes take men?" she asked. "What's the point?"

Her brother shrugged, and her mind raced. There seemed to be no strategy behind what they were doing.

"You said one of the men got away from them, didn't you?"

"*Seya*, but he's not right." Black swallowed.

"What do you mean?"

His quiet words struck the room like a hammer. "He lost his family when they took him."

He flinched at her stern tone. "Well, we've lost our family too, and I want to speak to him." He nodded, standing up, ready to leave.

"His name is Jannus."

Hadak was quietly talking with some of the village women outside. Nearby, a few women lingered. Occasionally, they gave him flirty smiles, and a part of her was fuelled by jealousy, just for a moment.

She could see Hadak's shock at her transparent jealousy when he looked at her. It didn't take long before her feelings for him were buried under an avalanche of hate, rage, grief, and despair. At the moment, she needed that to survive.

The expression on his face shuttered.

"Let's go," she said to Black in confusion. He looked between them with his eyes darting back and forth.

"It's not his fault," Black said, but her dark glare dared him to continue. He raised his hands in the air. "Okay, okay, not the time."

He flicked his head in her direction. Nasan suddenly appeared and followed them. In spite of the heavy fog, Black stopped before a house without lighting. The feeling of unwelcoming was the same as at the gates. She immediately wanted to run away, knowing something bad had happened.

But there would be no rest or running. It was important for her to understand why.

Approaching the rickety house - not that theirs was any better - she touched the broken wood. The materials they had weren't ideally suited to build with. Ignoring Nasan's curiosity, she tapped the door. It would have been better if they had *tepays* like the Horde, but they lacked the leather to make them.

Once again, her hand fell softly. Even though she intended it to be soft, her fist was balled up, and all her energy was poured into it.

A slurred and biting voice said, "Hang onto yer knickers."

She raised her eyebrows in irritation and anger. A cloud of noxious fumes enveloped her as the door opened. Her eyes watered as she smelled alcohol leaking from the man's pores.

"What do yer want?" he asked, slurring his words.

"Answers," she bit back, her feral grin defiantly refusing to accept "no."

"Don't we all?" He grumbled, then burped, the odour of stale smoke and alcohol almost overwhelming them.

He waved his hand sarcastically as if he was welcoming royalty and said, "Come on in." She was unsure whether he noticed Nasan or gave a damn about his presence.

"Are you Jannis?"

"Yer, an what yer want of me? I got nothin to give, lady."

They walked through the rubbish until they reached a group of chairs that looked like they were made of wood. She was about to sit on one with a cushion when he snapped, "Not there, that's my girl's chair." His painful grief-filled voice further ripped open her wounds.

As she moved gingerly from one stool to another, she waited to be snapped at again. When he didn't bite her head off, she plopped down. "When you were taken..." she began, only to be interrupted by a laugh from him.

With that mad laugh, tears flowed from his eyes. She wondered if he was sane.

"You don't beat around the bush, do yer girlie." Looking around, he frantically moved things before finding a glass, then another, and clutching a bottle in his arms as if it were something precious. "I won't talk about this wit'out drink."

As he poured two large shots, he shoved one at her without offering anyone else a drink. She got the impression that the others didn't even register with him.

If she returned to find her brother dead, would this be her? After considering this, she poured the entire shot into her mouth, the burn being a welcome punishment.

He laughed roughly. His laugh was grating and filled with the same dark sadness that was within her. In salute, he threw back his drink and then poured another glass.

"Wha' do yer want?" he asked, clinking the glass with hers as he drank his drink. The two of them mirrored each other and slammed the glasses down simultaneously.

"Tell me everything that happened?" It was nothing short of an order. Was she channelling Hadak when she said that? Without a doubt. Did it have any effect on the man? She had no idea, but he did start talking. She didn't care if he spoke because she ordered him to or because he wanted to. The result was the same.

"They came in t' early hours of mornin. In the end, they dragged us away and beat me." He swallowed another shot with her and refilled his drink, shaking it vigorously and looking at it again. While he spoke, the buzz under her skin was numbing, welcoming. "My daughter screamed bloody murder all the time. My wife, I don' know what happened to her. They wanted slaves."

Hold on, what? "Slaves?" Never heard of that before.

In response, he nodded, tilting his head for a moment before returning it to its normal position. "Jutin. One spoke our language." He shook his head, bewildered. "Said he needed slaves." Hiccupping, he downed a shot, wondering when she would do the same. "He put two men together and said tha' they would be slaves. As for women..." He burped and swung the bottle when he shrugged. "Not sure. He said he couldn't get anything from the used women."

"Used ones?" What the heck did that mean?

After downing his drink, he shrugged and expelled a long burp. When he began swaying forward, he lurched forward and clenched his fingers around her arms. Nasan shifted around, ready to intervene if he thought the broken man would harm her.

"Leave an don't come back, girlie. Risk the plains."

As Nasan attempted to free Jannis's tight grip on her, the inebriated man proved surprisingly strong; despite Nasan's larger size, he was unable to get him to release her.

"Leave," Jannis implored, his eyes sliding shut. "Please, leave," he said, completely slurred, slumping in her arms with his head on her lap.

"Get out," she instructed Nasan. "This man's grief deserves some respect, especially after what he told us just now. I don't want anyone to judge him. He's a man on the edge."

Having no idea what he would think of the warrior seeing him break down, and since she had no idea if he even registered that Nasan was there, it seemed only right for Nasan to leave and let the man slide into oblivion.

After nodding, Nasan left without arguing.

While she was able to see his shadow under the door, he gave them the space they needed to help make Jannis comfortable. Her sympathy rose as she stroked his hair back. With the assistance of Black, she laid him back on the sofa.

He was a shell of a man.

Standing, the room spun, and she held her hand and grabbed the chair to steady herself.

She began to clean up the mess as best she could. She felt numb, her limbs buzzing, and sad, just sad. Black assisted her without complaint, and when she shut the door on the man inside, her heart broke for him.

"Will he be okay?" Nasan asked her, his eyes focused on her arms. His gaze was drawn to the small marks on her skin as he flipped her hands to get a better view. There was a moment where he seemed to lose sight of the fact that she belonged to Hadak. Or did she?

Shrugging her shoulders, she looked up and found the beautiful starry night sky obscured by fog. An alcohol-induced chuckle escaped her lips. "No, he won't, but his grief is his own. Private. If he wanted help..." She sucked in her breath, hoping he might contact someone for assistance. "The people here are kind, and they'll give him whatever he needs when he asks for help."

Her answer was met with a nod of approval from Nasan.

"I would like to ask Hadak something. Could you come with me?" The needy question was addressed to her brother. She hadn't yet reached the point of being comfortable letting him leave her sight. He sighed heavily. She thought he was relieved, then he took her hand in a gesture of solidarity.

During the short walk back, the fog became heavier. Even with her hand raised, she couldn't see very far.

She felt her brother's hand jerk away from her. Worried, she moved with him, and it was then that she noticed a shadow above him.

He wasn't pulling away. He was being attacked, and as he screamed, she yelled, "Nasan."

"Keep calling out so I can find you," Nasan yelled when he lost his grip on her.

Laughter boomed around her.

Due to the dense fog, everything echoed, and it was nearly impossible to determine where his voice was coming from. It was no longer possible for her to hold on to her brother for long, so she was left with no choice but to shout loudly, "Nasan!"

They fought blindly in the fog, tugging at each other and trying to bring her brother closer to them. A rough tug of war. "Umph." A heavy weight fell where her brother dropped next to her, their hands still clasped.

Dropping down beside him, she opened her mouth to scream, but she was unable to do so. A knock on her head had her falling over him. Her only thought was to shield him from harm. Once she noticed a shadow, she clumsily launched herself at the moving figure.

While she may not be able to defeat them, she could confuse them.

If they followed her, they wouldn't be able to find her brother in the fog, and that was fine with her. Assuming it was a Jutin, she aimed low at the Jutin's long swinging arms but missed the target completely.

The shorter-than-expected arms encircled her, and she vaguely realized it was a Horde warrior. She did not know which one he held over her mouth, but he clamped his hand over it, preventing her from breathing.

Her attempt to identify them based on their smell was unsuccessful. She wasn't enlightened as to who it was by his touch because no one ever got that close to her except Furan and Nasan. She was sure it wasn't them.

Her nose was choked off by sweaty palms caked in dust from the plains.

There was a burning in her lungs, and her brain was getting sluggish.

As she drifted away, the wildest thought crossed her mind. Despite her snapping and snarling, Star knew Hadak would look after her brother. There was no doubt in her mind. Hadak would make sure he was alright.

As she slumped in her attacker's arms, a tear escaped her eye. Her vision was obscured by darkness.

Chapter 13

Nope. Her eyes slit open, and light pierced her eyeballs as she thought, no, *nen*.

Her heart sank when she noticed a group of Jutin standing nearby. Why would a warrior bring her there?

What happened?

Her mind immediately recalled images of her brother crumpled on the ground, as well as the sensation of a sweaty hand covering her mouth.

She swallowed down bile.

Suddenly, anger rose. Anger for Hadak and her. This was an insult. They believed that she was *Avae*, and if she wasn't, the sense of betrayal Hadak would feel would be unbearable. The traitorous little so-and-so. She would skin them for this.

Was it just her, or was she becoming violent?

No, she thought, it was simply the accumulation of crappy experiences over the past few weeks. Not to mention the violent murder of her parents that her brother witnessed. The whole thing had her sitting straight, her veins throbbing with courage.

There was no way she would sit there meekly. Vulnerable.

There was a warrior with his back to her. There was an urgent conversation between him and the Jutin, and she frowned, trying to catch it, but they were too far away.

She inhaled sharply as the traitor turned, surprised yet not surprised, as she should have recognized him immediately.

There was a smile on Intuk's face. It was a sinister act. His teeth flashed, and his black eyes glowed with glee. "Wakey, wakey, little *hak*."

That's fantastic! She enjoyed being referred to as a little shit. Not.

What was wrong with this Zandian? He was helping the Jutin who had invaded their planet to conquer them. If the Horde found out, he would most likely be dead after a long and lengthy torture, possibly by more than one Horde king.

It would be impossible for him to be punished or forgiven.

No matter how smug he appeared, he would be discovered. People like him always were. It might take years, it might take a few turns of the moon, but Hadak would figure it out in the end.

"You are a disgrace," she spat. "The Horde will kill you, and *Avayak* will kill you."

It came from nowhere, fast as a whip, but it was to be expected. Slap. After all, that was how he first greeted Star when he thought she was being disrespectful.

"Don't mention the Horde to me. How would an *Immani* like you know about it?" His sneer accompanied the shove that caused her to fall.

Not wanting to be under him, she shoved up onto her elbows.

"I know more than you if I know better than to cross them." It was a taunt, and a promise rolled into one, and his eyes flashed with a tiny gleam of fear, and a smile tugged at her lips.

She saw fear on his face, and if it was one of the last things she saw, she was pleased. "Why did you bring me here?"

Among the trees above them, there were at least six Jutins. She wondered how long she had been out and how far he had taken her.

Was anyone looking for her?

She resented Hadak's offer of protection when he offered it without hesitation. The last thing she remembered was the flash of pain on his face. When she thought the women were flirting with him, she didn't wish to see it, but he appeared hopeful. It was as if he was pleased that she had reacted with jealousy.

Afterward, his gaze shrank as she shut everything down, and harsh emotions swept over her. She had rejected him, which hurt him.

She judged him harshly and herself for leaving her family behind. However, he couldn't have known, and if she had to die, she would like to do so without either of them feeling bitter. The first male, alien, whatever - he was hers - and her first love, her first deep friendship with whom she felt she could share anything. Furthermore, he had held nothing back from her, being brutally honest and open.

She was dense and slow. She should have told him. Since she had given herself completely to him, she held onto the hope that he knew. She hoped that if she were to die, he would know all of that.

Her past fumbles; her small kisses and light touches were meaningless when she gave him her entire being, body, and heart. Star opened up to him in a way she had never anticipated. Until now, no one had tempted her to do so.

There is a lot of chatter among the Jutins.

She returned to the present moment when Intuk touched her cheek.

"You are here because you made me mad, which is not a smart thing to do." He laughed sarcastically, "You *Fhoked* with all the *fhalah's* in the food *tepay*, and guess who met a Jutin by the river?"

In an instant, she knew who it was. Bloody Illasay! "It's you she is sneaking off with," she replied, shocked and appalled. When he chuckled, she looked at him with new eyes.

"Don't be so *sako, Immani*. My brother is the unfortunate warrior who fell between that *fhalah's* thighs." He spat on the ground beside her.

"How did you learn about Jutin then?"

She could see him clenching his fists and fighting the urge to strike her. It was visible in his eyes. For him, violence and pleasure were like drugs mixed together. "She has his balls in her hand, controlling and pulling him along by his cock. He came running to me worried because, little *ryss* that she is, she told him to leave it alive. He didn't know what to do." His nose wrinkled, and his eyebrows furrowed. "The love-sick fool that he is, he would do anything for her."

"What for?" she asked, appalled.

"She wanted to sell you to the Jutin right away, so she thought they'd leave the Horde alone if she did that." He scoffed, "I'm not so stupid as to believe Hadak would've let you go. It would've looked too obvious after Hadak found out how they had been treating you in the *tepay*, but bringing you back here," he laughed as he stood above her. "Now, it'll look like some tragic accident."

"*Seya*," she said sarcastically. How will you explain that my brother was attacked and I disappeared at the same time? He's not here." She wanted confirmation from him.

With a loud laugh, he drew Jutin's attention to them. "He didn't see me; they'll assume it's Jutin."

Upon seeing them approach, she felt her breath leave her in a rush. They dragged their limbs across the floor.

There was a spark above their heads that caught her attention, like stars falling from the sky.

After crashing through the atmosphere, there was a long boom, followed by the fiery object crashing to the planet's surface. It was dark in colour and shaped like an egg. This red and shiny object looked as if it had been made fiery hot by the heat of entering. There were tales of that from humanity's past that she remembered.

She tracked it with her eyes. It wasn't far off. Was it more Jutin? That was all they needed!

The landing wasn't smooth at all. It looked violent. Clearly unhappy with the landing, Jutin scowled.

"You can leave," the voice was hazy and trilling, buzzing like an insect's wing. Jutin glanced nervously at each other and then at the landing site.

"Just remember, don't lose this one. We don't want to try to get her back," Intuk laughed harshly and left her there, surrounded by true *Immani*. A tremor ran through her body as she felt truly frightened for the first time since leaving the colony.

She was kicked and sniffed by one of them. "We can't do much with this one, no virgin ceremony," it buzzed to the others.

"What do you want?" Was that her? Oh my God, it was! Her mouth opened, and she spoke. What motivated her to do that?

Jutin's identical features twisted sharply as they looked at her. "It speaks, and I don't like it."

She could feel a tick in the corner of her eye. She could see it and feel it. The reason was that every bloody man or alien she encountered got angry at her for speaking. One of them approached. She flinched when it touched her leg.

It didn't do anything threatening, just touched her, but that was enough. Something inside her collapsed when she felt that cold, clammy touch.

As it stroked her hair and rubbed the gold strands together, it said, "Look how shiny it is. We don't have anything like this colour. It's a shame it can't do the ceremony."

"What kind of ceremony?"

It buzzed and let her hair go.

They stood together for a moment, speaking in their languages. There was a debate going on between them about something. Their hands were waving up and down, indicating their agreement.

Watching their hands fly up and suddenly slap back down like jelly when they hit the ground was almost comical.

Their conversation was suddenly cut off by a sharp buzz.

As she watched them, she noticed that they were closing their eyes and concentrating in an unnatural way.

A cold shiver ran down her spine as they nodded together. It was as if they were being moved like puppets. All of them spoke at once '*sssi*,' the buzzing and hissing rose and rose until her ears felt as if they were bleeding. While covering them, she watched as they all responded as if something was speaking to them.

Their communication was telepathic. While attacking the colony or fighting the Horde in the trees, it certainly appeared they coordinated without speaking. Considering running for it, her brows furrowed in thought, but what chance would she have?

She wanted to tear their heads off their bodies and dance on their scaly backsides as her newly awakened fierce side demanded blood for blood. She rubbed her thighs with her hands, feeling exhausted from her inner mental bitch.

There was a side of her that wanted what it wanted without caring what others thought, and right now, bloodshed would work.

Sighing, she pondered the possibility of going back to how things were. There were no parents for her. There would be no pleasure in playing strings for others. Her life had been lived for everyone else half the time.

She felt a measure of comfort when she touched the choker still on her neck. It was what she wanted. He liked being hers, and she liked being his. Her only chance at taking what belonged to her lay in finding a way out of this mess.

Like a balloon being released, the Jutin suddenly deflated. The whole thing gave her a creepy feeling.

She stumbled as they dragged her up. Oh, she thought as she stumbled.

Combined with oxygen deprivation, Intuk must have hit her harder than she thought, leaving her lightheaded.

"The only thing we need from you is to release us, not to breed you," one hissed.

Trying to figure out what he meant - or what she meant, her stomach flipped. She thought it meant that they couldn't or wouldn't breed her. Release them, though. While she hoped it wasn't sexual, she had a bad feeling it was. As she examined their scaly bodies in an attempt to locate any discernible sexual appendages, she shuddered, terrified. Let her be wrong, please.

She doubted it, given the way things were going.

"You're all murderers. What was the point of coming here in the first place? The sound of her voice was hoarse and reedy. "You can't defeat the Zandians," she taunted, though it didn't seem to have much effect on them. "What will you do after all the humans are wiped out?"

One hissed, "Shut up."

Upon opening her mouth, she felt a hand grab her head. Looking deeply into her eyes, it cooed and hissed. There was something fascinating about the way it moved, and she felt like she was floating. As they walked, the Jutin who had touched her earlier stroked her waist, guiding her.

He buzzed her, putting her down in the dirt like a well-trained animal. "It's too bad it's not clean," he said.

"It can't do the ceremony now. You'll have to claim a different one," another said.

Across from her, a Jutin hissed. "I like the hair. I wanted it to be mine." It stroked the strands of her hair with its palm, catching and pulling them.

One of them buzzed back at him, "You should have kept it the first time you had it."

"I didn't have it; my brother did. He was killed for it by the crazy Hordes," he hissed, the tugs increasing in intensity.

"Put it out while we wait for the rest, hopefully, they'll find some more clean ones."

Clean ones?

"Sleep," he hissed, and his eyes hypnotized her. She fell like a puppet whose strings were cut, just like they did before.

"Get up!" Her eyes peeled open once again as she heard the frantic call in a voice that was so clear and so true. How did she keep finding herself in these situations? Oh yeah, the Horde. That was why. Still, the Horde was going to be home eventually if she could get back.

In confusion, her eyebrows furrowed as a musical voice rang out. That didn't sound like Jutin.

The thought made her peel her eyes open, struggling to wake up just in time to see the strangest thing she had ever seen.

A blue woman with pointed ears, a roped muscled spikey tail swishing behind her. She used it to whack the Jutin that was creeping up on her, and it was a she. Her breasts were firmer than Star's. They didn't sway, and had no visible nipples - Just a few shiny discs covered them, and two firm globes held them in place. There were two belly buttons on her toned stomach.

Her vivid pink hair hung just below her shoulders. What most surprised her about her hair was the deep pink spikes with their flexibility and softness. These spikes started at the top and finished somewhere between her shoulders, similar to a Mohican.

Her hair was plaited tightly to her head at the sides, finishing above her breasts. Dark blue downy hair started at the base of her spine and became thinner until it ended in a spiked whip on her tail. There was no doubt she had toned legs and lithe curves in her shorts that moulded to her body.

She must have taken a really bad knock.

In an attempt to clear her vision before her, she blinked her eyes. When she opened them, she was still standing there.

As she cut her way through the Jutin, she was a blue tornado of speed and raw-edged steel, whirling with power. There were five Jutin left, and they took to the trees in fear. The blue and pink alien laughed like she was having the best time of her life.

A high-pitched growl of pain emitted from the Jutin after she slashed over its arm, causing it to fall. Grabbing the branch it had just abandoned, she wrapped her tail around another branch and swung fast. In awe of her dexterity, Star's mouth fell open. In the trees, she moved as if she was made for them, giving her the same advantage as if she were one of them.

Two bodies fell on her blade. Dead before they hit the ground. The Jutin above dropped, leaving her as the only one to attack.

It was the Jutin who wanted Star, who scuttled forward. Apparently, he was planning to leave with her while he could. It didn't occur to him that she would rather die than let him harm her like that.

While gritting her teeth, she looked around for something she could use and saw a short sword dangling from a blue hand. She was startled by the fangs in the blue alien's mouth as it grinned at her. Using one arm to swing the blade, the blue alien used her tail to keep herself atop the tree.

Grabbing the sword, sure that she could stab if needed, she swung it up more confidently than she felt. Her mother's words whispered back to her, yes, she could be strong.

She bared her teeth in a fiery snarl, channelling Hadak, the terrifying Horde warrior. The Jutin hesitated, trying to catch her gaze. She wouldn't fall for that, as her gaze dropped. Her eyes fell on a patch that appeared vulnerable.

She stabbed it as hard as she could while screaming in rage. Her muscles burned from the effort, and sweat beaded on her neck. Perhaps because her muscles were weak, it was more difficult than she thought it would be.

Jutin's blood spurted out and fell back with her on top. Grunting, she tried to pull it out, making more of a mess in the process. Dark green and thick blood rushed out faster. After gagging, she pulled in her breath and stopped breathing through her nose.

"Will. You. Just. Die?"

Her words were punctuated by a heave as her weight pulled the sword, jolting the Jutin's body. The sight of blood pooling around it was one of the most revolting things she had ever witnessed and satisfying in a slightly worrying way.

It may have been the murderous revenge side of her that had her grinning like a lunatic.

The sword was making its blood flow faster as she tried to get it out, and it looked as if she had nicked something vital. The Jutin stopped wiggling, going still, and it died in a quietness that was almost peaceful but unsatisfying.

In place of white, the blue woman's golden eyes were surrounded by a light blue tint as she dropped down. Her veins were a darker blue under her skin, and the little blood vessels in her eyes were also darker. It was striking and unusual, but then again, she was blue, so it made no difference. The gold eyes of the woman rolled over the blood and the mess she had made trying to remove the sword from the leg.

With a savage smile on her face, she pulled the blade out with a slicing sound. "I approve of the blood thirsty hacking, though it would have been easier to remove it if you had nicked the vein here." She tapped close to her shoulder. "If you nick it and apply pressure to it, you can draw it out."

Her mouth dropped open as the blue female started cleaning her weapons, sliding them into their homes with ease of practice. Star's interest was sparked by the fact that she understood English, and her voice seemed so pure for the words she just used.

"You speak English?"

"I have made it my business to understand the languages of places I need to visit. Currently, I have a translator installed from another plant, Gitar."

"You've been to other planets?" Why did Star sound so surprised when she was looking at a blue woman who was clearly not a native? Star's eyes followed her hands as she pushed herself up, and she noticed her six blue fingers flexing.

"I'm following the Jutin. They attacked my home world, Clanen. They have a new weapon that melts flesh." She rubbed her arm, flicked her tongue, and her skin pulsed with what seemed to be a nervous or upset light. "The weapon annihilates completely and is easily replicable. They are trying to replicate it on a larger scale so that they can destroy planets."

There was an unsteady rhythm to her heartbeat. It wasn't a dream. It was impossible for her to dream of such a scenario.

In an attempt to stabilise herself, she gripped the nearest tree with both hands. "My name is Star."

After considering her for a moment, the blue woman leaned forward. She kept her head still as she wondered what was happening. She touched her head against Star's. It was a quick and brief greeting. "I am Jilaya Pul'atur, twin to Kilaya Pul'atur, daughter of house Saar."

Despite the grim situation, she smiled at the woman and said, "It is a pleasure to meet you." She meant it sincerely. Jilaya laughed softly when Star gazed pointedly at the bodies.

There was only one way to describe her voice - it was so beautiful. Soft, melodious, and set at a soothing pitch, it was soothing to the ear. Jilaya stretched out and flitted her tail from side to side, her eyes searching about. "Are you native to this planet?"

"*Nen*, eer...no."

As her eyes shifted and moved, Jilaya replied, "I understand all languages, including Zandian."

"Is there more to a translator than translating languages?"

"Yes, it can change my tongue to produce foreign languages. It's a clever piece of tech, and it's supposed to aid the reason I'm here. I've been sent to warn other planets."

"What else does it do?"

"It has basic information on every planet and will supply it once it hears the language."

"That's handy. You came to tell us about Jutin?"

"Yes, are you authorized to pass things along?"

In surprise, she burst into laughter. Grinning, she thought about how the Horde kings would react if she passed the message from another *Immani* to the *Avayak's*.

"Yes, I thought this place was more..." Her mouth flattened for a moment. "Barbaric. According to my research, the people are ruled by travelling warriors who rule the planet."

"You're right." Her eyebrows rose at the information she already knew. "Some things are old fashioned." For example, the way they interact with the Horde's women, but in other ways, they are doing fine.

Despite not understanding how out of her control everything was when she first arrived in the Horde, Star secretly loved the way Hadak looked after her. She wouldn't readily admit that to him, but a small part of her appreciated how in control he was. "You've landed here. How far can you travel?"

Star flicked her eyes over to Jilaya, and her muscles twitched. She wasn't asking for her...but the colony might want to leave if they heard about it. Especially now, in fact, she almost guaranteed it.

"I can't take travellers; my ship can only hold me." Jilaya's watchful eyes constantly scanned the area. Star was sure they weren't about to be attacked, but she didn't feel confident and started approaching the treeline with a vague idea of where she was.

Grimacing, she added, "I will warn you, though, one of them won't be too kind to you. Apparently, he hates foreigners, including my kind."

"You are not conquerors like Jutin?" I know something of your plight. It was recorded in our history."

Laughing, she slapped at the branches around her as they tangled in her loose hair. "No, we are nothing like that," she said with a sigh, giving her a quick summary. "When we landed here, we got stranded with no way to repair our exploratory vessel. Our colony eventually grew, but the natives of the planet wouldn't let us roam. It is mostly comfortable where we live now." There was a gap up ahead, a thinning of the trees. Quickening her pace, she asked her, "What about your planet?"

"Clanen, we are all close in the Drak system."

She nodded as if all this was normal for her. In some respects, it should have been because they were originally aliens from another planet, so it wasn't a surprise. However, seeing a blue alien was still a little unsettling. "Do you have transport?" Jilaya asked.

"No, we might have to walk for a while. I have no idea how long I was unconscious or even where they took me. There's something familiar about this."

"There's a camp a few miles up there." Jilaya pointed to her right, squinting her eyes as though she could see it.

"That must be the Hordes camp. Were there many people?"

"There was a small army, and I initially thought they might be Jutin, so I landed away from them."

"The ship!" God, she was so slow. That was the ship she had seen. "Yes..."

"It's yours, the one that came down today? So that explains why the Jutin looked unhappy and why they were rushing."

"It is. I was stunned when I saw how many were orbiting the planet, preparing to land. I altered my course to come here first."

Her tail whipped out to grab a branch, gently moving it out of the way. She was so graceful for a being with an extra limb. Although she seemed thin, there was a lightness about her as if she could float. Jilaya caught a strand of her hair. She scrutinised it carefully.

"What?" Star asked, then gave her a small smile because she realised Jilaya might be as curious as she was.

"This colour is strange but beautiful, just like the material of our homes on my planet." Her smile was wistful, small fangs peeking over her bottom lip. Her magical eyes moved to her hair, glistening with curiosity as she gently touched the strands. "Different, but I like it."

"We have a lot of blondes, browns, and blacks, even some golden or orange colours. You don't have this colour on your home planet?" Though looking at her pink hair, she doubted it.

Her lips twitched as she said, "No, only a few eyes." Star gathered it was an expression of distaste.

Before Star could ask, Jilaya rushed on, "Most on my planet have skin colour like this, in all shades of blue. Our hair has various shades of blue, pink, and purple. This colour on your head reminds me of home, of what I'm doing here."

Jilaya obviously needed a moment to collect herself, so she left her to gather her thoughts. Her thoughts were on how long it would take Hadak to find her. She had no doubt he was making himself mad looking for her despite her lashing out at him.

The discovery of Jilaya almost made her forget why she felt fresh fury as she rubbed her hand over her eyes and sighed.

She lost something she loved to the Jutin.

Jilaya stopped and noticed her rubbing right above her heart. "Are you hurt? Is it serious?"

Her mouth pursed as Jilaya whacked a branch away. "No. No," she said more firmly when she appeared uncertain. Coughing, Star said, "I lost my family, not all of them, since my brother is still alive, but it happened very recently, and I might have hurt someone I care about."

A thoughtful Jilaya gazed up at the stars and spoke. In her melodious voice, she spoke softly, "On my planet, we believe that everyone goes to the stars when they die." Her smile was wistful, and it tilted as she spoke. "However, before that, there is the staying. Two Clanen's from beyond watch over you until you pass. When you go on to be with the ancestors in the stars, it's your duty to watch over the next generation until they pass. Our ancestors are connected to life even more so in death."

She sincerely hoped that was true, as it seemed oddly beautiful.

"Your friend will understand. Everyone loses something of themselves when they lose someone. There is now a void in your family. We all have to shuffle around and get used to our new places. It's never easy or comfortable, like slipping into another's shoes."

"Yeah, I've always had a dual role with my brother, so that's nothing new. All I want is to take comfort from someone I shouldn't have pushed away."

In a comforting gesture, her tail rubbed against her arm. It was soft and light. Star thought there would be a heavy weight to it after seeing how lethal it was in a fight, but it was as light as it looked. The thought of stroking it made her feel as though she was treating her like an animal.

Unsure of etiquette, she let her pet her as they got to a clearing, and her relief at seeing the stream was palpable. "We're close. The stream runs into the colony, and it's also near where the Horde kings set up camp."

"Good, I don't know when they plan to ignite the weapon or if they have brought the weapon to the surface. The sooner we warn your people, the better."

Hadak's choker hung snugly around her neck, so she didn't dispute that they were her people.

If we follow this path, we shouldn't have to wait long to find them. At least we're on the right track." Star hesitated and froze in her tracks. Jilaya stopped, her hands on her weapons, fast and swift, no hesitation. Frowning at her, Star worried about her bloodthirstiness. "They might mistake you for taking me?"

Jilaya scoffed, and her body uncurled from the fighter's stance she had adopted. "I'll take cover until you explain. I'll stay close; just let me know when you want me to drop down."

Nodding and watching her climb the tree, nimbly without fear, she was completely confident in her abilities.

Star's feet moved her in the direction of where the Horde was, and Star hoped Hadak wouldn't take Jilaya's head if he found her before Star could explain.

While she bounced from tree to tree, Jilaya was completely silent, her footsteps as light as feathers.

Star glanced up when she noticed the trees starting to thin again, expecting to see Jilaya, but all she saw were rusty brown leaves. Astonished at how well she blended into the background, she shook her head.

It was then that her feet began to ache, reminding her that they were still healing and not to abuse them. Mentally berating herself for getting caught, she stared at her toes as she walked.

It was instinctive for her to protect her brother, the only family she had left. She would consider Hadak and the Horde to be her family. Her throat was filled with a lump of emotion as she touched the choker.

The sudden tears blurred her vision, and she was able to see figures in the distance. Her breath coming out of relief, she whistled up into the tree to let her know she'd seen them.

In no time at all, her feet were pounding the ground beneath her, eating up the distance to the Horde.

It took her a moment to catch her breath as she looked into the empty space. Then there was a horde shout, the sound deafening as it echoed. Upon seeing the lump on her cheek, the first warrior who stopped her must have recognised who she was. Taking his time, he examined her cheek before guiding her to a seat.

Footsteps and then a familiar face. "What happened to you, fierce one?" Tenek asked with an easy smile, but his face turned darker when he saw the mark on her cheek. "Send a rider out to Hadak, he'll want to know that she's been found." He crouched beside her, his strange eyes rolling around, the white mark shifting as he looked at every bruise. "Well then, what have you been up to?"

Star knew it wasn't an accusation because he stayed firmly planted in front of her, protecting her from the Horde's gaze. "Intuk..." Shaking her head, she trembled as she tried again. "You need to grab him before he tries to flee. He did this. Grab him, don't let him see me."

His eyebrows slashed across his eyes sharply. "He went to the colony and hasn't returned."

Grasping his arms tightly, her hands tightened. "My brother is there. What if he hurts him?" Her eyes flicked about. In her mind, the only thing she could think of was getting a *Guyipe* and rushing back there.

Intuk may have meant to finish what he started if he returned to the colony instead of staying there. Because he hated her so much, he would kill Black simply for that reason.

His hand flipped over as he grasped hers, linking them and grounding her. Trust your *Avayak*, he won't let your family be harmed." He smiled, then touched her choker lightly before saying, "He won't let you down. The moment he found you were missing, I promise he didn't let your brother out of his sight. He'll be even more vigilant."

"How do you know that?" Her racing heart began to calm as he talked. Slowly, the panic began to subside.

"Because that's what I would do, and we are both good kings." His grin held a teasing edge, and a sharp laugh escaped her. Smugly, he added, "Extremely good kings."

"Modest, so modest," she laughed. He chuckled softly in response.

Standing close to her, he shrugged. "Rest first. I'll call when I see him approaching. He'll no doubt ride like a devil."

After accepting the plate of food, her eyes scanned the trees, searching for any flicker of blue alien, but all she saw was the endless sky. As soon as she'd finished eating, she grabbed a tub of water and began washing off the grime.

She poked at the tender spots on one foot, checking to make sure she hadn't aggravated them. The wounds looked okay to her, even though she was no healer. They should be fine after a little rest. She had been careful with her hands, so they were fine.

A smile spread across her face as she pulled up the fur Tenek had laid over her shoulders and wrapped her arms around her knees. These Horde kings were quite courteous.

Whether it was two hours or three, or maybe it was only one hour, the time felt longer, and so when she heard pounding, and Tenek touched her arm to shake her, she unwrapped herself from the position she was in and looked at the horizon in the direction of the human colony. Seeing four riders, she felt relief flow through her.

She felt a small thrill of fear because she knew one of the riders was Intuk. Jutin tried to kill them after he sold them to him.

She cringed at the thought of the punishment he would receive as a severe, angry-looking Paken stepped up to join them. When she saw Paken's lined face, she frowned, realising that his Horde had never supported him. It was noticeable that they stood apart from each other, unlike Tenek and Hadak, who stood together.

Hadak threw everything into his *Guyipe*. As he got closer, she noticed a deep, worried line between his eyes. Concerned...worried about her. A pale hue appeared over his knuckles, his grip so tight on the *Guyipe*. His face was like a hard mask. There was no relief on his face like she expected.

Black's excitement at the chance to see her around Nasan's wide shoulders almost caused him to tumble off his *Guyipe*. When they found her, his eyes lit up. He had an infectious grin on his face, and it caused her cheeks to strain in response. He waved, tilting to the side, and she lifted her eyebrows at him.

He was clumsy sometimes, and those gangly limbs didn't help. He was hoping to grow into them, and Star was hoping he did too. She didn't want him sliding off the *Guyipe* every time he felt the urge to look at something if he was going to travel with the Horde.

Funny how the thought of staying with the Horde came so easily now. The moment he saw her, Intuk slowed down, fearing his destruction was just around the corner.

He didn't turn and ride away, he approached them slowly. Perhaps he was trying to keep things from exploding for as long as possible. It was impossible for her to feel sorry for him because of the plans he had for her.

Tenek shifted closer to her, offering safety. A moment later, Hadak's eyes caught the movement, and he considered both of them. Whatever Hadak saw had him stiffening on his *Guyipe*, his shoulders tightening imperceptibly, his hands now a death grip on it.

He knew something was up.

With a thin line of sweat on her forehead glistening in the sunlight, she licked her lips, feeling both hot and cold at the same time.

Hadak flipped off his *Guyipe* and stormed toward her, but she instinctively retreated, making him furious. He reached out with balled-up hands. Seeing him stop, her fingers twitched with a desire to touch him as her heart beat a crazy rhythm.

As a result of her bone-deep terror of being handed to the Jutin, she needed his arms around her, holding her. They weren't, and she wondered why.

"Hi," she said in a small and uncertain voice. Biting her lip and looking behind him, she watched her brother slide off with no grace at all. He pushed past the *Guyipe*, almost running Hadak down in his excitement. Hadak's finger twitched as if he was going to catch her in spite of the slight impact of her *Brathar's* body.

She breathed in the misty forest scent that was her brother's scent, hiding a pleased smile on his neck. Under the sweat and cleaning fluid, he always smelled slightly wild. While his natural scent was too much for his young body, it was a glimpse of the man he would become if given the chance.

He choked out, "*Sithar*, leave me some breathing space." As she cradled him tightly, her arms tightening around him.

Her eyes were searching as he pulled back to look at her while grinning wetly. Even though she had made an effort to appear happy, she knew he could see what she was really feeling. When she returned home last time, both her parents were gone, leaving him alone. It was still lingering in the back of her mind. It might last for a long time.

As she glanced behind him, she caught sight of Nasan and Hadak. "Cut him some slack," Black whispered. He's been going crazy worrying about you."

"How long have you been best friends?" she hissed back at him quietly.

"Since I saw how erm...can I say devastated?" His lips quirked. He smiled, his words still low. "I'm not sure if I want to say that where he might overhear." With a frown, he searched for another word. "He was definitely unhappy." His hushed explanation made her laugh. "Horde kings aren't supposed to feel anything soft, at least not where humans see it."

Hadak's subtle movement toward them, inching himself toward them in a protective manner, drew her attention back to him. Intuk wasn't unaware of Tenek's shift closer to him.

In full view of the other two Horde kings present, Hadak surprised her by grabbing her in his arms. Despite Paken's scowl, she relaxed into Hadak and dug her nose into his shoulder, sighing in pleasure.

"What happened?" His growl had her hair standing on end, and her eyes were drawn to the rippling fury on his warrior's face.

Intuk.

Chapter 14

"Can we sit down? This is going to be a long story, and I need to rest my feet."

He picked her up, nearly knocking over a disgusted Paken, and set her on some furs around camp. Her heart died a little there as he took her boots off, and under the watchful eye of everyone present, he dutifully checked every toe.

She whispered, "Hadak," as his warriors grinned and puffed up as if they had just won the greatest *Avae* in history.

After Intuk, she was in need of it.

"Intuk attacked us," she blurted out without finesse, then she wanted to slap herself for not easing into it more gently. This was his warrior. A betrayal. She should have been more gentle. His eyes flashed, and his expression became frozen.

With great care, he lowered her foot. Putting her boot on with precision, he seemed to have all the time in the world. Then he spun around to face his warrior. "Tie him up," he ordered his warriors without further explanation. She fell for him because of his trust in her.

In a soft voice, he ordered, "Tell me."

"A shadow moved in as the fog got thicker..."

With a wave of his hand, he interrupted her. The look of concern in his eyes softened his words. "This bit, I know. Skip to the part about where he took you. I have been looking around the human colony and the plains for two days."

Really! It was that long.

"He took me to a group of Jutin." Hisses started up, and her brother cursed a blue streak. While frowning at Black, he tried to open his mouth, but her disapproving glare toward him made Hadak chuckle, causing her to lose her train of thought. "What?"

"You'll be a great mother," Hadak said, and her cheeks burned.

After ignoring it for a moment, she told the rest of the story. "...I have no idea why he did it, only that Illasay asked him to. She doesn't like me," she frowned. "And he doesn't like me..."

Hadak got up and approached Intuk, who was bound to a tree nearby. He bent low to him and said, "You can tell me now or later, but we both know you will tell me." His savage grin made all the warriors around him smile. Their eyes were filled with bloodshot anticipation, masking their feelings of betrayal.

You didn't threaten or try to hurt the *Avae*, obviously.

When Hadak punched Intuk in the stomach, he coughed up a laugh. He spat out, "I know...the *Immani*," and Hadak punched him again. Intuk grimaced and spat out a loose tooth. "She made me lose my position as a first warrior. All the warriors talked behind my back, even the *fhalah's* wouldn't approach me."

"Selfish *hak*," Tenek said through gritted teeth. "You sold out your *Avae* to Jutin for pride," harsh, angry words accompanied by a heap of disgust. There was no flinch on the part of Intuk.

The clearing was filled with Hadak's fury.

Star approached him so that she could get away from Intuk and complete her task. After all, Jilaya was waiting for them in the trees, and they didn't have enough time to decide Intuk's fate now. Her hand slid into Hadak's before he could draw back. He startled and pulled her away from Intuk. "There's more?"

Trying to explain the next part as clearly as possible, she nodded, knowing that it would be difficult but not impossible.

Everyone's eyes were on her when she spoke about Jilaya introducing herself. Intuk looked furiously amazed, as if he couldn't believe his bad luck that she had escaped again, and this time, it was another alien helping her.

She thought luck wasn't in it.

There was so much she had lost here, and she wouldn't allow someone like Intuk to take it from her or let her future be affected by Illasay's petty jealousy.

Suddenly, two spots in the sky flared, and more ships descended. Before she had the chance to stop him, Hadak stepped away from her.

He growled, his hand wrapped around Intuk's throat. "They are a plague, and you wish to align yourself with them." Hadak threw Intuk back against the tree and spat on him.

"It was to get rid of her. She is not fit to be *Avae*; she is a human, *Immani*. Our Horde deserves better." With that rush of words, his voice was filled with a loathing that made them all glare.

"Did you blacken her cheek again?" the quiet, loaded question rang through the clearing. When Nasan moved closer to Intuk, it appeared as if he too wanted to have a go at him. Hadak grinned when Intuk didn't respond. Hadak hit him, and because their bones were thicker and their skin more impermeable, it took a long time and many blows for a bruise to appear. She gripped Hadak's hand as he swung once more, concerned. Star didn't want everything between them to be about revenge or punishment.

"Tell your friend to come down," he said calmly, then looked back at Intuk. "I'm gagging you because another word against her could get you killed. You're not fit to breathe the same air as my *bryd*. My *Avae*."

Star felt a rush of pleasure when he said that. Taking his hands, she blotted away the blood, checking he hadn't done any damage to himself. She called up into the trees, "Jilaya?" Noticing as she tended their *Avayak*, several of his Horde members looked at her with self-indulgent grins.

Everyone's eyes flew upwards when they heard a rustle. It was apparent that the tops of the trees were moving as she descended. A blue streak of colour and confident of her landing, her tail helped lower her and slowed her movement just before she crouched and then straightened.

"Greetings." She bowed low as the warriors took her in. Another alien on their planet. "My name is Jilaya Pul'atur, twin of Kilaya Pul'atur. There's a threat I came to warn you about."

"*Seya*, we've been told you arrived on the planet at the same time as other ships." Paken's accusation caused her to stand straight up.

"My planet agrees that a messenger should be sent; females rule my planet, an unbroken line of matriarchs from the Pul'atur line. I fought to get her to help you." Her breath escaped her, and she flicked her tail, perhaps agitated. "I have an Ebadisc." Their confusion must have been evident since she replied, "I have an Ebadisc; it will show what happened when Jutin used the weapon, but it is only on a small scale. I have intelligence on them too."

Hadak's eyes found Star's, and she nodded at Jilaya to show them. Hadak took her hand, shifting slightly in front of her, shielding her. Her heart raced so loudly that she was afraid someone would hear or see it.

With a smile on her face, she leaned into his arm. When Jilaya brought out a piece of metal large enough to fit in her palm, she looked around him. By using her sixth finger on the other side, which acts much like a thumb, she began tapping it.

An orange glow emanated from it before small ghostly figures appeared. A gas substance consumed the air behind the blue figures as they leapt into the trees, fear driving them and leaving their mouths open in horror and stunned silence. Her people were instantly disintegrated, turning to dust and then disappearing altogether. Once the devastation had been completed, Jutin began arriving.

Suddenly, an army of her people began to battle them, accompanied by a voiceless cry. They were evenly matched, swinging around the treetops while using the branches as offensive and defensive weapons.

It was even more striking because there were no voices to be heard. In her mind, Star could almost hear the words and sounds they would be uttering. A ring of clashing swords echoed in her head as a reminder of what the battle would sound like.

Clearly, her people had an advantage over Jutin's in that Jutin possessed no skill with swords. Therefore, it wasn't long before they began cutting through their scales and decimating their numbers. They faced the Jutin with less ease than the Horde warriors, but they still managed to take down all but one of them.

In some sort of ceremonial attire, Jilaya twirled her sword while surrounded by blood. From the corner of the square, she emerged with a savage smile on her face. The tip of one sword was pointed at the remaining Jutin.

As Jilaya in the present touched the square, the picture disappeared, and silence followed what they had just seen. Touching the edge of the square with her lips, she watched the light wobble around its edges.

"What did he tell you?" Star asked since nobody else was eager to find out what had happened. She knew that they would have questioned it.

"It took days for it to crack," Jilaya stated in a ruthless tone. The smile on Tenek's face was swift and approving. "I received more information than we could have hoped for. Every planet has been invaded by them in small numbers. I was instructed by my people to visit each planet in turn with a warning, and I hoped that I would make you aware of their presence and help you defeat them so that you would be able to avoid the machine they use." Shaking her head, she shifted the Ebadisc back into her bag. "I wasn't supposed to be here first."

"Where were you headed?" Hadak asked.

Her curiosity about other planets was piqued. When the colony became stranded in space, they hailed planets whose orbits were close to their ship. They received only one response from Zandar.

Star wondered if the other planets had received the call and ignored it or were unable to receive it due to technological limitations.

Perhaps a visit to another planet would be exciting, or it would have been once, she thought, her fingers stroking Hadak's sun-kissed skin, and knew she wouldn't leave him. As she leaned heavily on Hadak, she decided there were enough interesting places - specifically people - on her planet for her to want to remain there.

"Inurn, which is a green planet with one large city and a forest with many hiding places, was supposed to be my first planet. Trying to track Jutin there would take time." Jilaya rubbed her spikey hair, and the hair snapped back up. "I saw the ships surrounding your planet." Jilaya shook her head and stared at the two objects still approaching the surface.

"How many?" Hadak asked in a serious tone. In response to his tightening grip, Star ran her hand along his side in a soothing manner.

Jilaya exhaled and spoke, "Many, so many that I abandoned my original mission to Inurn, turned back here, and made it the first planet on my list. It isn't clear to me what their plan is, or if they even have one, but I am aware that humans on this planet are of interest to them."

Hadak swung Star around. His arms were tightly encircling her waist, and his head rested on hers. Even if she tried, she wouldn't be able to move. "Why?" he asked through gritted teeth.

"They perform a ceremony involving the first blood of women who were compatible with them. The women are tied to Jutin, and if they attempt to leave, it is excruciatingly painful and can result in death in most cases. It is a link that binds them together."

"The virgin ceremony," Star whispered, recalling the conversation with the Jutin who wanted her.

"What's that?" Hadak asked, tilting her head so that she could see his black eyes.

"The Jutin who wanted me, who tried to take me back when we first met, was told I could no longer perform the ceremony." Her cheeks burned, but she carried on regardless. "They knew."

Her brother coughed behind her. Nasan looked crushed, and she felt her heart twist.

Jilaya nodded in agreement. "After that, they use you as slaves, as nannies for their growing nursery. They prefer human women because they are guaranteed six or more children every time."

As her body stilled, her head began to shake back and forth. "That can't be right. For my kind, it is extremely rare to have more than three children, and even twins are uncommon."

"Something about the ceremony..." she shrugged uncertainly, flicking her tail again. "It is possible that they have some technology to accomplish this. When they possess the technology to wipe out my people in such a manner, who can say what else they might be capable of?"

"We kept wondering why they killed some women and took others. It's because they're still untouched. What about the men?" Star's mouth dried when she thought of Jannis' daughter and his wife. Their fates were nothing short of horrific.

"Slaves," Jilaya replied.

While Tenek bombarded her with questions about what she saw from above, how many she thought might be there, her mind was whirring with what she had said.

"Slaves..." Her whisper trailed off as she plucked at her furs. It was her father who they tried to take as a slave, but... "They came back for me."

She was responsible for their parents' deaths. They came back because of her.

"What's that *Avae*?" Hadak lifted his hand to her hair, playing with the strands. "Who came back for you?"

She saw understanding in Black's eyes, and her heart broke. The thought had already crossed his mind way before all this happened, and he didn't blame her. A part of her blamed herself, however. As she rubbed her chest, she tried to still her frantic heartbeat. Her emotions felt trapped inside her, trying to escape, and there was no time to let them. There was no time to grieve properly.

"That Jutin wanted me. He knew I was untouched, so they came back for me," she explained, her voice trembling, her lower lip wobbling as Hadak touched his thumb to it. He turned her to face him. He placed his forehead on hers so he could look her straight in the eye.

The fact that they were being watched didn't seem to matter to him.

"It's not your fault, not then and not now," he said fiercely, gripping her neck in a familiar hold to keep her from looking away. "*Nen*, look at me." Lifting her eyes from the dusty ground, she looked at him, aware of the Zandians surrounding them, trying to give them the illusion of privacy by looking somewhere else. "It's not your fault."

Shuddering, she nodded as much as his hand allowed. Burying her face in his chest, she hid for a minute, knowing the pain wasn't going away. Getting over it would take a long time, if she ever could. Perhaps, getting over it wasn't the right approach, and maybe just moving on was enough. No matter what, she knew Hadak would be there for her.

A warm hand landed on her shoulder, and she turned to see her brother staring at her without a hint of accusation. She wrapped herself around him after Hadak let her go.

Would they approve of her hacking at a Jutin or allowing herself to become lost in a moment of rage? There was a possibility that her brother would be shocked. Hadak would be pleased until he recognised the danger it placed her in.

"Do you know what their plans are?" Tenek asked, his voice rising above the squabble among the others. Jilaya squinted at him. "Their plans for this planet?"

When Jilaya grinned, it was tinged with sadness when she said, "Apparently, you're not easy to kill. They called for Zandar to be the first planet they overthrow." Tenek tilted his head at her. "I have a feeling my planet was a test run."

While Tenek frowned, Star's mind kept wandering to the water. They were always near it when they were attacked. When they discovered Illasay, she was by the river. Jilaya found her with Jutin near the river. They dragged her father off and went upstream. They attacked the human colony constantly, and the river ran straight through it in a narrow stream.

Taking Hadak's hand, she squeezed it, pointing to the river. "We've never seen Jutin anywhere else, right?"

"What do you mean?" he asked.

As she turned to include the *Avayak's* in her conversation, she looked at each of them in turn. It was with a slight hint of envy that Tenek watched Hadak and her casual touches.

"There aren't any reports of Jutin near the city or anywhere else the Horde travels?" she asked urgently.

"*Seya Avae*, in one other area," Hadak replied, and Tenek nodded in agreement.

With a small hitch in her voice, she asked. "Where?"

"By the Flavue lake," Hadak said, a wrinkle forming in his eye as he put it together.

"Every time they attack or take people, it is by the water. As far as we know, they are nowhere else on Zandar, right?"

"There are none found on the ice plains, nor are there any on the dusty plains."

"If I'm right, then they'll be along this stretch of river and by the lake since coastal areas are uninhabited."

"No, these places are not suitable for living, but we should send an *Avayak* along the coast with Horde warriors to inspect them." Hadak's smile was bloodthirsty and eager.

She rolled her eyes at the male's response to fighting and then turned her attention to Jilaya, who was flicking her tail in irritation.

"You are right," Jilaya told her, her unusual eyes staring at her with deep sadness. "Maybe if we had known beforehand, we could have searched our waterways and killed them before their machine set off." Jilaya shrugged and ruffled her hair before settling back down. "This is a fight for all of us. I will join you," she told everyone.

The Horde king's negative shaking caused her to hiss, and her sharp teeth flashed in the light, allowing them to see her fangs for the first time.

Paken spoke first; as expected, he had something nasty to say. "You're a *fhalah* and a feeble one at that. You'll be of no use to us."

Silence followed by her indrawn breath as she straightened her spine and positioned her hands near her swords. "It appears that you mistake me for asking for permission."

"Your people died in battle against them. What can you do but fall on their swords for us?"

Star was astonished by his vicious and cutting words, and her eyebrows rose.

Jilaya's skin glowed with a pearlescent shine that moved below her skin like pastel rainbow lights. Star assumed that it was a normal response, one of anger. This shine appeared to happen when Jilaya's emotions were heightened.

"It was my people who tore through their forces and sent me farther than we had ever attempted to go before. To. Save. You."

With each softly melodious word, she advanced on him. The soft tone made the statement even harsher. "And what kind of greeting do I receive, insults?" Her skin brightened as she swung her sword around, and before Star could blink, Jilaya had it up against his neck.

It was only after she had placed her blade at his neck that the Horde warriors gasped in surprise at her speed. The look in her eyes dared anyone to step closer. "I lost family members to share this news with you, now twin without a twin. The bond may be beyond your comprehension, but you must understand this." Her sword drew blood, and she licked one of her fangs. It was at this point that Star noticed a clear drop of fluid. "If you voice the insult again, I will gladly cut you in half."

The sword moved swiftly through the air, leaving a line of blood on his skin as it passed. While tucking it away, she looked at Star with exasperation, as if she couldn't believe her desire to be with one of them.

Attempting to convey the depth of her feelings for Hadak through one glance and how he was worth the effort, Star raised one eyebrow and curled the corner of her lips. The moment Hadak saw her look, he gripped her chin and placed a quick, passionate kiss on her lips, leaving her breathless and craving more.

Jilaya laughed outright at their play while Star's silly smile remained on her lips.

Everyone was stunned by the sound. It was pure and so angelic that she had no words to describe it. There was an innocence to her vocal sounds that contrasted starkly with the way she wielded a sword. Her curiosity was piqued as she wondered what other talents she possessed.

When her laughter tinkled off, she noticed everyone was stunned, including Paken, whom she sneered at. "We work in teams. I'm on his." Jilaya pointed at Hadak with her sword, and no one disagreed with her, although Paken looked extremely put out.

Hadak laughed against Star. "She's a fierce warrior. We should have children like her," he said as his hands rested on her stomach. "Little *fhalah's* who look like their *Mathar* and fight like their *Fathar*."

"Hey!" She pushed him a little only because he let her.

He grinned in reply. "Okay, and fight with the heart of their *Mathar*," he amended.

"That's better." She placed a soft kiss on his chin as everyone around them began to move.

"It seems you've decided to stay then?" he asked, even though she felt both of them had already decided Star couldn't go back.

"*Seya*," she whispered happily.

"*Seya*?" he asked with joy as he swung her around. "I fight for you today, then."

"*Nen*. It is a fight for all of us, and I know you'll protect us." She said hesitantly, "Just be careful."

"I'll gather my *Guyipe* and ride with some warriors to the human colony. I want you behind the walls and behind my warriors."

"Okay," she agreed.

"No argument." His brows twitched, and his black eyes seemed to grow brighter.

"No argument. I'll arm everyone as much as possible. I'll explain what's going on." Her next question died on her tongue. Hadak waited patiently while she grabbed Black when he finished talking with a warrior. She brought him into the conversation. "Should we tell the colony what happens to the human women they've taken?"

Hadak breathed sharply, and Black wrinkled his brow as if he hadn't even thought of that. "I don't know, *Avae*, it's something you have to decide together." He thought for a moment before nodding. "If it were my *fhalah's*, I'd want to be aware, but I'd also want to know if there's any hope of getting them back."

She looked at Black to see if he agreed with her, but he was lost in thought as well. "Right now, we don't have a way, and telling them would just torment them," she decided with a heavy heart.

Black shrugged. "We can't outright lie. There are some things we can't reveal right now until we know more. We don't want them to harm the people they have." He thought for a moment, then said, "Tell them everything about the new threat and about Jilaya. She might provide a glimmer of hope. The fact that all the planets in the Drak system are fighting the Jutin will give everyone hope."

"When did you become so wise?" she jokingly asked.

In a dramatic gesture, he flourished his hand. "Black the all-knowing, all-seeing..." The effect was somewhat marred by him tripping over a root behind him. Hadak burst into laughter.

Black grinned at them, and she shook her head in despair and said, "You are so clumsy!"

Jilaya approached them, staring at Star's brother in confusion. "He is your sibling?"

"*Seya*, he is."

"Hmm." Jilaya offered him a hand. When he was standing, Jilaya examined his thin shoulders and wiry arms. "He should start practising with a sword."

A grin spread across Hadak's face, and she had the impression that something was already in the works for her brother. Whatever Black's feelings may be, Hadak would at least help him become more comfortable with self-defence. Star knew that he would do everything he could to train Black so that he would be able to save himself.

"Let's leave now," Hadak said, and his second warriors gathered.

Tenek joined them, leaving behind his seconds and keeping pace with Jilaya while chatting animatedly with her. Despite their differences, they liked each other.

Paken, thankfully, remained behind with his warriors. Star wasn't sure how long they would support him. None of them moved to defend him from Jilaya's blade.

She felt her body react to the sound of everyone getting ready as if it were a warning signal. Suddenly, she became hyper-alert, twitching at every sound. Her head whipped back and forth with every too-fast movement. She had a tight ball of anticipation inside her; her nerves were on fire.

They walked together along the river, searching for Jutin along the way. Star didn't expect to find any. It was unlikely they would stick around when they knew that three Horde kings were close at hand.

The fourth *Avayak* should be arriving any day now. He must have been delayed. Since Hadak was not concerned, neither was she. Her mind was already full of worries without adding yet another. She was confident in their numbers, particularly since she was aware of the fierce nature of the *Avayak's*.

Jilaya stood on the *Guyipe*, her hands resting on Tenek's shoulders. For balance, she held her tail behind her, and her two braids whipped around in the air as she laughed. With her shoulders back and arms wide, there was no sign of fear.

Tenek shared her laughter.

Madness. She smiled and thought they were both mad.

Chapter 15

They rode with the wind against them for the entire day.

She relaxed into Hadak. She felt dejected and wondered whether she was wrong about water being a source they needed to stay close to. She felt her arms becoming heavier, her eyes closing, and she trusted Hadak wouldn't allow her to fall.

Sleep had become something she treasured wherever she could find it. Since Jutin had taken her father, Star didn't think she had experienced a peaceful night's sleep. In the evenings, Hadak cuddled up to her as they travelled, but even then, she slept on hard, uncomfortable ground with thin fur covering her hips and shoulders.

Her thoughts drifted to the night in his *tepay* as she drifted to sleep.

She awoke to the sounds of shouts, and her eyes took a moment to adjust to the new surroundings. It was at this point that Jilaya threw herself over Tenek's head and pushed her sword into a Jutin. With a grin on her face and her skin glowing, she swung the sword rapidly, ready to respond with deadly force in just a few seconds.

Bloody hell. Where did they come from?

The sight of more than thirty Jutin blocking their path by the stream sent a chill down her spine. They were only a few miles away from the human colony. Her hands firmly gripped Hadak's waist, his fingers clenched against her own, exerting a cold, hard pressure against her palm. Taking what he was handing her, she brought it close so she could inspect it.

When she realised he was handing her his blade, her fingers curled around the cold, hard metal. It was shorter than his long blade. She gripped it tightly, knowing she would do whatever it took to survive.

Her fear for her scrawny brother prompted her to whimper, "Black." Her eyes darted about until Hadak lifted his chin to the right.

Black's hands were white and clenched tightly around the handle of a blade. He looked sick, and she only had a moment to dwell on Black's fear before the Jutin attacked.

It became chaos when Jutin's rushed them.

In a violent rush of bodies, the sound of swords striking swords could be heard.

Hadak slipped off the *Guyipe*, keeping one hand on her while striking a Jutin with the other. As he thrust his sword low, he was aiming for the same soft spot that she had noticed earlier. After slicing his lower abdomen and legs, he let out a low growl as she was pulled away from him.

"Star!" She heard the shout reverberate over her head as she was dragged through the collision of bodies.

Her eyes were drawn to Black. Holding back a Jutin, he stood with his back bowed, his sword trembling in his hand.

She struggled, throwing all of her weight into her body, letting it fall, then turning her sword, she slashed at it. She was being held by a Jutin who raised its lips.

Immediately, the hairs on the back of her neck stood on end.

It held his hand next to his mouth, its fist closed tightly, and took a deep breath to blow.

After throwing herself away from him before the powder touched her, she flinched when it touched a warrior's arm, and her horror increased when his arm folded over.

It looked like the flesh was being sucked inward. It took some time for the skin to slowly sink into the hole as if it were disappearing into itself. Goosebumps covered her whole body as he let out an almighty howl. Muscles were exposed, then they shrank and folded.

Bones broke and got sucked in until he was left with nothing but a stump.

Warriors close by watched in shock as the powder quickly consumed the flesh of the warrior.

It was Jutin who roared out a victory and renewed their attack.

With a furious Horde cry on his lips, Tenek charged the Jutin. It was pointless for her to use her puny sword skills in this fight, so she moved as far away as she could. Her goal was to get back to Hadak.

Stumbling over a body, she noticed brown skin and dark hair. It was all she had time to see before Jutin's scaly body fell on top of it. A nervous system response caused the fingers to twitch. Her gorge rose as his furry hand fell off and flopped into the dust, still twitching.

The battle was a blur. To keep herself safe, she swivelled around and drew her sword up to protect herself.

Jilaya swung her tail, gripping a branch near Star. Jilaya flipped into the air, straddled a Jutin's shoulder, and pushed her sword through its brain.

Guess they found another weakness...eww, Star shuddered.

His legs were hit by Jilaya's tail, which whipped out and beat them until he fell. In a smooth move, Jilaya whipped the sword out to strike a Jutin as it closed in on her.

Her blow was deflected by his scales, but she wasn't stopped. When she whipped her tail to catch his hand, she aimed low and uttered an enchanting sound that was possibly meant to be a powerful shout.

The Jutin seemed entranced by her voice. When she delivered the fatal blow, he froze. There was almost a sense that he had been waiting for it for a very long time and was pleased to die in battle.

She flinched when someone clashed nearby, spraying blood over her. When she lifted the sword, her arms struggled. Holding it for so long wasn't as easy as it seemed. The weight of it was heavy. It was heavy enough to affect her balance if she didn't put it down soon.

She worried that they might have more of the melting powder.

There was a safe distance between everyone and Jutin. They checked to see if they had closed his fists before moving in. There was a more hesitant nature to the fight as they remained back and then darted in to attack Jutin when it was safe.

A Horde cry caused her eyes to scan through the melee, and she saw Hadak standing tall in the middle of three Jutin. His powerful arms swung repeatedly without hesitation or pause. After putting all of his strength into his blade swing, he was able to bring down the two on his left.

It was mostly ducking and trying not to get caught up in the fighting as she made her way to him. Black stumbled into her, and she grabbed his arm as her mouth dried. He swung his sword in the air. "Black," she yelled. "Black, Black, it's me."

"Thank God!" He looked at her, making sure she was uninjured. She was doing the same to him. It appeared that he only sustained a cut to his upper arm. The area around his mouth was red and swollen, like he had been punched. He was also covered in blood, but it was from someone else.

Nasan was engaged in a fight with his own Jutin close by when Hadak noticed her and threw the Jutin without even attempting to wound him.

His attention was focused on her, so he narrowly avoided being hit in the gut. Jumping back, he roared at his opponent before slicing him in half.

With each thudding step, he drew closer. She went on the offensive with her brother at her back until he was able to join them. While keeping her sword up, she wanted to ensure he had as much assistance as possible, even though her skills were rather limited.

It filled her heart to see her brother, trembling from fatigue, hold up his blade in readiness to defend them if necessary.

They formed a triangle, with each of them slicing at any attacker they encountered. Having better aim, Hadak was able to take down the Jutin while she and Black injured or otherwise prevented them from reaching his back and sides.

After hearing a cry beside her, she felt a slice to her arm, then another to her arm. The moment she turned, Black was sliding to the ground. "Black!" her shout drew Hadak's eyes. After a glance, he altered his stance, defending them while she checked on Black.

Turning him over, she observed that his face was deathly pale, and his eyes were filled with pain. While he held his hands over his stomach, she noticed red seeping between his fingers. She emitted a strangled sound. Her trembling hands reached for her mouth in an attempt to contain her sobs.

Stuck in combat, two people brushed by them, and they bumped into his legs. A pained whimper escaped him. When it appeared that they were about to topple over, she threw herself on top of Hadak. She jerked back up as she heard him groan in pain as they collided with Tenek and Nasan.

Her eyes shifted back to Black when he doubled up. "We need to move you, Hadak is being distracted by us."

She wasn't wrong in her assessment. It was as if he was trying to be everywhere at once. Hadak's broad shoulders and arms enabled him to swing his sword fluidly. He was fast; he was trying to protect both himself and them at the same time.

Seeing their dilemma, Jilaya fought her way over as she frantically attempted to stop more of her brother's blood from spilling.

When she applied pressure to her *Brathar's* wounds, who was getting his hands all over the place, she snapped at him, "Will you move your hands?" He wouldn't allow her to do so. The only thing she could see was a bright red line running between his fingers. In her anxious mind, it resembled a gushing river.

"My insides are falling out," Black groaned, lines of pain appearing around his mouth. There were goosebumps all over her body as she froze. She immediately began to think of the worst case scenario. As she unpeeled his fingers, the breath she was holding abruptly escaped her mouth when she saw the thin line.

"Your insides are not falling out, you idiot." She pinched him on the arm in a state of relief. He moaned as though he was dying. "I can't believe you." She had thought for a moment that he might actually be dying.

Upon hearing the clash of swords, she flinched back. Jilaya had struck another Jutin, leaving a trail of blood in the air.

"Well, I feel like my insides are falling out," he complained.

Star shook her head in disbelief. "Come on, I need to get you away from here."

Hadak met her gaze and nodded in agreement. She and Jilaya bundled Black under their arms and backed away from the main fight.

Hadak remained vigilant against any approaching Jutin. There was a roar of clashing steel and a shout of exhalation as the battle raged. It was difficult for her to ignore the dying screams she heard.

She hurried them to the far end of the clearing towards the trees.

Not that the treetops gave them any cover. Even though Jutin lived in the trees, Jilaya was equally as dangerous from a height. Black's feet were stumbling as they approached the edge, and his breathing was harsh.

"Star!" A hand grasped her arm, pulling her away from a blade aimed at her throat. Jilaya's skill was evident in her ability to throw with precision. The blade in her hand penetrated a Jutin's neck up to halfway through.

A rage-filled Hadak yelled as he pulled Jilaya's knife from Jilaya's grasp. 'Star!' he shouted, his teeth bared in rage.

He grabbed both her brother and her, spun, and sprinted for the trees. Jilaya ran beside them, twirling her sword in a carefree manner, as if she weren't in the thick of battle. As his feet hit the ground, she was jolted and felt sick to her stomach. He put them down as if they weighed nothing, then went back to defending them.

Using her hands, she moved Black's. Her entire attention was focused on his wound. There was a deep slash across his midsection. "I'm dying; my insides are falling out," he groaned. He insisted that his insides were spilling out, but they weren't.

"They are not. You're not dying," she replied with a grim smile despite the horror around her. She tried to ignore the grunting and clashing behind her.

"*Seya,* I am."

"Will you stop being such a baby?" she scolded, absentmindedly brushing back his hair. As he lifted his hands again, she examined the wound. There was only a thin layer that had been cut through. Thankfully. Her eyes burned from tears, but she blinked them away and moistened her lips.

Since she didn't have anything to wrap around his middle, Jilaya pulled a thin scarf and a light-weight shirt from deeper within her bag.

Star nodded in thanks.

She ripped it with her hands and applied pressure to it. "Sit up," she instructed him, and groaning with pain, he moved mechanically until he was upright and rigid.

With the scarf in hand, she wrapped it around his middle in order to secure the temporary bandage. It was the best she could do right then. As soon as she was finished, he sat back and uttered an expletive.

Her gaze flicked nervously to the fight now that she had seen to Black.

It was slowing down. There were four Jutin left, and Tenek fought furiously to take down two of them. Jilaya's hands twitched as she swung her sword as if she desperately wanted to be involved.

Nasan suddenly charged out of nowhere, taking the head of one of them. She let out a cry as the fourth crept up on him as if it had been planned. Furan appeared over its shoulder, pushing his blade in before it knew what was happening.

Tenek's shoulder muscles tightened with tension as he approached the heap of dust that once held one of his warriors.

He hovered his hands over it. After hanging his head for a while, he threw it back and roared. It made her flinch. There was anguish in the sound.

On her knees, Jilaya bowed her head, and a soft lilting melody floated out of her, and it felt like a wave of peace.

In the clearing, the silence was heavy with loss when Tenek rose from the ground and walked over to Jilaya. "*Behku* for your help," he told her sincerely.

"It is an honour to sing your warrior into the next life." She bowed and climbed into the trees, perched on top of a branch.

Star's eyes followed her, but whatever she was doing must be of importance to her because she bowed her head and whispered to herself.

"*Kussa*," Star whispered, her voice heavy with guilt. It was his warrior who jumped into action to protect her, and he didn't deserve that. "I didn't know what would happen," she explained, tears trembling on her lashes. "He just jumped in front of me."

Tenek gently pulled her fingers apart and waited until she had his full attention. The way Hadak looked at him made it appear as though he would kill him if he said the wrong thing.

"He protected another *Avayak's Avae*. His family will be proud of him. Until the very end, he was a warrior, and that is what we all hope for. You couldn't have faced Jutin alone; he would have been a coward to leave a *fhalah* battling for her life." He took a deep breath in. His smile, when it came, was strained. He squeezed her fingers before letting go. "*Nen*, he made a decision he knew to be right, and we won't dishonour his memory by feeling guilty about it."

She sucked in her breath and nodded her head in his direction. In agreement, Hadak grunted.

There would still be sadness in her heart. The thought that someone in the Horde deemed her worth the price of his life moved her and frightened her at the same time.

Hadak took her shoulders as they watched Tenek gather his warriors. There had been a great deal of loss, too much loss. She felt Hadak gently squeeze her hand as though he knew she was thinking of the deceased. His soft kiss was followed by a smile of understanding. His gaze was wistful as he caressed her collar.

"We need to take my brother to a healer."

"I sent for my *Mathar* before you disappeared. She should be here by now. We may find her if we return to the camp." She opened her mouth to object, not wanting to leave him out in the open, wounded while they travelled a greater distance. "If we return to the colony," he said. "Then it may take another day or two."

"Oh, right."

"I won't let you down, and I will look after your family," Hadak promised her as he gazed tenderly at her *Brathar*, Black. "We need to get him fighting fit if he's going to be a warrior."

There was a flicker of light in Black's eyes, and he groaned in pain. Her mind was able to picture him swinging his sword about cockily and then accidentally cutting his toes off. He grinned and stroked her arm in a soothing manner.

"Let's go. Help him up slowly," Hadak said to his warriors. He left her to talk to Tenek.

Jilaya dropped beside Star and made her jump. "Jeez, a bit of warning."

"I apologize." Jilaya shrugged and ran her hand through her braids. "I will accompany you. You are very close to my ship."

The Warriors had just lifted her brother, and he was trying valiantly not to groan in front of them. She smiled when she recalled how he cried like a baby when he saw her.

As the blood-splattered fur stuck to her, she grimaced. She tried not to think about whose blood she had been covered in.

Turning her arm, she noticed a few cuts on her back and some dirty scrapes on her knees. As long as she bathed it properly, she wouldn't have any problems. She could only imagine how annoyed Hadak would be if she succumbed to another fever.

It didn't take Hadak long to finish his conversation. He gripped her hips and pulled her into a tight hug. "I don't like seeing you in battle."

Laying her head back against him, she rubbed his arm reassuringly. "I knew you wouldn't let anyone hurt me."

She stared at him with seriousness as he tilted her head back. "Does that mean you are definitely?"

"Does that mean I'm definitely staying? Yes." How could she not?

It was him who defended her brother. When she struggled through the worst tragedy, he stayed by her side. When they were alone, she knew he'd be there for her when she broke down. She always had her big, strong Horde king looking out for her. He was willing to train her brother. He wanted to have children. She wasn't touching that thought at the moment, but he was planning a life with her, and she wanted that.

"*Seya*," he said with a grin. "But I was determined to keep you by any means necessary." He placed his hips against her, and she felt his hard length. Her chest was filled with laughter as she shook her head.

"You're insatiable." They hadn't been together for a while, and she felt the same need after their near-death experience.

"*Maye* Star?" He rubbed his hands over her arms, trailing his fingers along the inside of her elbows as he pulled her away from the crowd.

How could it be so captivating and mesmerising about such an innocent thing? He held her shoulders and kissed the side of her neck. He lifted her. She clasped her hands behind his neck, straining to reach his lips on her tiptoes. She yelled in surprise as he lifted her.

"Are you going to send me back to the food *tepay*?"

Illasay was a matter she was confident he would handle, but he stiffened at the reminder. When she wasn't around, the other *fhalah's* might be more relaxed. She had a feeling they would be friendly if they weren't squashed by Illasay's powerful, err...personality. *"Nen*, you belong with me, *maye Immani*."

A small smile spread across her face as she replied, *"Seya*."

"Seya," he said with one hand tight on her hip and the other on her arse.

"Seya, I'm your *Avae*. I'll stay with the Horde." And they would all mourn together. She needed something solid and real at that moment. Her arms tightly gripped his.

He tightened his arms around her and kissed her until she was breathless. With a smile on her face, she held onto him and kissed him as if their lives depended on it. "How about a lesson in the river while your *Brathar* is being patched up so we can wash all this filth off?"

"A lesson, *Avaye*?" she asked, watching his eyes go molten with desire at her use of the word, 'my king,' although she thought it was an odd time for a lesson.

"Seya." With an unrepentant grin, he thrust his hips and said, "A naked one."

Laughing softly, a huge smile spread over her face as he led her to the river.

More books from May

<u>Paranormal Romance</u>

Series - Numbers

Cain

Drey

Mallen

Samiel

Perdy

Nick

<u>Sci romance</u>

Series - Drak System

Warrior of Zandar

<u>Fantasy Romance</u>

Series - Ignis

Blackfire

May Doyle

About the Author

May Doyle has a weakness for biscuits and can often be found sitting amidst a pile of crumbs while writing her latest paranormal romance. As a mom of two young kids, May discovered that their time at school could be spent writing. She has been composing every school day since.

When she's not writing, May enjoys time with her three King Charles Cavaliers, who make the perfect lap dogs. She also loves reading about characters who overcome obstacles to get to their happily ever after.

May would love for you to drop her a line at maydoyle30@gmail.com or visit her at Https://maydoyle30.wix.com

Read more at https://www.maydoyle30wix.com/.

Milton Keynes UK
Ingram Content Group UK Ltd.
UKHW040641091023
430221UK00001B/45